What Happens Between Friends

Beth Andrews

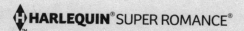

Recycling programs
for this product may
not exist in your area.

ISBN-13: 978-0-373-60790-7

WHAT HAPPENS BETWEEN FRIENDS

Printed in U.S.A.

ABOUT THE AUTHOR

Romance Writers of America RITA® Award winner Beth Andrews set her latest series, In Shady Grove, in a fictional town based on her own small hometown in northwestern Pennsylvania. A few of her favorite friends-to-lovers characters are Harry and Sally *(When Harry Met Sally)*, Monica and Chandler *(Friends)* and Keith and Watts *(Some Kind of Wonderful)*. Beth firmly believes love conquers all and Elvis is a great name for a dog. Learn more about Beth and her books by visiting her website, www.BethAndrews.net.

Books by Beth Andrews

HARLEQUIN SUPERROMANCE

Other titles by this author available in ebook format.

For Andy

CHAPTER ONE

No, NO, NO.

Lightning flashed, a dazzling display that crackled the air with energy, made the hair on Sadie Nixon's arms stand up. Ten seconds later, thunder boomed, vibrating through her moving Jeep.

She leaned forward to look through the windshield at the rapidly darkening sky. Clouds rolled, merged together. A strong gust of wind buffeted the Jeep, had her fighting to keep it on the road. She pressed down on the gas, strangled the steering wheel. Please, don't do this to her. Not this time.

She passed the road leading to Knapp's Creek. Glanced out the driver's-side window. She wasn't going to make it. She could turn around, she thought frantically. She was barely in Shady Grove, had just passed the city limits. She'd head west, maybe spend the night in Pittsburgh then come back tomorrow.

It was a good plan—and for someone who preferred to let life happen to her instead of bending it to suit each situation, that was saying something.

Yep, it was a solid plan. And it probably would have worked...if she hadn't run into Jessica Gardner at Miranda's Market. Jessica wasn't a gossip, but what were the chances she wouldn't tell anyone she'd seen Sadie a full day before she'd returned to her hometown?

Probably somewhere between zero and in Sadie's dreams.

She didn't have a choice. She had to keep going. Maybe, if luck was with her, the wind at her back and all that jazz, she would make it to her destination before it rained. Or, better yet, the clouds could pass right over Shady Grove, just...keep going. Wait to unleash their fury on some other unsuspecting town.

Yes, that was it, think positively. She'd use the power of her mind and her good intentions to keep the storm at bay.

She could have sworn she heard the Fates laugh in delight—seconds before the sky opened and a torrential rain came down so hard, so fast, the drops bounced off the hood, sounded like rocks hitting the roof.

Stupid Fates.

Scowling, she continued down Case Boulevard, her fingers tapping the steering wheel to the beat of Mumford and Sons' "I Will Wait." The dark seemed to swallow the beams of her headlights before they could do more than reflect the next twenty feet or so. Her windshield wipers put up a valiant, yet pretty much useless battle against the downpour as she sped along the familiar road.

It was coincidence, of course. One of those freak-ishly weird anomalies that had a thunderstorm appearing as she happened to return to town for the first time in three years.

Just as it was coincidence, and only coincidence, that had some natural disaster occurring every time she returned home.

Every. Single. Time.

Rainstorms. Floods. Hail. A tornado. And that memorable freak spring blizzard when she'd driven in from Dallas back when she'd been twenty-two.

Maybe the Fates could hit the town with hordes of locusts or an earthquake next time. Just to mix it up a bit. All these rainstorms were getting predictable.

And she hated being called Cyclone Sadie.

Oh, and of her grandmother genuflecting every time Sadie came to visit.

Jeez, an ancient tree limb happens to fall onto her gram's beloved Cadillac at the exact same moment Sadie knocks on the front door for an impromptu visit and suddenly Sadie's the spawn of Satan.

Bringing evil omens.

Which was ridiculous. There were no such things as omens—evil or otherwise. Sure, a person could follow the signs, but Sadie preferred to trust in her own instincts. So when those instincts had told her to get the heck out of Dodge—or in her case, New Orleans—she'd packed up her worldly belongings and skedaddled.

Not slowing, she turned the defrost up to high

and leaned forward, squinting to make out the white center line dissecting the road. If only she could remember to check the weather forecast before any actual skedaddling took place, she'd be golden.

As for her current streak of bad luck... Well, it had to end sometime. Her fortunes would turn around soon. They always did. Highs and lows and all that. Such was life.

It was like being on an endless roller-coaster ride. The slow, jerky ascents, quick, stomach-tumbling drops and body-shaking twists and turns made getting out of bed each day worthwhile. Interesting. Exciting.

She wouldn't want it any other way.

The flat, straight, in-the-middle times were so calm. So...boring.

She might be at rock bottom, but she'd had fun on the way down. And now, there was nowhere else to go but up.

Telling herself she felt better about the whole crappy situation that was her current life, Sadie reached for the coffee she'd picked up at Miranda's Market. She took her eyes off the road for a split second—barely a *fraction* of a split second, really—but when she glanced up, the cup to her mouth, a huge dog stood in the middle of the street.

Her heart leaped to her throat. Time seemed to slow as she stomped on the brakes and yanked the wheel hard to the left. The Jeep fishtailed, the force causing the back end to shake violently before hitting a patch of water and skidding off the road. The vehicle spun once…twice…before the rear driver side slammed into what felt like a brick wall, jerking Sadie hard to the side. Her seat belt cut into her shoulder. Her head snapped sideways, hitting the side window with a sharp thud.

Her vision blurred, then went black.…

She couldn't have been out more than a minute because when she came to, the same Rihanna song that had started when she'd been spin, spin, spinning, was still playing on the radio.

Sadie peeled her eyelids open, breathed deeply then winced at the pain on the side of her head. Gently probing the area with her fingertips, she brushed against a rising bump. Ouch.

She glared upward—at the approximate spot where she was sure the Fates were gloating down at her.

She slowly stretched then squirmed, flexed her toes in her sandals, curled and straightened her fingers. Other than the bump on her head and what was sure to be a lovely mark on her chest from the seat belt, nothing was broken.

The song had reached her favorite part, but at the moment, the notes jarred her teeth, ran over her already ragged nerves. She shut the radio off, her hands and breathing both unsteady. Leaning to the left, she stared out the driver's-side window. She could see now that she hadn't hit a brick wall, but a four-foot-wide brick pillar, one of two holding the large, cheery sign towering over her.

She couldn't make it out clearly, not with the rain and her windows fogging up and all, but she already knew it showed a deliriously happy family of four enjoying a picnic alongside the river. In the background, boats dotted the water, the sky was clear, the sun shining brightly. An ornate steel bridge led to the town of Shady Grove.

On a red plaid blanket spread over the grassy bank, the mother—a testament to the eighties with her acid-washed shorts and big hair—read to her cherubic daughter. Off to the side, father and son tossed a baseball. And across that incredibly blue sky, written as if the words had been spun out of fluffy white clouds, was a simple salutation.

Welcome to Shady Grove—where everyone feels at home!

It was the same sign that had greeted her over twenty years ago when she and her mother had moved here. Her first glimpse of what life was going to be like in this small, western-Pennsylvanian town nestled amidst the rolling hills. Traditional. Idyllic.

Sheltered. Tedious.

A far cry from how they'd lived when Sadie's father had been alive, when each day brought with it a new adventure—be it a trip to the zoo or a spontaneous move to another state. Life with Victor Nixon had been unpredictable, unstructured and always, always exciting.

She missed him. After all these years, she still missed him so much.

Sighing, she shut her eyes and willed the headache pressing against her temples to subside. What the heck had sent that dog out on a night like this anyway?

Her eyes flew open. Crap. The dog.

Unbuckling her seat belt with one hand, she turned off the Jeep with the other, then grabbed the small flashlight from the glove box. She bolted out into the rain. Her feet slid out from under her and she went down on her knees.

Double crap.

She glanced at the heavens—and almost drowned from the deluge. She lowered her head, but rain still stung her face, plastered her hair to her cheeks, the back of her neck.

Didn't whoever was in charge upstairs have any idea how hard it was to get mud out of cotton? You'd think they could cut her some slack, at least until she found the dog.

A bolt of lightning lit the sky. But it didn't strike her dead.

She'd take that as a sign she could safely continue on her way.

Staying in the beams of her headlights, she carefully made her way to the side of the road. No dog. Of course not. That would be way too easy.

Thunder rumbled, echoed across the valley.

She rolled her eyes and turned on the flashlight.

Yeah, yeah. She got it. She was a puny mortal, help-less against the whims of fate and the wants of a higher authority. Whoop-de-freaking-do.

As if she wanted to be an all-powerful entity. Please. There was way too much responsibility in-volved.

When she screwed up—as she was wont to do—she only had herself to worry about.

At the other side of the road, Sadie peered into the woods but couldn't make out much, other than trees, trees and more trees. She tucked the flashlight between her arm and side and clapped her hands. "Here, doggie."

From the corner of her eyes, she caught move-ment to her right. She stilled. There it was again. A flash of white, the glint of two eyes.

"Hi." She smiled and stepped forward, kept the light aimed at the ground. The dog startled and slunk off into the shadows. "I'm not going to hurt you. That's it," she continued when the dog ap-proached again. She extended her free hand. "Come on, gorgeous. I don't bite. Unless you bite me first, then all bets are off."

The dog cocked his—or her—large head, con-sidered Sadie's hand for a moment then delicately sniffed her fingers. She took the opportunity to check under the hood—so to speak.

Boy.

"You're a handsome fella, aren't you?"

He inclined his head as if to agree.

Then again, most males who were good-looking knew it, so why should a dog be any different? He was mostly black with a white chest and face, and a black left ear and patch around his right eye. Definitely a mixed breed, but she could see some boxer in his square face, the shape of his pointy ears.

Sadie rubbed his head gently. He didn't wear a collar. "I bet your name is Patches or Spot or something equally uninspired and unoriginal. But a true king like you deserves something much more majestic, don't you think?" She cupped his face in her hands. "And, as there's only one king worthy of being christened after, I hereby name you Elvis."

He licked her wrist.

"I hope that means you like your new name and aren't trying a taste test before chomping on my arm. I'm rather fond of it. My arm. And your new name, actually." She straightened. "My mom always said I didn't know enough to get out of the rain and I'd really like to prove her wrong—for once. What say we head into town? How do you feel about birthday cake?"

Elvis looked her up and down, then obviously finding her lacking, sat.

"Yeah? Well, let me tell you something, Your Majesty, you don't look so hot right now, either. And you stink."

The dog turned his face away, his black-and-pink nose lifted in the air.

"Oh, don't be so sensitive. Just speaking the truth

here. Look, my Jeep has a brand-new dent—which means I'm going to hear, yet again, how careless, reckless and hopeless I am—all because of you. But you don't see me holding a grudge, do you? You have two choices here—you can come with me, get something to eat, get cleaned up and spend the rest of the night warm and dry. Or you can stay here, wet and miserable and, yes, smelly. What's it going to be?"

Elvis looked at her, then the woods, the road and then her again.

"Really? This is something you have to think about?" Her hair was dripping and she was soaked through to her underwear—which was sticking to her skin. She blinked water from her eyes. "You know what? Maybe I should rescind my offer. After all, it looks as if you're doing just dandy without any help from me."

Elvis got to his feet slowly and, it seemed to Sadie, with a great deal of resignation, and crossed to her. Nudged her thigh with his head.

"Yeah," she said. "That's what I thought."

He followed her to the Jeep. She opened the passenger-side door and he hopped onto the seat, lifting and lowering his legs—all the better to spread muddy paw prints over the light gray fabric.

"You missed a spot," Sadie told him, but he ignored her sardonic tone and sat, looking very much the regal ruler ready to be driven to his castle.

She shut the door and hurried around to the driver's side. "I bet you're starving," she said as she started the engine. "After birthday cake, we'll order a pizza. Double pepperoni."

Shivering, she buckled up and blasted the heat. Thanks to the Jeep's four-wheel drive, they were on the road a minute later, heading toward Shady Grove—and all the memories, conflicted familial relationships and emotional baggage that went along with going home.

"WELL?" JAMES MONTESANO'S mother asked as she measured grounds into the coffeemaker.

Through the open window over the sink, the scents of rain and wood smoke drifted into the kitchen. When the rain started twenty minutes ago, the birthday guests had abandoned the fire ring set on the lower tier of the three-level deck to settle inside, either in the living room, where James's grandfather played the fiddle, or in the game room in the basement, from where bursts of raucous laughter—along with the occasional good-natured curse—floated upstairs.

No matter what the occasion, the time of year or the weather, his mom threw one hell of a party.

"*Well* what?" He eyed the leftover sheet cake. They'd done the whole singing thing—though he'd gotten out of the candle tradition by letting his seven-year-old nephew, Max, blow them out. James had already had two scoops of ice cream plus two servings of the German chocolate cake with coconut pecan frosting.

Aw, what the hell? If a man couldn't have extra cake on his birthday, what was the point of getting another year older?

Stretching onto her toes, Rose reached over the sink and turned the handle, closing the window. "What do you think of Anne?"

James cut a large square of cake and set it on one of his mother's fancy dessert plates. He licked frosting from the side of his thumb. "Who?"

"Anne." His mother snapped the lid of the coffeemaker shut and turned it on. "Anne Forbes. The pretty brunette in the dark blue dress?" He shook his head and she sighed heavily. "The new painter?"

Right. Kloss Painting and Wallpaper's newest hire. Brunette. Blue dress. Early thirties. "She seems capable. Has some good ideas for the kitchen and dining room at Bradford House."

Montesano Construction was nearing completion of their renovations of the one-hundred-year-old Victorian. Still, there was quite a bit to do before they moved on to the next job, and if James wanted to keep them on schedule—and James always, always wanted to keep his father's company on schedule—he needed to check on the delivery of that claw-foot tub.

He pulled out his phone and opened the calendar function.

"Ahem."

"I'm not calling anyone," he said, not bothering to so much as glance over at her. He didn't have to. He'd been on the receiving end of his mother's do-not-mess-with-me look often enough that he could feel it—he didn't need to see it. Moms. Nothing diminished their kick-ass powers. Not even celebrations of their child's birth. "I'm just making a note."

His entire family ragged him endlessly about how often he was on his phone. How the hell did they think so many things got done if he didn't have his notes and reminders and schedules to keep the company on track?

He put the phone in his pocket, picked his cake up again only to freeze—the fork raised halfway to his mouth—to find Rose staring at him as if his brain had leaked from his ears and oozed onto the custom-built butcher block topping the center island.

"What?"

"I can't believe you spent a good twenty minutes in conversation with Anne and the only thing you can say is that she's—" Rose's mouth twisted "—capable."

He ate the bite of cake. Silently urged the coffee to hurry up and brew. "What's wrong with capable? You want us to work with inept subcontractors?"

She grabbed cream from the stainless-steel fridge, slammed the door shut. An attractive woman despite the extra pounds in her hips and thighs, her face was a softer, rounder version of the beautiful girl she'd once been. Her chin-length hair was still dark, her face showing only faint signs of age. "I want you to notice when there's an attractive, intelligent, interesting, *single* woman right in front of you."

He narrowed his eyes. "You said you invited her because she's new in town."

"She is."

"And because Kloss's recently hired her."

"They did."

"And because you wanted us to get to know her, since we'll be working with her so closely at Bradford House."

Rose added her delicate china sugar bowl—the one James and his brothers had bought for Mother's Day a good twenty years ago to replace the one they'd broken during an impromptu, and ill-advised, indoor game of soccer—to a large serving tray. "I'm well aware of what I said."

"You forgot to mention you were setting me up with her," he said in a thoughtful, patient and completely reasonable tone. He was nothing if not a thoughtful, patient and reasonable man, damn it.

He stabbed another bite of cake.

"No one has set you up. All I did was invite Anne to the party for all the reasons I mentioned and you so helpfully repeated. If you two hit it off, great. If not…" She shrugged, though the look she shot him clearly said if he didn't hit it off with Anne, he was an idiot. "No harm done, then."

"You're sneaky."

"I prefer to think of it as multitasking. I help

someone new to town feel welcome, introduce her to a few friends and possibly help you find your future wife."

He set his empty plate aside. "Sneaky and scary."

"Relax. No one's forcing you to the altar. I'm just showing you an option."

Thunder boomed and his sweet-natured dog, Zoe, a German shepherd/husky mix, whined and nudged the side of his leg. He patted her head, but kept his gaze on his mother. "Anyone ever tell you you'd make a hell of a used-car salesperson?"

"I'll take that as a compliment." She set cups and saucers on the tray. "Why don't you open a couple more bottles of wine and take them around to the guests? Make sure one is merlot."

He went to the other side of the square island and searched through the well-stocked, built-in wine rack. Pulled out a bottle of merlot along with one of pinot blanc. "Don't tell me, Anne prefers merlot."

Beaming, Rose patted his cheek. "You always were a bright child."

Bright enough to know arguing with his mother would do him no good. The best way to handle this was to grin and bear it.

He opened the bottle of white, set it aside to breathe. He didn't have anything against Anne, or pretty brunettes in general. But he could, and often did, get his own dates. He didn't need his mommy setting him up.

"Dad wants to know if the coffee's ready," James's

younger brother, Eddie, said as he came through the kitchen door.

"The regular is about done," Rose said, "but the decaf is going to take a few minutes."

Eddie grabbed a cup from the tray and reached for the pot. "He won't know the difference."

Rose slapped the back of his hand. "If you give him regular, he won't sleep. And when your father doesn't sleep, I don't sleep. Mostly because he keeps me awake until the wee hours of the morning with all his tossing and turning. You'll give him decaf or I'm sending him home with you and Max tonight."

"No need for threats. I'll give him decaf." He turned to James. "Meg Simpson's looking for you. Said she wants to discuss us doing an addition at their cottage on the lake next year."

"She'll have to wait," he said mildly, lifting the merlot bottle. "I'm getting my future wife a drink."

Eddie raised his dark eyebrows. Shorter than both James and their youngest brother, Leo, but broader through the shoulders, he had their father's muscular build and their mother's hazel eyes. "Future wife?"

Nodding, James pulled the cork from the merlot. "It's all thanks to Mom. She got me a girl for my birthday."

Rose shook her head. "Now, James. Really. A girl?"

"Sorry. Woman."

Eddie helped himself to a strawberry from the

fruit-and-cheese tray Rose was putting together. "She got me a watch for my last birthday."

"Maybe she'll get you your very own woman for Christmas," James said.

Eddie gave one of his reticent shrugs. "A man can hope."

"Meg Simpson wants to talk to you," Leo told James as he came in carrying dirty dessert dishes.

"Yeah. I got that memo."

Leo put the plates in the sink. "A customer wants to talk to you about doing a new job and you're not racing out there with your handy schedule and charts and whatnot?" He studied each of them, his dark eyes narrowed. "Okay, what's going on?"

"Mom got him a girl for his birthday," Eddie said.

"Yeah?" Leo grinned, slow and wicked. "Which one?"

"Kloss's new painter," James said. "Tall brunette in a blue dress in the living room."

Leo and Eddie exchanged a glance then both walked out only to return less than thirty seconds later. "She's hot," Leo said. "Excellent legs, nice ra—"

Rose slapped him upside the head.

"Shoes," he amended quickly, holding his hand over the spot she'd slapped. He stepped out of range. "Really nice shoes. Good choice, Mom."

"Thank you," she said, pouring the regular coffee into an insulated carafe. "I'm glad one of my sons appreciates my efforts."

"Guilt?" James asked. "That's beneath you."

Leo smiled, the same smile that had made fools of hundreds of women. Females. Always falling for a pretty face. "If he doesn't want her, can I have her?"

"Absolutely not." Rose turned to James. "My goodness, the way you're acting, you'd think I bought you a Russian mail-order bride and had you legally wed without your knowledge. All I did was invite a lovely, interesting, nice woman to your party. Is that so wrong?" she cried with the dramatic flair he'd come to know and love.

Eddie pursed his lips and, as usual, wisely kept quiet. Leo rolled his eyes.

James showed his appreciation with quiet applause that had Zoe lifting her head, her tail wagging. "That was true Oscar material. Bravo."

Leo snorted. "I've seen her do better. It was lacking something. It needed more…action. Drama. Maybe next time," he told Rose, "thump your fist over your heart. Gnash your teeth. Rip at your hair. Don't hold back."

Rose gave him one of her patented disdainful sniffs. "Everyone's a critic."

"Hey, you know my motto—go big or go home."

"I wish you'd go home," James said with feeling. He turned to his mom. "And I wish you wouldn't set me up, especially without asking first. Especially on my birthday," he added.

Guilt may have been beneath his mom, but he wasn't above using it himself.

Sometimes a man had to fight fire with fire.

Rose rounded her eyes. "It's your birthday? Today? Why, that must've completely slipped my mind, which is strange as I'm usually good with dates and things. Oh…wait…" Frowning, she pressed her fingertips against her temples. "Is today the twenty-first? Because I'm getting this vague memory of being in labor on this date years ago for…let me see…"

"Twenty-nine and a half hours," James, Eddie and Leo said in unison.

Rose's hazel eyes gleamed, but her expression remained as serious as a heart attack. "Yes, that's right. It's all coming back to me now. Then again, it's hard to forget twenty-nine—"

"And a half," the brothers added.

"Twenty-nine and a half hours of excruciating pain. And that's not even including pushing you—and your rather large head—out."

Wincing, feeling more than a little sick to his stomach, James rubbed the back of his regular-size head. And conceded defeat. "I appreciate it. I think. Next year, I'm throwing you a party."

"The flowers you send every year are more than enough, thanks." She laid her hand on his arm. "Can't you give Anne a chance? Just talk to her. Get to know her a bit. That's all I'm asking."

He sighed. He knew his mom wanted him settled. Married.

Hell, he wanted that, too. Wanted a family of his

own, a wife in his bed, a couple of kids running around his house. He'd always figured it hadn't happened yet because it wasn't meant to, but that it would. Someday.

Since he had no control over when, exactly, that day would arrive, he didn't bother worrying about it. It was useless, and a waste of energy, to fight the ebb and flow of life. Better to focus on keeping your head above water and just ride the waves out.

But maybe, this one time, he could try paddling and get where he was going faster.

Even if his mother was doing the steering.

"I'll talk to her some more," he said. What could it hurt? "But I'm not making any promises."

"No promises. Got it."

She hugged him. Looking over her head, James glanced at Leo who mouthed, "Sucker."

James flipped him off.

"Leo," Rose said as she broke the hug. "Please make another pot of coffee while Eddie and I take these trays out."

"If you keep feeding people," Eddie grumbled, "they'll never leave."

Rose handed him the coffee tray. "Your unsociable side is showing again."

"Does he have any other side?" Leo asked.

"God, I hope so." At the door, she looked back at James. "Don't forget the wine."

She swept out of the room, as regal as a queen, as formidable as a Navy SEAL.

"Yeah," Leo said, rinsing the coffeepot. "And don't forget the engagement ring."

James stepped forward, ready to dunk his brother's fat head under the running water, when his phone buzzed. He took it out, checked the caller ID. And, grinning, answered.

"Well, what do you know?" he said, crossing his ankles and leaning back against the counter. "It's trouble come to call."

Sadie Nixon laughed, the light, tinkling sound warm and as clear as if she was standing next to him. "I bet you say that to all the girls."

"Only the ones who've earned it."

"What's life without a little trouble?"

"Peaceful."

"I think the word you're searching for is *boring*."

"With you around? Never."

"Flatterer. Now stop trying to charm me, I'm on a mission here. Guess where I'm at?"

"Jail?" he asked, earning him a curious glance from Leo.

"After that New Year's Eve incident in D.C. you made me promise never to ask you to bail me out again, remember?"

"Hard to forget." He'd left his date—a very friendly blonde—and driven the four and a half hours from Shady Grove, Pennsylvania, to D.C. in a blinding snowstorm. It had been worth it. Being with Sadie was always worth it. "Not jail, then."

"You'll never guess—"

"Then why did you ask me to?"

"—so I'll just tell you...." He was surprised she didn't tap out a drumroll during her drawn-out dramatic pause. "I'm in Shady Grove."

"No kidding? You at your parents' place?" Dr. and Mrs. Ellison had left the party less than an hour ago and they hadn't said anything about Sadie coming home.

Then again, most of Sadie's trips to Shady Grove were unexpected. She was like a summer storm—you never knew when she would strike or how long she would stick around. And when she took off on her next great adventure, it was as if you'd been swept up in a tornado, your head dizzy and aching, your thoughts and feelings twirling.

"No, I had a stop I wanted to make first. Say, when did your mom have that stone retaining wall put in out front?"

"Two years ago. Eddie, Leo and I did it for Mother's—" He straightened. "Don't move."

He shut off the phone, stuffed it into his pocket and walked through the house toward the front door. If he happened to glance in the living room, just to see if Leo's assessment of Anne's legs was correct—it was—no one could fault him.

And while he had every intention of keeping his word to his mom, he kept walking. But he didn't want Anne Forbes. No matter that his mother had deemed her future-wife material. What he wanted,

what he'd always wanted, was outside right now
waiting for him.

He wanted Sadie Nixon.

CHAPTER TWO

THE RAIN HAD stopped, and beyond the Montesanos' two-story brick home, a crescent moon glowed brightly against the dark sky. In the driveway, parked behind a long line of cars—when Rose Montesano threw a party, she didn't mess around—Sadie clicked off her phone.

"He's coming," she told Elvis, stroking his head, and his eyes squinted in pleasure. "I can't wait for you to meet James. He's the best." The best friend a girl could ever have and the second greatest guy she'd ever known.

The number-one position was reserved for her father, the late, great Victor Nixon. Bigger than life and handsome as sin, he'd done more, seen more and had gotten more out of his thirty years than most people did who lived three times that long. Most importantly, he'd lived life on his own terms, thumbing his nose at his family's wealth and rigid standards to forge his own path at the tender age of sixteen, following his dreams wherever they took him.

He'd taught her that each day was an adventure waiting to be experienced.

She rubbed a hand over the ache in her chest, just above her heart. God, but she missed her daddy. She still missed him so, so much.

The front door opened and James stepped onto the wide porch and jogged down the stairs.

"I'll be right back," she promised Elvis before climbing out of the car.

Holding the top of the door with one hand, she waited while James approached in all his six-foot, darkly handsome glory, his stride purposeful. She knew the moment he spotted her. She never tired of the way his face lit when he saw her, of how, out of all the people she knew and loved, he was the only one who never got frustrated with her lack of planning, her decisions. Never lost his patience with her or tried to change her.

With a whoop of joy, she launched herself at him. His arms came around her, strong and steady. Comfortable. No matter what the circumstances, no matter how she messed up or how fast she was falling, James always caught her before she hit rock bottom.

She could always, always count on James to catch her.

Laughing, Sadie squeezed him tight. Yeah, Shady Grove was where she'd spent the majority of her formative years, the town where she'd first completed an entire school year without the disruption of another move. It was where her mother had grown up, where her mother, stepfather and sister all lived. But it was just a place, just another town.

This, she thought, clinging to her best friend, was home.

"You're soaked." Settling his hands on her hips, he pulled back and frowned at the mud on her pants, the wet spot on his light blue dress shirt. "You look like a drowned rat."

"Oh, James." She simpered, batting his chest. "You sure do know how to sweet-talk a girl. I'm shocked, shocked I say, that you're still single."

"And I'm shocked, shocked I say," he said in a seriously decent imitation of her, "that you manage to get through each day without causing yourself—or others—bodily harm."

She lifted her hand to the side of her head. "Who says I didn't cause any bodily harm?"

He brushed her hand aside and lightly probed the area above her ears, his touch incredibly gentle. The tips of his fingers trailed across the sensitive goose egg. She bit her lip to keep from hissing out a sharp breath.

"What did you do?" he asked.

"I had a little accident—"

"How bad?"

"Not bad," she told him quickly, knowing how he worried about…well…everything. "I was on Case Boulevard and skidded off the road and hit the pillar holding the Welcome to Shady Grove sign."

The front door opened, and a couple she didn't

recognize descended the porch steps, lifted their hands in farewell to James before getting into their car.

James walked to the driver's side of the Jeep. He crouched to study where the pillar and vehicle had, briefly, become one.

"You," he said, straightening, "are a menace. And a threat to brick pillars everywhere."

She grinned. How could she not when it was such a James thing to say, his words spoken with so much resignation and fondness? "None stand a chance while I'm behind the wheel."

"You sure you're okay?"

"I bumped my head. It's nothing." And no way would she tell him she'd momentarily blacked out. He'd insist she go to the E.R. when all she wanted was a hot shower, something to eat and a few hours in his company.

Being with James was always so easy. So relaxed. No matter how long they'd been apart, when they got together again it was as if they'd seen each other the day before. He didn't lay guilt trips on her if she didn't call or text him for months on end. He may not understand the choices she made, and he often teased her about her mistakes, but he never judged her. Better yet, he was always the first one to congratulate her on her triumphs.

He believed in her and accepted her for who she was, no questions asked. He loved her without reservations or expectations.

Some days she thought he was the only person who did.

Tears stung the back of her eyes. To hide them from James's intense gaze, she stretched onto her toes and hugged him again. He stiffened, his fingers digging painfully into her hips as if to push her away.

As if to set her aside.

A crazy thought. James would never do that to her. He'd never be done with her. The mere idea of it was absurd. Irrational.

Inconceivable.

Still, panic tightened her chest, made it impossible to breathe. She squeezed him harder. He sighed heavily, his breath ruffling the damp hair at her temple, the exhalation seeming to shudder through him. He slowly shifted closer, slid his hands around to settle at the small of her back, his warmth seeping through her wet clothes.

A pebble of unnamed emotion lodged itself in her throat and she pressed her face into the crook of his neck and simply held on. She inhaled deeply, and his spicy cologne and the underlying scent of sawdust only made the urge to bawl stronger.

God, she must have hit her head harder than she'd thought. Sure, her life was in the crapper right now, but it was temporary. A rough spot, one she'd eventually get over. "This, too, shall pass" and all of that. Good times and bad times, successes and failures... they all came and went.

And eventually she'd get back to looking at the bright side—but right now the glare was giving her one hell of a headache.

"Hey," James said, his soft, gruff voice causing goose bumps to rise on her arms. "What's this about?"

"Nothing." She cleared her throat and prayed she didn't sound as needy and unsteady as she felt. "I'm just...I'm really happy to see you."

She leaned back and studied him. His handsome face was as familiar to her as her own: soulful eyes the color of rich chocolate, heavy eyebrows and shaggy dark hair that had the tendency to curl at the ears and nape. His Roman nose bent slightly right, thanks to his taking an elbow to the face when he went up for a rebound during a basketball game their sophomore year.

Yes, he was the same. Same mouth with the full bottom lip. Same square jaw. But there was one difference....

"What's this?" she asked, tapping his chin. She had the strangest, strongest urge to leave her fingertips there, to trail them across his dark whiskers, to rub the thick, triangular patch just below his lower lip.

She dropped her hand back to his shoulder.

He stroked his thumb and forefinger across his neatly trimmed mustache and goatee. "Chicks dig it."

"No doubt."

Then again, females of all ages dug the Montesano men. James may not have Leo's panty-melting looks or Eddie's sexy intensity, but he was handsome, kind and when you were with him, he listened—really listened—instead of patting your head or giving you unwanted advice. A woman could trust him—with her thoughts, her secrets and her heart. He was sweet. Safe.

A good catch, her mother had deemed him way back when he'd been fifteen.

She'd been right. Irene Ellison was always right. It was her third most-annoying trait.

"You've never had facial hair before," Sadie said, musing aloud. "I mean, other than that scraggly thing you tried to pass off as a mustache when you turned eighteen."

He smiled, one of his easy, warm grins. The whiskers may be new, somehow making him seem harder, edgier than he truly was, but inside, where it mattered, he hadn't changed.

And thank God for that.

"It might have been a little…patchy."

"Patchy? It looked like you'd taped a molting caterpillar to your upper lip."

He shrugged, the movement causing his chest to rise and fall against her inner arms. Tingles of heat pricked her chilled skin.

She stepped back. "I sure missed you, pal o' mine."

"I missed you, too. Though I'd miss you more if

you didn't bring mayhem with you every time you came back to town."

"You know what they say. One person's mayhem is another's good time."

"No one says that."

"They should. Think I could get it trademarked? I'd make a killing with needlepoint samplers."

"I thought you were going to make a killing selling organic beauty products."

Heat crawled up her neck. Thank goodness it was too dark for him to see her blush. "Surprisingly, there wasn't as big a market for them as I'd hoped."

And, if she was honest with herself—something she tried very hard to avoid—her products weren't good enough to be competitive in an already very competitive market. It'd been a whim, one of many she'd followed through on.

"That is surprising," James said mildly. Bless him, he never bad-mouthed her ideas or told her they wouldn't work. "So, what brings you to town?"

"I didn't want to miss your birthday."

"You've missed plenty in the past fifteen years."

"But I couldn't miss this year. Such a special milestone."

"Yes. Turning thirty-four is very significant for most people." He crossed his arms, the movement pulling his shirt open at the neck, showing a sprinkling of dark chest hair, the strong line of his throat. "What's wrong?"

"What makes you think anything's wrong?"

"Because you're standing in front of me, wet, muddy and bedraggled—"

"Ooh…breaking out the big-boy words. I'm so proud."

"—which I'm going to guess means you're flat broke, unemployed or without prospects. Or all of the above. No offense," he added.

"None taken."

How could she when he'd pretty much summed up her situation? And quite succinctly, too.

At least he wouldn't hold any of those items against her.

"Actually," she continued, "I prefer to think of it as financially challenged, between jobs and open to life's many possibilities."

"To each their own." He stepped closer, gave her one of his searching looks, as if he could see inside her head. Too bad she didn't let anyone, not even her best buddy, get that close to her. "What can I do to help?"

Those damn tears were back. Here she was, slinking into Shady Grove with her tail and her failure tucked firmly between her legs. But with James, there were no recriminations or smirky looks—oh, man, she really hated those smirky, I-expected-so-much-more-from-you looks.

Her mother was an ace at them.

He didn't list all the many, and varied, ways Sadie had gone wrong in her life—conveniently forgetting the times she'd been successful. Didn't insist she'd be happy and fulfilled only if she stopped chasing foolish dreams and married some dentist or lawyer, birthed two-point-five kids and spent the rest of her days locked in a three-thousand-square-foot Cape Cod house, complete with inground pool, gourmet kitchen and white picket fence. He didn't expect her to stay in Shady Grove.

Didn't expect her to follow in her mother's footsteps.

Irene had given up her freedom for security. She'd traded in spontaneity and excitement for schedules and monotony, had tossed aside her independence for a life of entitlement, one she hadn't even earned. She'd settled.

Sadie never would. She had too much of her father in her. Would rather die than to be…ordinary.

And James knew it. He knew her, better than anyone.

She squeezed his forearm. "Thanks, but right now, all I want to do is get into some dry clothes, have a huge piece of your birthday cake and then drown my sorrows with a bottle of wine."

"I think we can manage that."

"I'll get my bag." As she passed the passenger side, Elvis, previously lying across both front seats—the better to spread his muddy paw prints around—sat up, his ears perked. Sadie let him out and he raced to the front of the Jeep, his body vibrating. He barked three times, sounding like some vicious beast ready to tear a man's arm off and use it as a chew toy, then sniffed the ground, lifted his leg and peed on her front tire.

James blinked. "There was a dog in your car."

"Sherlock Holmes has nothing on your deductive powers."

"You got a dog?" he asked, sounding as shocked as if she'd hog-tied good old Sherlock and painted his toenails bright pink.

The strap of her bag slung over her shoulder, she shut the rear passenger-side door. "Sort of."

"Is that like when you *sort of* had a job as Bill Gates's personal assistant?"

"I told you, Bill and I had a real moment at that restaurant. We clicked." She linked her hands together to show her and Bill's connection. "He probably misplaced my number, that's all."

James's snort made her think he didn't believe her.

"I never pictured you with a pet, especially one that big."

"He's not technically mine. I found him."

"What do you mean, you found him?"

"I'm not sure how to make that statement clearer. He was in the middle of the road, I swerved to avoid hitting him, hit that stupid sign then went back and found him on the side of the road."

"You went back to rescue a stray dog? By yourself?" James asked, incredulous. Worried. Well, it was one of the things he did best. "What if he was rabid?"

She and Elvis exchanged an amused look—okay, so it was definitely amused on her end. As if he'd understood every word they'd said, Elvis hung his head and slunk over to James, where he sat and lifted his paw quite adorably.

"Yes," she said, her tone all sorts of wry, "clearly he's the next Cujo."

But James didn't hear her, he was too busy shaking Elvis's paw with one hand, petting him with the other as he murmured to the dog about what a good boy he was, how smart.

"Aww…there's nothing quite as heartwarming as a boy and his dog," Sadie said.

"No."

She blinked innocently at him. No one did innocent like she did—even if she had to say so herself. "What?"

"I'm not taking him off your hands. I already have a dog." He straightened. "Unlike this one, she's never pissed on anyone's tire and she doesn't stink. And don't try to tell me you got him for me for my birthday."

Shoot. That had been her next tactic.

See? That was the problem with someone knowing you so well. No sense of surprise. "So you won't take him in, raise him as one of your own," she said.

"That about sums it up."

"But you will help me find out if someone is searching for him?"

He kept silent, as if he was thinking that one over.

Silly man. Didn't he realize she knew him just as well as he knew her?

Which was how she knew he was going to agree even before he nodded.

Grinning, she linked her arm with his, hugged it close to her side. "I knew I could count on you." Always. Forever. "Come on. Let's go see about that cake."

JAMES GLANCED AT his phone. By his calculations, Sadie had been back in his life for approximately twenty minutes and he'd already agreed to help her with her latest problem. Which meant he'd be taking on the responsibility of finding the damn dog's owners. Twenty minutes. Must be some sort of record. Leo was right. He was a sucker.

He never could refuse Sadie anything.

It was his cross to bear, his greatest weakness.

She was his greatest weakness.

He stopped just inside the doorway to his parents' room, flipped on the four recessed lights in the vaulted ceiling, casting the room in a soft glow. The walls, a deep olive green, were offset by low-pile beige carpet and white trim. Filmy, tan curtains with splashes of darker brown hung open, leaving a clear view of the crescent moon trying to break through the clouds, the hills a dark shadow in the distance.

Sadie pressed against his back. "You sure your mom doesn't mind me hopping in the shower?" she asked, her breath washing over the sensitive skin at the side of his neck.

He made the mistake of glancing at her. Damn it, she wasn't beautiful, not classically so, anyway—her chin was too narrow, her cheeks too wide, her nose on the thin side. But if you put all the elements together—her mouth with its sharp cupid's bow, her milky-white complexion and ice-blue eyes—she was more than lovely. More than just another pretty blonde.

She was stunning. Effervescent and sparkling, like the finest champagne.

And like champagne, if you weren't careful, you could get drunk on her.

His hands fisted. Need for her was like an itch between his shoulder blades. One he couldn't reach, couldn't rid himself of no matter how hard he tried.

Story of his goddamn life.

He forced his fingers open and stepped forward. "It's fine."

Hesitating at the door, looking unsure and vulnerable—neither of which suited her—she rolled her eyes. "It didn't seem fine."

True. His mother had been less than welcoming and gracious—both of which were unlike her. "She's probably just tired. Plus she's stressed about her classes starting next week."

"Classes?"

He crossed to the antique, marble-topped table his mom used as a nightstand and turned on the lamp. Better, but the room still seemed too cozy. Too intimate.

He blamed the king-size bed.

"Mom's going to attend Seton Hill part-time."

The Catholic university was one of a dozen or so colleges located in Pittsburgh, a forty-minute drive from Shady Grove.

Sadie finally stepped into the room. "Yeah? That's great. You must be really proud of her."

He was. Of course he was. If his mom wanted to get a college degree, to pursue a career in social work, then he was all for it. But it would mean changes. Adjustments. Not to their family life as much as to Montesano Construction. From the time Frank had started the company, Rose had managed the office. She planned on continuing in that capacity while she earned her degree part-time, but eventually, she'd leave to follow her newly formed dream.

It just proved you were never too old to change course.

Though James was too firmly entrenched—in his life, his father's business, his place in his family—to even think about changing his.

Why would he? he thought, flipping on the light on the tall dresser, then the one on the round table in the seating area. He was right where he was meant to be, working a job he was good at and enjoyed, surrounded by family and friends he loved.

He was content.

And how many people could truly say that?

"Shower's this way," he said, walking into the large bathroom, Sadie following.

"Oh, dear, sweet Lord," Sadie breathed. She turned in a slow circle, her eyes wide as she took in the room. Dark woodwork, free-standing sinks on Italian marble, a separate area for the toilet, large whirlpool tub and walk-in shower. Not to mention the heated tiles beneath their feet and a closet the size of most bedrooms.

James grinned. It was one hell of a room, one of Montesano's best. They'd redone his parents' master suite five or so years ago, completely gutting what had been a utilitarian bathroom and turning it into what his mother deemed her oasis.

Women and bathrooms. He may not completely understand why they went so crazy over them, but he could appreciate their enthusiasm over a well-designed room.

He leaned against the vanity as Sadie opened the door leading to the closet and peeked in at his parents' clothes. She'd slipped off her sandals downstairs, had mud splattered across her bare, narrow feet and up her calves. Her bright orange top—one of those wide-necked ones with flowing sleeves that reminded him of something a gypsy would wear—was wrinkled, her yellow pants ruined.

She was a mess. A walking disaster.

She'd grown her hair out from the short bob it'd been three years ago. It reached past her shoulders, the wheat-colored strands streaked with thin stripes of pale blond. But even with it frizzing to twice its normal size, and mascara smudged under her eyes, she was the most beautiful thing he'd ever seen.

For the past twenty years, he'd been wishing like hell that she wasn't.

Sadie pressed her nose against the glass-encased, walk-in shower.

"Did you just whimper?" he asked.

"It has three showerheads," she said, turning her head to the side, her arms wide as if giving the shower a hug. "Three. It deserves a good whimper. Maybe even a moan or two. And this…" She stepped to the side, sat on the edge of the tub. "It's huge. Big enough for a small family. Or a large dog."

"Not going to happen."

"What's not?"

"You giving that dog a bath in my mother's tub."

After drying him off, they'd left Elvis in the garage with blankets and a bowl of water and a plate of roast beef Rose had given them.

"What is this world coming to?" Sadie asked, setting her bag on the floor. She bent to dig through it, her long hair falling forward, her top gaping, giving him a glimpse of her lacy, white bra, the curve of her breast. "It's so a person can't even *think* about something without getting shot down."

Straightening, James jerked his gaze up. "Trust me," he muttered. "Some thoughts are better nipped in the bud before they can fully form. Besides, you

can give the dog a bath when we get to my place."
He pretended great interest in rearranging the hand
towel on the pewter ring next to the sink. "You have
any idea how long you'll be in town?"

She set a pile of clothes at the end of the counter.
"I'm not sure. A couple of weeks? Maybe a month.
But no longer than that," she added firmly.

A chill swept through him. A month?

Aw, hell.

As they'd gotten Elvis set up in the garage, Sadie
had asked if she could bunk with James. She often
stayed at his place, preferring it over going home to
her parents' house—she and her mother got along
better if they weren't in constant contact with each
other. But usually, Sadie's trips home were a few
days, a week at the most. Now he was stuck with
her for only God knew how long.

Stuck with having her underfoot. With her warm
smiles and nonstop chatter and the way she hummed
all the freaking time. With her floral scent following him from room to room, with her barefoot in his
kitchen, using every clean dish he had just to make
scrambled eggs and toast, her lithe body in nothing
but a tank top and shorts.

He'd be insane in two days. Three, tops.

Something major must have happened to have
her staying in Shady Grove for so long. He'd suspected that out in the driveway when she'd clung
to him. Sadie wasn't the clinging type. She didn't

let mistakes or failures slow her down, let alone get her down.

He wanted to ask again what was going on with her, but he'd wait. He had a party to get back to and she was wet and probably cold, though she hadn't complained. There would be plenty of time for her to tell him what was wrong. Why she'd come back.

If she meant what she'd said about staying for a month, there would be plenty of time for him, too. Time for him to get used to having her around again. And to prepare himself for when she left.

He stepped to the door, held on to the handle. "I'll let you get cleaned up. Towels are in there," he said, nodding toward the narrow linen closet to his left. "Let me know if you need anything else."

She stopped him with a hand to his forearm, her long fingers cold, her short nails painted a sparkly dark blue. "Thanks, James. For everything. I don't know what I'd do without you," she said, her voice soft and unsteady, her gaze sincere. "You're a good guy and a really good friend."

Unable to speak, he nodded, forcing his lips into the semblance of a grin. It wasn't until he'd slipped into the bedroom and shut the bathroom door behind him that he let his mouth flatten. He tipped his head back and exhaled heavily.

A good friend. That was all he'd ever been to her. All he ever would be.

It was his own damn fault he wanted so much more.

CHAPTER THREE

CHARLOTTE ELLISON HAD a life plan.

She'd thought this through in its entirety, had weighed the pros and cons, dissected each aspect, considered all the consequences and any and every possible outcome. This wasn't some flighty whim of fancy or a childish fantasy. This was real. Important. Possibly the most important thing she'd ever done.

She applied soft brown eyeliner in the small bathroom off the Montesanos' kitchen, capped the liner and tossed it into her small makeup bag. Leaning over the sink, she swiped on mascara. She was nothing if not pragmatic. Realistic. Centered and grounded. From the time she was sixteen she'd known exactly what she'd wanted out of life. She'd written it down, then had broken those goals into smaller, manageable steps—just like all the gurus preached. Over the years she'd changed or adjusted those steps accordingly.

She'd already achieved so much. Valedictorian of her high school class? Check. Admitted to the University of Pittsburgh's school of nursing, graduate at the top of that class and gain employment at Shady

Grove Memorial? Check, check and check. Buy her dream home by the time she was twenty-five? She had her eye on an adorable 1920s cottage that had an awesome kitchen, a view of the river and plenty of potential for the extra bedrooms and playroom she'd need once she had her three kids.

A boy and two girls—God willing—all twenty to twenty-four months apart, the first coming along sometime between Char's thirtieth and thirty-second birthday.

She slicked on a pale peach gloss, rubbed her lips together. Straightened to study her reflection. Sighed. There wasn't much she could do about the sprinkling of freckles on her nose and across her upper cheeks, the ones that went with hair that was as bright red as her father's.

The ones that had doomed her to a life of being cute and adorable when all she'd ever wanted was to be sexy and beautiful.

And her hair—dear, sweet Lord, her hair—could have used some serious time with a heavy-duty conditioner, blow dryer and flat iron. That was what she got for coming here straight from work. After a ten-hour shift and that summer storm, the smooth waves it'd taken her an hour to achieve that morning were now back to their original form. Wild, springy, frizzy curls.

She would pull the whole mess into a ponytail except, call her crazy, she didn't think passing for a sixteen-year-old would help her cause.

At least the rest was acceptable.

Her favorite dark jeans made her legs seem endless, and the emerald-green top she'd splurged on last summer, but had never worn until now, brought out her eyes and clung in all the right places, making it seem as if she actually had a curve here and there. Not an easy feat.

Twisting, she rose onto her toes and checked out her butt. Pursed her lips. Not bad. Not bad at all. Possibly even better than top-notch.

Resolutely turning away from the mirror, she dropped her lipstick into her purse before opening the door and stepping into the short hallway. Voices, laughter and music drifted to her from the living and dining rooms. She turned right, away from the party and majority of people, her back straight, head held high, steps determined.

She was on a mission here. Because while she fully realized some things were out of her control, there was still plenty she could do to make her dreams come true. And if she wanted to be married by the time she turned twenty-seven—after a year of dating and a two-year engagement, thereby enabling her plenty of time to plan the perfect wedding—she needed to get a move on.

And let the man of her dreams know she was interested, available and, most important, ready to be in a serious, long-term relationship.

The first thing Char had done when she'd arrived was to seek out Rose Montesano—best to get on her future mother-in-law's good side right from the start. When Char had heard that her prey was in the kitchen with his brother, she'd quickly excused herself to freshen up.

She was as ready as she'd ever be. Had psyched herself up about this ever since she'd received the party invitation two weeks ago. In mere minutes, what was destined to be a lifelong love affair would have its beginning.

Her steps slowed. She pressed a hand against her roiling stomach. There was no need to be nervous. No need at all. All she had to do was walk into the kitchen. Make idle chitchat. It wasn't as if she'd never spoken to the man before. They'd had plenty of conversations, had known each other for, well, her entire life, practically.

Char rubbed her fingertips against her palms. Inhaled a deep, calming breath, blew it—and all the tension and worry she held—out.

Sending up a prayer she would be successful, she stepped up to the doorway.

James and Leo Montesano were the only two inside. Could she really be blamed if she stood there, just out of sight, and took in the sight of two tall, dark, handsome men? If her heart sighed at knowing one would, soon enough, be hers?

They both had on jeans, but while James was dressed for the party in a blue button-down shirt, Leo had on a black V-neck T-shirt that clung to his muscular frame. James leaned against the counter near the stove, his arms straight, his fingers curled around the curved edge. At the sink, Leo—tall, broad-shouldered and handsome as sin with his floppy dark hair and sexy grin—was up to his elbows in soapy water. James said something and smiled as Leo laughed, the sound deep, masculine and enticing as all get-out.

Warmth bloomed in her chest. Glancing up, she mouthed *thank you* for her prayer about to be answered.

"Need any help?" she asked, making sure her voice was light and bright.

Both men glanced over. And being pinned with those dark eyes made her mouth go dry.

"Hey there, gorgeous," Leo said, rinsing a large tray under the running water at the sink. "How do you feel about washing dishes?"

Char smiled widely—the better to show the dimple in her left cheek to its full potential. "I've got nothing against it."

Leo gave a masculine whoop, quickly dried his hands on the towel tucked into his waistband and crossed to her in a few long strides. Before she realized what was happening, he wrapped his arms around her waist, lifted her as if she weighed no more than a five-year-old and spun her around. Laughing, she gripped his shoulders, the muscles bunching and flexing under her hands.

"You're an angel," he said in his husky voice. "The answer to my prayers. A—"

"Guest," James finished. He scowled. "Quit twirling her around like a rag doll and stop trying to weasel your way out of your chore."

Leo stopped and set her back on her feet, but her head still spun. "I don't mind," she said breathlessly.

Leo slung his arm around her shoulders, pressing her against his side. "Yeah, she doesn't mind."

"She might not, but Mom will," James said.

Leo winked at Char as his pager beeped. "Unlike birthday boy here, I'm not afraid of my mother."

"Better come over here," James told her, wrapping his fingers around her upper arm and tugging her to his side as Leo read the pager's screen. "It's only a matter of time before lightning fries his lying ass."

"Three-car accident on Jefferson Street," Leo said, grabbing a set of car keys from the windowsill. "Who's on tonight?"

Char worked in the E.R. and saw Leo, a firefighter and EMT, often. Most firefighters had their favorite and least-favorite doctors. At the bottom of Leo's list, she knew, was Dr. Nathan Hamilton.

Hamilton, an obnoxious, sexist creep, was at the bottom of most people's list, including hers.

"Wertz was there when I left," she said, "but Goldberg is taking the night shift."

Nodding, he slapped James on the back. "Gotta run. Happy birthday, bro." He sent her another devastating grin. Her knees went just a little weak. Hey, she was human after all. "See you around, gorgeous."

"When did you get here?" James asked as Leo went out the back door.

She crossed to the sink. "A few minutes ago."

A few minutes. Twenty minutes. What was the difference? Had he been waiting for her? Looking for her? Could she get that lucky?

"None of that." This time he encircled her wrist and led her to the island. "You are not doing the dishes. Don't let Leo sweet-talk you into...anything. Ever." He squeezed her hand, his touch leaving tingles of sensation against her skin. "Now, let's get you a drink. Wine?"

Since speech was impossible, she nodded. When he turned his back to pour a glass of deep red wine, she rubbed the pad of her thumb over the area where he'd touched her, could have sworn she still felt the heat of his fingers.

"Leo's a flirt," she finally managed to say, "and he doesn't discriminate based on looks, age or marital status. All the women in the E.R. are half in love with him."

He raised his eyebrows. "All?"

Was he jealous? She could only hope. "Maybe not all," she said huskily, sending him a look from under her lashes.

"Good." He handed her the wine, didn't seem to notice her sexy tone or seductive look. She would have to work on them. "You're way too good for my brother. Don't ever forget that."

She wanted to giggle like a schoolgirl. Wanted to swear to James—as in, cross her heart and hope to die—that she had absolutely zero interest in becoming the next woman to warm Leo's bed. "I won't."

It was an easy enough promise to make. Sure, Leo had that whole charming, playboy thing going on, and he resembled a Roman god with his sharply chiseled face and dark eyes. But he wasn't the kind of man a woman could count on. Wasn't the type of man Char wanted to spend the rest of her life with. She wanted a husband who was smart and responsible and successful. A man who would be there for her and their kids, who would be committed to his own career and supportive of hers, and active in the community they both loved.

James Montesano was going to make the perfect husband.

"I hear you're looking to buy a place of your own," he said.

She sipped her wine, hid a grimace. Yuck. She couldn't stand the stuff. No matter what kind she tried, it always tasted like cough syrup. But if James drank wine, then she'd drink it.

And wish it was a beer instead.

"I've had enough of renting. It's time I had something that's mine, you know? A home, not just an apartment where I happen to sleep. And with

Jenn getting married next spring, it seems like the right time."

"Your roommate's getting married? Isn't she a little young?"

"She's my age, so not so young."

"Your age is plenty young," he said, as if he was ancient.

Char pretended to take another drink. She'd wondered if the age difference would bother him. While she couldn't say it thrilled her to have him think she was *a little young,* at least she now knew where she stood. And knowing was half the battle.

"You sound like Daddy." As she'd hoped, he frowned at being compared to a middle-aged man. Good. Maybe that would help him realize he was still in the prime of his life. And having a wife ten years younger would only help keep him young.

"He wants me to move back home," she continued, "which is so not going to happen." Holding her glass with two hands, she let out a very put-upon-sounding sigh. "I just wish it wasn't so hard finding a decent house. The last two I looked at in my price range were horrendous. I swear, I thought they were going to fall down around my ears. Luckily, I found one I think will work, but I have no idea if it's worth the asking price or how much I'll have to put into it. The real-estate agent said it needed a new roof, but what if there are other problems, ones that aren't as easy to spot? The building inspector said he couldn't get to it for at least a month and there's no sense asking my dad." She gave an exaggerated eye roll. "He's no help whatsoever."

"Tell you what," James said, glancing at the doorway as if looking for someone, "why don't I check the house out for you?"

Triumph flashed, hot and heady, inside her. That was easy.

The heavens really were on her side.

Still, she injected the right amount of hesitation in her voice when she said, "Oh, I couldn't ask you to do that...."

"I'm offering."

She nibbled on her lower lip. "Well, if you're sure you don't mind...I'll take you up on it. This Friday work for you? Say, six?"

She held her breath while he took out his phone, checked his schedule. "Friday it is."

"Great." Taking her courage in hand, she stepped closer, touched his forearm. "Thanks."

"No problem," he said, patting her fingers.

Their gazes met, and though she hadn't planned on their first kiss taking place so soon in their relationship, she couldn't pass up this perfect, breathless moment. All she had to do was let him know he could take the initiative. But how? Maybe if she slid her hand up to his bicep, rose onto her toes, he'd lean down and—

"Lottie!"

Startled, feeling as if she'd been caught molesting the poor man, Char whirled around. Blinked.

"Sadie? Sadie!" she repeated and, with a laugh, ran to envelop her sister in a hug, keeping to herself how much Sadie had sounded like their mother. "What are you doing here?"

Sadie rocked them both from side to side then leaned back and held Charlotte by her upper arms. "It's so good to see you. Oh, my God, you're so grown up!"

Char glanced at James as her face warmed. Curse her fair complexion. At least the blush would camouflage her freckles. "I've been a grown-up for six years now."

"Yes, but now you look like an adult instead of a college coed. And this is the first time I've seen you live and in person since you flew down to visit me in Memphis. That was what...two years ago?"

"Two and a half." Though they did text almost daily and video chat once every few weeks. "Come home more than once every few years and my turning into an adult won't be such a shock."

Sadie waved that away. "I'm here now."

Yes, but for how long? She wouldn't ask. Lord knew Sadie didn't share Char's love of plans, schedules and goals. "Why didn't you tell me you were coming?"

"It was a spur-of-the-moment decision."

"Naturally." All of her carefree older sister's decisions were spur-of-the-moment. "Did you know?" Char asked James.

He shook his head. "Not until an hour ago when

she showed up in the driveway covered head-to-toe in mud with a dog in her front seat."

Char laughed. "Oh, I have got to hear this story."

She hugged Sadie again. Her sister was home and Char had taken those first, all-important steps in her plans to get James Montesano to fall in love with her.

Best. Night. Ever.

THE NIGHT WOULDN'T end.

Not that it was a bad party, Sadie thought as she let cold dishwater out of the kitchen sink. She just wasn't in the mood for the whole celebration thing and the act that went with it. She'd played her part, though. No sense disappointing anyone or, God forbid, have them asking her questions about what was wrong, what was going on with her. So she'd made the rounds, flitted from group to group, bringing laughter and making a good time even better.

She was, after all, the life of any party.

Just like her father.

She wondered if it had ever worn him out.

"Sadie," Rose said as she came into the kitchen, her tone less than friendly. She set down the almost empty fruit-and-cheese platter on the island. "You don't have to do that."

Sadie wiped out the sink then turned the water on hot. "It's no problem."

"Don't be silly," Rose said, smiling tightly. "Go back to the party. Enjoy yourself."

If Sadie didn't know better, she'd think Rose was trying to get rid of her. "Really. It's okay. I want to help."

"I insist."

And to go along with her insistence, Rose snatched the bottle of dish soap from Sadie's hand.

Sadie raised her eyebrows. She could go back, she supposed, as Rose nudged her aside and squirted soap under the water. The party was winding down, but there were still quite a few guests milling about.

That was the problem. She didn't want to entertain people. Didn't want to be friendly. Didn't want to try to charm everyone, entertain them all with more stories of her adventures. She wanted to stay here, right here. She wanted to hide.

And that was the ultimate sin for someone who was always, always the belle of any ball.

"I realize you don't need any help, but do you...?" She cleared her throat. Tried again, this time adding a pleasant grin so Rose wouldn't see her true intentions. "Would you mind if I stayed in here anyway?"

Rose stared at her as if she'd asked if she could strip naked and roll around in the leftover cake.

Not that that was a bad idea. It was really, really good cake.

"You want to stay in the kitchen," Rose said, studying her much the same way James often did. Trying to look into people's souls must be a family trait. "You do realize there's a party going on outside of this room?"

"I guess I'm just tired." Yeah, tired of explaining how her latest idea had tanked and that she had big plans once she was back on her feet again. Of pretending her life was going exactly how she wanted. Of feeling as if every person she'd spoken with had more going for them than she did—careers and spouses, kids and contentment.

She snorted softly. As if she'd want any of those things. Okay, maybe the career wouldn't be too bad, but only if it was one that let her come and go as she pleased. One that didn't tie her to a desk in some closed-off office in a town where the most exciting thing to happen was when the local high school football team made the state playoffs.

One where she had the freedom to be herself, to live life on her own terms instead of blindly following the expectations of others. Where she could breathe.

One that wasn't Shady Grove.

"I could dry," Sadie offered when Rose remained silent.

Not looking too thrilled with that prospect, she nonetheless handed Sadie a clean towel.

The window above the sink was open, bringing in a crisp breeze. Shutting her eyes, Sadie inhaled deeply and held it, held in the scents of wet grass and fresh, clean air. "I love how it smells after a summer rain. Like everything's been wiped clean."

Like anything was possible.

Rose made a noncommittal sound.

"I can't believe how big Max has gotten," Sadie said of Eddie's son as she accepted a dish from Rose. "What is he now? Five?"

"Seven."

"It seems like just yesterday he was a baby."

"Yes, well, you've been gone a few years now. Things tend to change. Children grow. People get older."

"I'm getting older, too," Sadie sang, but her "Landslide" reference fell to the ground with a resounding splat. "Sorry. I can never resist a chance to do my Stevie Nicks impersonation." Nothing. Not even the faintest hint of a smile, no glimmer of humor lit Rose's hazel eyes. "Uh…James, he, uh…" Sadie set the plate on the counter, took the next clean one. "Mentioned you're going back to school."

"Yes."

"That's so great. Really great. What are you taking up?"

Rose sighed, as if dealing with Sadie was more than one person could handle. "Human services."

"Wow, that's—"

"Great," Rose interrupted, rinsing another dish. "So you've said."

Okay. James was right. His mom really was stressed.

And grumpy, too.

Zoe padded into the room, crossed to Sadie and nudged her legs. Sadie slung the towel over her shoulder and kneeled to take the dog's face in her hands. "Hey, there, beautiful. Did you have fun playing with your new boyfriend?"

Almost immediately after James had first introduced Zoe to Elvis, the two dogs had fallen in love with each other.

"I'm glad you two are getting along so well," Sadie continued. "And I promise, while we're at your house, I won't let him eat out of your food bowl or sleep in your bed."

Rose inhaled sharply. "Are you…are you staying with James?"

"It's so much easier," Sadie said, washing her hands. "I hate to impose on my mom and Will—they're used to being empty nesters." Not that her mother and stepfather would complain about having Sadie there. They would probably love it. But it reminded her too much of when she'd been young, of how her life had taken a sudden turn after her father's death. Of how close she'd come to losing herself.

Like her mother had lost herself.

Sadie took a hold of the serving bowl Rose held out. "Plus, with Will's allergies, there's no way I could bring Elvis there. And there's barely room for Lottie and her roommate in that cramped apartment, so I asked James to put me up for a little while."

Rose looked as if she'd sucked a lemon then chased it with a shot of drain cleaner. And she still hadn't let go of the bowl. "How long is a little while?"

Sadie frowned, considered yanking on the damn thing, but resisted. Barely. "A few weeks or so."

Rose shut her eyes. "Lovely," she murmured.

"Is that a problem?"

"Why would it be?" As if realizing she was in a subtle tug-of-war, Rose let go of the bowl. "Like you said, it's only a few weeks. And then you'll be off again."

At least that thought seemed to cheer her up.

Sadie hummed "Landslide"—now that it was stuck in her head, resistance was futile—and stared blindly out the window. Luckily, the storm had dissipated almost as quickly as it had formed. After the last of the rain, the clouds had shifted, blowing away to find some other poor town to soak. Best of all, only three people had called her Cyclone Sadie.

One of them being her sister, so that didn't even really count.

Frank and Rose's house sat back from the road on top of a small knoll. Frank's father, Leo—or Big Leo as he was known to family and friends—occupied the small cottage on the corner of the property. James's only sister, Maddie, lived with her daughter across the street. Even Eddie lived on the street, though a block away, while Leo had an apartment two streets over.

Only James had separated himself from his family, choosing to build his house on the outskirts of town.

As if conjuring him out of thin air, Sadie heard

the familiar deep tone of his laugh moments before he stepped into the soft glow of the lanterns spread across each tier of the deck. Smiling—she'd always loved the sound of his laugh—she opened her mouth, ready to call out to him only to have the sound die in her throat when she realized the reason he was so jolly. He was with someone. A woman. An attractive woman in a deep blue wrap dress that showcased her curvaceous body and killer legs. A dress that made Sadie feel decidedly underdressed in her floor-length, multicolored skirt and black tank top.

They stopped next to an SUV, one of the few vehicles that had circumvented the traffic jam in the driveway by parking in the yard near the back corner of the house. James said something that had the brunette smiling and swatting his arm, her hand lingering there longer than necessary.

"Eddie's heading home," Frank said as he came into the kitchen. In khakis and a green polo, he was still as trim and fit as when Sadie had first met him as a child, the only signs of age a few lines around his brown eyes and a liberal sprinkling of gray in his short dark hair. "He's going to drop Dad off on his way."

"Are Maddie and Bree still here?" Rose asked.

"They're saying good-night to Gerry and Carl. It was nice of you to invite them."

"They are almost family."

"Almost." He came up behind his wife and kissed

the side of her neck. "You outdid yourself, Rosie. As usual."

She tipped her head to the side so that it pressed against his. "Thank you. I think James enjoyed himself."

"He seems to be enjoying himself now," Sadie murmured, wondering at the bite to her tone, the tightness in her chest.

Rose and Frank both followed her gaze out the window. The brunette had her head close to James's, said something as he typed on his phone.

Putting her number into his contact list.

Sadie cleared her throat. "I don't recognize her. Is she a friend of Maddie's?"

"That's Anne Forbes. She works for a local painting contractor," Frank said, picking up a clean towel and drying the next dish. Raising his bushy eyebrows, he nudged Rose with his elbow. "You must be pretty pleased with yourself."

"You know I hate to brag," Rose said. "But since you mention it, yes. Yes, I am." She glanced at Sadie. "Very pleased."

"Is this one of those family secrets?" Sadie asked, forcing her tone to lighten, her lips to curve.

"No secret. Rose here decided to take matters into her own hands and find our eldest a wife."

Sadie's scalp prickled. Her hands tightened on the towel, twisting the fabric until her fingers went numb. "A wife?"

"No one's booked St. Theresa's for a wedding

mass yet," Rose said drily. "I just thought he might be interested in meeting a lovely, intelligent woman."

"As opposed to the ugly, stupid women he's usually interested in meeting?" Frank asked.

"Well, he did go out with Melissa Alden," Sadie said, glad her voice had returned to normal. "She was cute enough, but dumb as a rock. Then again, James was fourteen and, I believe, hypnotized by the sight of Melissa in her cheerleading outfit."

"Many men have had their better sense stolen by short skirts." Frank winked at Sadie. "How do you think Rose managed to nab me?"

"I'd take exception to that," Rose said, "except it's true. And it worked."

Frank leaned down, whispered something in Rose's ear that had her laughing.

Wanting to give them privacy, Sadie crossed to a different window, looked out as James opened the door to the SUV. Anne climbed into the driver's seat, her dark, straight hair swinging above her shoulders. She really was lovely. Sadie had seen her earlier in the living room when she'd been chatting with Maddie and Big Leo. Sadie had envied the other woman's red, open-toed shoes, the way her side-swept bangs fell perfectly.

Sadie lifted her hand to her own hair, tucked an errant curl back into the messy bun at the top of her head.

James shut the SUV's door and Anne turned on the ignition. A moment later, she backed up then pulled forward. James watched as she drove alongside the driveway.

So, James had met someone. Sadie rolled her eyes. Obviously he'd met Anne, but they'd exchanged numbers. Had maybe even made plans to meet for drinks. Or dinner.

A date.

Good for him. Maybe it would work out and he and Anne would fall in love, get married, have a couple of little Montesanos, kids who had James's easy grin, his love of schedules and his anal tendencies. There was no one more suited for marriage and family life than James. He deserved to get everything he wanted. Deserved to be happy.

Hadn't Sadie always known he'd find someone? It might not be Anne, but eventually he'd meet a woman he could love and spend the rest of his life with. And when he found that woman, it would mean the end of Sadie's relationship with James.

Oh, sure, they would always be friends, but things would change between them. How could they not? No longer would she be able to stay at his house when she returned to town. She'd have to stop calling him whenever she wanted, night or day, just because she wanted to hear the sound of his voice. Because she'd missed him.

No longer would she be first in his life. That spot would belong to his wife, his family, the way it was supposed to.

He wouldn't need her at all. He'd have what he'd always wanted.

And she'd be left alone.

CHAPTER FOUR

JAMES SANK ONTO a lounge chair on the deck, opened his bottle of water and took a long drink. He wanted to get home. Though tomorrow—he checked his phone's clock—though *today* was Sunday, he still had to work. He needed to finish that estimate for the Websters' addition, catch up on some billing and put in a few hours working on the design for Mrs. Kline's kitchen.

The door opened and Maddie, the youngest Montesano sibling and only girl, sauntered onto the deck, followed by her eleven-year-old daughter, Bree. Zoe, lying at James's feet, rose and walked over to Bree.

"I thought you left ten minutes ago," Maddie said to him.

"I'm waiting for Sadie." It seemed as if he'd spent his entire life waiting for Sadie. "She wanted to double-check if Mom needed any more help cleaning up."

He wanted to follow her back to his place in case there was more damage to the Jeep than they initially thought.

"God help her." Maddie glanced through the

door's window, her white summer dress like a beacon in the dim light. "We're heading out before Mom can give us something more to do."

"We waited until Nonna went into the living room and then snuck out," Bree whispered excitedly, her hand on Zoe's head. "Poppa kept watch."

James pulled her down beside him and put his arm around her shoulders. "You're taking your lives in your hands doing that."

"Desperate times, my friend," Maddie said. "You know how she gets after a party."

"Crazy," Bree said solemnly.

He squeezed her. "That's my girl."

"When I told her I'd come back in the morning to run the vacuum, I thought her head was going to explode. And that I would have to clean that up, too." Maddie shook her head. "I think this school thing really has her freaked out."

"She'll work through it."

"I know. But it's tough when she's the one we can always trust to be practical and responsible. Well, other than you, that is."

"You make practicality and responsibility sound like negative traits."

"Did I?" she asked sweetly. "So sorry."

She wasn't. She was rarely sorry, even when she knew damn well she was to blame. And there wasn't much sweet about her, either. Growing up with three older brothers had made her tough as nails. Her stubbornness, competiveness and bordering-onobsessive need to prove she was equal to the men in her family in every way was due to the prickly, pugnacious personality she'd been born with.

Was it any wonder they all adored her?

Maddie tugged Bree to her feet. "Come on, kiddo. Let's get out of here before Nonna realizes we've escaped." When James stood as well, Maddie hugged him. "Happy birthday."

"Thanks."

She stepped back and Bree moved into his arms. "Happy birthday, Uncle James."

He held her close. She was a shorter, rounder version of her mother with her tanned skin, dark hair and heavy eyebrows. He pressed a kiss to the top of her head, surprised to realize she now reached the middle of his chest.

When the hell did that happen? *How* did it happen?

It seemed like just yesterday she'd had pigtails and a wide, empty space in her smile where her two front teeth used to be. Those teeth had long ago come in, and she'd traded in the pigtails for a supershort pixie cut that accentuated the fullness of her face. But that would change soon, too. She'd get taller. Thin out. Grow up.

But she still smelled like a little girl, like clean sweat and baby powder. She still hugged him fiercely as if she never wanted to let go.

Love for her swamped him and he hoped she never did let go.

"Hey," he said, leaning away so he could look down into her pretty face. "How about on Tuesday we go to that new bakery that opened up downtown?"

She stepped back, sent her mom a worried look. "Tuesday?"

"That's the first day of school, right?" He pulled out his phone. He could have sworn he'd made a note that school started on the twenty-fourth.

"Yes," she said slowly, sidling closer to Maddie, "that's the first day, but—"

"Or we can stick with Rix's Diner if that's what you'd prefer. What?" he asked when he realized they were both staring at him, Bree rubbing her eyebrow, a sure sign she was upset or nervous.

Standing behind her daughter, Maddie placed both hands on Bree's shoulders. "Actually, Neil is coming into town Monday night so he can be here for Bree's first day of seventh grade."

Neil Pettit, NHL star and original Hometown Boy Done Good, was also Bree's father.

"Okay," he said. "What does that—"

"He wants to take her out," Maddie said softly. "He wants to take us both out. You know, start a new tradition."

A new tradition.

Ever since Bree was a precocious, chubby three-year-old preschooler, James had taken her out to breakfast on the first day of school. Every year. It was *their* tradition, one he'd thought meant as much to her as it did to him.

"We could do something else, Uncle James," Bree blurted. "The two of us. Like, start a new tradition."

She looked so worried, he couldn't even get angry she was throwing him a bone. Besides, she was just a kid. A sweet, quiet kid who'd had his heart from the moment he'd first laid eyes on her as a squalling, red-faced infant. Her entire life he'd done his best to be there for her, to fill the void Neil had left when he'd walked out on Maddie twelve years ago.

James had given her time and attention and, in the rare instances she needed it, discipline. For eleven years he'd been the biggest male influence in her life. Had been more of a father to her than her real dad.

Until two months ago when Neil had returned to Shady Grove and decided to be a part of his daughter's life full-time—or as close to it as possible when Neil played for the Seattle Knights and spent half his time on the other side of the country. Though he still had over two years left before his contract with the Knights was up, he'd made his desire to be traded to an East Coast team sooner rather than later clear. It was only a matter of time, and getting the right offer from another team, before the Knights let him go. But even though Neil wasn't with Bree on a day-to-day basis, the results were the same. He was Bree's number-one guy now.

Leaving James to be demoted to favorite uncle.

Change happened. James accepted it, rolled with it.

But that didn't mean he had to like it.

"Sure," he said, trying to smile. To reassure her. "We can do something different. You pick."

"Do I have to decide right now?"

She loved to weigh her options, to take her time and think things through before making any decision, whether it was what kind of ice cream to order or what she thought of the latest book she read. She sure as hell hadn't gotten that from her mother.

"No hurry," he said. "You just let me know whenever you're ready."

"Why don't you wait for me in the truck?" Maddie asked, giving Bree a gentle nudge toward the steps. "I'll be there in a minute."

"Good night," Bree told him.

"'Night."

As soon as Bree was out of earshot, Maddie turned to him. "James, I—"

"It's fine, Maddie. I'm glad Bree is spending more time with her father."

He almost meant it, too.

Sure, he wanted what was best for his niece, and Neil was showing that he could step up and be the kind of attentive, loving father Bree needed. But it changed things.

It changed how much time Bree spent with James, how involved he was in her life.

Not that he could complain about it or even let it get him angry or upset. A good guy, wasn't that what Sadie had labeled him? She wasn't the only one. Usually, he took it as a compliment; he liked being the kind of man people could turn to, someone they could trust. But there were times when doing the right thing was annoying as hell.

The good not only died young, but they also didn't get so much as a day off from other people's expectations. Not even on their freaking birthday.

"Thanks," Maddie whispered. "Really. I know not everyone agrees with me and Neil getting back together, so your support means a lot to me."

"I've always got your back," he told her. "No matter what."

It was what big brothers did. Even if he wasn't sure *support* was the right word for how he felt about her reuniting with her high school boyfriend, the man who'd gotten her pregnant at sixteen and left to pursue a professional hockey career.

But, unlike Leo—who'd never liked Neil—James was keeping his opinions to himself. He would sit back and let events unfold, as he always did. And if things went bad, he would be there to pick up the pieces.

"I appreciate that," Maddie said, giving him another hug.

He sat in the chair, Zoe by his side as they watched Maddie drive down the long, winding driveway and across the street to her own house.

The door opened, but he didn't turn, didn't need to see who was there. He easily recognized the sound of her step, the light, citrusy scent of her perfume.

"I hope you're not still pouting," Sadie said, sitting at the end of his chair.

"I don't pout."

"No? Well, your bottom lip said otherwise." She took the water from him, sipped. Laid her hand on his knee. "It's only a game, James."

Swinging his legs around so they sat side by side, so her hand fell away from his leg, he grabbed his water. "I realize that."

Though having her wipe the pool table with him was humiliating.

But he hadn't pouted, damn it.

"It really shouldn't bother you so much to lose to me. You know no one beats me at eight ball."

"That's why no one else will play you," he reminded her. Not once they learned she'd spent a couple of months in Vegas making her living as a pool shark.

She sighed, as if the entire world was against poor, little ol' her. "I know. It's not fun. I'm just glad I can always count on you."

That went without saying.

Sadie braced her weight on her arms behind her and tipped her face up. Eyes shut, she inhaled deeply, her full breasts rising and falling under her silky tank top.

His throat dried. His fingers twitched with the

need to stroke the long line of her throat, to flick over the pulse beating at the base of her neck. Even when she was still, there was an energy about her, like an electrical current, one pulsating with life.

It called to him, had always called to him, pulling him in, daring him to touch, to feel that zing coursing through his blood, just once.

Tearing his gaze from her, he held his water between his knees, stared at the floor. But he could feel her next to him, the brush of her leg against his outer thigh, the shifting of the seat when she stretched, arching her back. Could hear her soft breathing, the low, melodic tune she hummed softly.

He'd sought her out tonight. He hadn't wanted to, but it seemed no matter where he was, what he was doing, who he was talking to, he couldn't stop from seeking out the sound of her laugh, the sight of her light brown hair. She was like a butterfly in her bright, colorful clothes, in how she fluttered from a conversation with his grandfather about how to make a foolproof marinara sauce to entertaining a group with tales about tending bar in the French Quarter to coaxing his seven-year-old nephew to dance.

She captivated him. He wondered if he would ever get free.

"You ready to go?" he asked, his voice gruff.

She sat up. "Sure."

They walked down the driveway and rounded the front of the house.

"It's good to be home," Sadie said as they crossed toward the garage, her tone soft. Hesitant. "But the best part about being home is being with you. I just…I wanted you to know that," she said quietly.

She sped up, leaving him to gape at her as she went into the garage for the stray dog.

He wasn't sure what that had been about, wasn't sure he wanted to know.

It's good to be home.

He'd never heard her admit that before. Never would have believed that she could actually mean it. But even it was true, it was only temporary. Everything with her was temporary. Her jobs, her relationships, her goals and dreams—they changed based on her whims, on where she was living and who her friends were at any given moment. She may be glad to be in Shady Grove, but she wouldn't stay.

Her leaving was the only reliable thing about her.

SADIE PADDED INTO James's kitchen, Elvis at her heels, the wood floor cool under her bare feet. She flipped on the pendent lights over the center island and crossed to the refrigerator.

Good Lord, even the inside of his fridge was immaculate and so organized it could be in an appliance commercial, with a place for everything and everything in its damned place. Well, she thought, helping herself to a Golden Delicious apple, at least she didn't have to worry about catching some deadly disease by eating his food.

Unlike when she spent the night with Doug, her last boyfriend.

She was glad to be rid of him and all those penicillin samples he grew in his refrigerator.

She just wished she'd been the one to end things.

Washing the apple, she looked out the window at James's side yard. When she'd first seen his house, she'd been surprised. Not by the workmanship; she'd expect nothing less than the best from him and Montesano Construction. No, what had shocked her was that instead of a traditional, two-story house with an attached garage—and the same boring floor plan as half the houses in town—he'd gone with a log home design.

Guess even lifelong friends could surprise each other every now and again.

And, yes, he'd explained how his house combined contemporary design with waterfront, coastal and cottage elements and blah, blah, blah. Biting into the apple, she leaned against the counter. All she knew was that it was gorgeous, with vaulted ceilings, dozens of tall, narrow windows and a stone fireplace. A house that reflected well James's love for rich woods, deep colors and simple furnishings.

The first floor consisted of a master suite, a small bathroom and laundry room and a country-style kitchen that opened into a huge great room. Upstairs, a loft overlooked the great room with a bedroom on each side, along with another bathroom. In the kitchen, he'd chosen wide, rough-hewn pine beams for the ceiling, narrower boards for the floor. Whitewashed, glass-front cupboards and slate-gray counters.

He had a good eye, she thought as she opened an upper cabinet and took out a jar of peanut butter and a box of crackers. At least architecturally. When it came to interior design, he still had a lot to learn.

It was like you were in a plywood box—wood, wood and more wood.

If this was her place, she'd switch things up. Add some color and visual interest with a tile design on the center island, fill the cupboards with thick, white ceramic dishware. She munched on a cracker, her eyes narrowed as she studied the room. A throw rug under the high-back wooden stools and a window treatment for softness, both with hints of burgundy…maybe even yellow for warmth.

Yeah, she thought, eating another cracker, that's what she'd do. She'd turn this boring, bland house into a warm and welcoming home.

The cracker tasted like sawdust. Her scalp prickled with unease. With a sense of foreboding.

The sense that she was missing something by not having a place like that for herself.

Which was ridiculous. She didn't want a home. Not a permanent one, anyway. Roots were well and good for her mom and sister—they didn't mind being stuck in the same town, surrounded by the same people, doing the same things over and over again. Day after day. Year after year.

You might be able to have both roots and wings, but you couldn't fly, couldn't have true freedom with your feet planted in the ground.

That's what she had, she assured herself, digging a spoon out of the utensil drawer before taking her food into the great room. Freedom. Choices. The ability to take off for new adventures or opportunities whenever the mood struck her.

The ease of leaving behind a crappy apartment, friends who were barely more than acquaintances and men she'd never really loved anyway when things went belly-up.

"Things always go belly-up," she whispered to Elvis as she settled onto the couch.

With a sigh that was made up of more oh-woe-is-me than any self-respecting, independent woman should experience, she curled her legs under her.

The moon shone through the bank of floor-to-ceiling windows and cast dappled shadows across the braided rug in the middle of the room. Like the kitchen, this room, too, was a study in browns—plush leather couch and two armchairs the color of chocolate, russet-and-tan oval braided rug, oak coffee and end tables.

The man really needed some color in his life.

Built-in shelves filled with books and framed photos lined both sides of the fireplace and a large, flat-screen TV hung on the opposite wall. When they had gotten to his house after the party, James had helped her give Elvis a bath before calling it a night. Though she was exhausted, Sadie had tossed and turned for hours on the comfy double bed in the guest room upstairs.

"What are you doing up?"

She squeaked and almost dropped her spoon. Sticking it into the peanut butter, she glared at James. "You about gave me a heart attack, sneaking up on me in that ninja way of yours."

"Please tell me I'm sleepwalking," he said from his bedroom's doorway, his deep voice gravelly, Zoe at his side, "and you're not really eating my peanut butter straight from the jar."

"I'm not really eating your peanut butter from the jar," she said around the spoon in her mouth. "You're sleepwalking. It's all just a dream. A horrible, horrible dream."

James crossed to the floor lamp and turned it on—the better to illuminate his adorable scowl. He was so cute, trying to be all stern and angry with her.

Thank God that would never happen. He was too sweet, too even-tempered and well, too dang nice to lose his cool, much less get mad at her.

He towered over her. "If you let that dog lick the spoon then put it back in there I'm tossing you both out."

He seemed…bigger somehow. Broader. His faded Pittsburgh Pirates T-shirt clung to his shoulders, his sweatpants hung low on his flat stomach. He should have looked harmless, funny with his dark hair sticking up on one side, his eyes heavy with sleep.

Her breath shouldn't be stuck in her throat just from looking at him. She shouldn't want to smooth his hair, keep her hand there to run her fingers through the strands.

She swallowed hard. "Do people really eat after their pets?" She used the spoon to scoop out more peanut butter. Ate it, though she wasn't sure she could get it past the tightness in her throat. "That doesn't seem very hygienic."

"You're like a teenage boy," he grumbled.

She choked back a surprised laugh. "Not sure that's an accurate assessment, but seeing as how it's so late, I won't hold it against you. What are you doing up? Couldn't sleep?"

He grunted.

"Do you happen to have a pocket translator I could borrow?" she asked. "I don't speak caveman."

"I heard footsteps."

Instantly contrite, she sat up straight. "I'm sorry. Elvis and I thought we were being very stealthlike."

"You probably were, but Zoe hears every sound. She woke me, I heard you moving around and here I am. What's your excuse?"

She wished she knew. For weeks...months...she'd been restless. On edge.

Unhappy.

No, she corrected quickly, not unhappy. More like...dissatisfied. Unsure of what she should do next, where she should go. Sometimes she was even unsure of who she was anymore. Who she wanted to be.

"Elvis and I just wanted a snack."

"How can you be hungry? My mom had enough food at the party for two hundred people."

"I didn't get a chance to eat much."

"That's because you didn't stop talking long enough to take a breath, let alone eat."

"I'm sociable and people want to chat with me. It's a burden. Hey," she said, remembering her earlier promise to the dog, "want to order a pizza?"

"Where are you going to find a pizza parlor open at two forty-five in the morning?"

Good question. Panoli's, her favorite pizza place in Shady Grove, was probably long closed. "We could drive into Pitts—"

"Sadie." His voice was soft, his gaze patient. "What's wrong?"

His kindness undid her. "I screwed up," she admitted, injecting a lightness she didn't feel into her tone. "Nothing new there."

Nothing new except that this time—for the first time—screwing up, failing so spectacularly, bothered her. It had been weeks, and she still hadn't been able to shake off the sense of malaise, of disappointment in herself.

She shook her head. Tried to smile. "Hey, I have something for you," she said. "I'll be right back."

She hurried up the stairs and into the room on

the left, dug through her suitcase until she found the brightly wrapped package. When she returned downstairs, he was on the couch, his legs straight, his head resting against the back.

"Happy birthday," she said, holding the present out.

Looking from her to the gift and back again, he sat up.

But he didn't take it.

For some stupid reason, nerves settled in her stomach. "I hope you don't mind that it's technically late—though I'd like to point out only by a few hours."

Finally, he took the present. "You didn't have to get me anything."

"Of course I did. It's your birthday. Besides, I'm hoping this'll make up for not getting you anything the past few years."

He stared at the package in his hands. "I don't expect anything from you, Sadie."

He didn't. Never had. She appreciated it. Counted on it. "I know, but I saw this and I had to get it for you."

James was so thoughtful, always sending her flowers or her favorite chocolates on her birthday while the most she usually did was give him a call. It wasn't as if she didn't think about him—she did. Often.

"Besides," she continued, "this isn't the first gift

I've given you. Two years ago I sent you that subscription to *National Geographic*."

"It was four years ago. And you sent it a month late."

"I did?"

Not seeming upset about it, he nodded and unwrapped the present. His smile bloomed, slow and warm. "This is great."

Relieved, she sat next to him. "You like it?"

"Are you kidding?" He opened the first-edition copy of *The Adventures of Tom Sawyer,* his long fingers smoothing the aged pages. "I love it." Wrapping one arm around her shoulders, he gave her a quick hug. "Thank you."

She had to force herself not to lean into him for longer than necessary, but he felt so good, so solid and warm and strong. Steady. She may not want steadiness in her life too often, but it might be a nice change of pace now and again.

Brushing her hair over her shoulder, she eased away and swung her legs up so she sat cross-legged. "I'm glad you like it."

Silence surrounded them, the quiet hush of night, the only sound their breathing, the dogs' nails clicking as they walked across the floor. It was peaceful. She'd never craved peace before, had always preferred the exhilaration of the next adventure, the surprise of jumping off that cliff, seeing how far she could fly before having her wings clipped.

But this, being with James in his overly drab house, was nice.

It was also dangerous. Sitting so close to him, wearing nothing more than a pair of cotton shorts and a T-shirt. He shifted, his knee brushing her bare thigh. He stiffened at the contact, but didn't pull away. His gaze flicked to her chest before jerking up to her face again.

Her breasts grew heavy. Her heart pounded in her ears.

Dangerous. Exciting.

Two of her very favorite things.

Afraid he'd go to bed, that he'd leave her, she blurted, "So, what's been going on with you? How's work?"

"You know me," he said, setting the book on the coffee table. "Same old, same old."

"That's good. I mean, that is how you like things. No surprises. No…bumps in the road."

"That what happened in New Orleans? You hit one of those bumps?"

He knew her well. Too well.

She almost didn't answer. She was feeling too vulnerable now. But this was James. He'd never take advantage of her weak state. And she was still strong enough not to give too much of herself away.

"Actually, things were going great in New Orleans. Really, really great."

"And yet, here you are."

"Yeah, well, I wouldn't say I hit a bump. More

like the bottom dropped out. I wasn't able to make enough tending bar and Doug—"

"Who's Doug?"

"My boyfriend. Ex-boyfriend."

"What happened to Tim?"

"We split up a year ago." He'd dumped her for not being adventurous enough in bed to agree to bring in a second woman. As if she'd subject another woman to Tim's clumsy hands and short…stamina. "Doug worked on an oil rig, but that was only until he got his big break."

"Don't tell me," James said blandly. "Doug is a musician."

"Artist." Though he'd had that whole rock-star vibe to him. Long hair, scruffy facial hair, a penchant for wearing ripped jeans and his battered leather jacket. And then there was his Harley. Man, don't get her started on that—talk about sex on a stick. Doug was perfect for her.

Until he'd found another muse.

Oh, well. Easy come, easy go.

"Anyway, Doug and I split a few months ago, and since the whole organic beauty products weren't working out, I decided to come home."

Had *wanted* to come home. To be home.

"That's it?" he asked, studying her in that way she hated, as if seeing through all her bullshit, right to her soul. A girl had to have some secrets, didn't she? "There aren't any warrants out for your arrest? No ex-boyfriends you owe money to?"

"Of course not," she said primly. "You know I don't borrow money."

It was a line, one of few that she refused to cross. Fail or succeed, she did it on her own.

He linked his hands together behind his head, causing the muscles in his arms to bulge and flex. "What are your plans?"

"I don't know." She didn't do plans. It'd never been a problem before. If something didn't work out, she moved on to the next venture. If she got bored, she packed up and heeded whatever new idea called to her.

Except the idea fairy must not be able to get through because she was blank. She had no clue what she wanted, where she should go. It didn't help that her choices were limited, thanks to her bank account being depleted, her two credit cards being maxed out and her wallet holding exactly sixty-three dollars and forty-seven cents.

"I guess I'll stick around here for a while," she said. "Get a job or two, save up until I have enough to start over. Phoebe—you remember me telling you about my friend Phoebe? From Austin?" He nodded. "She and her partner moved to Napa and have a vineyard. She said I was welcome there anytime."

"Head West, young woman?"

"Maybe." Though the idea of being on the other side of the country from her family and friends gave her a twinge of panic. "Not that I know anything about working in a vineyard."

"When has that ever stopped you?" He took her hands in his. "So you didn't set the world of organic beauty products on fire. You'll find your niche."

She snorted. "I barely made a spark." Hadn't made her mark yet. Was starting to wonder if she ever would.

"Doesn't matter. Listen to me, you're one of the most capable, smartest people I know. You're able to adapt to any situation, find the good in just about everyone and you're fearless. You took off when you were barely eighteen and you've made your way across the country and back again on your own. You're not afraid to take chances." His thumb brushed the back of her hand, shooting sparks of awareness up her arm. "I admire that."

She glanced down at their hands, his large and tan and work-worn, hers pale and soft in comparison. "You do?"

His lips curved. "I do."

Her entire body warmed. She exhaled, felt as if it was the first time she'd been able to breathe freely in weeks. Months. Because of James. He believed in her. He saw more in her than she even saw in herself.

And when her wings failed and she fell to the ground, he was her soft place to land.

CHAPTER FIVE

SHE WAS HIS own personal addiction, one who tormented him, kept him awake, made him crazy. One he couldn't overcome, no matter how hard he tried.

And she didn't even know it.

James slid his hands away from Sadie's, pretended to look at the book she'd given him as an excuse to put a few more inches of space between them.

Space he desperately needed.

He never should have come out of his room. He'd just dozed off when Zoe's whining had woken him up, and he'd heard Sadie moving around out here. But he should have left her alone. Should have turned and walked back to his room when he'd seen her curled up on his couch, her toned legs bare in a pair of pink shorts. She was braless, her small breasts round and enticing under the thin material of her shirt, her nipples pressing against the fabric.

Sweat broke out along his lower back. He curled his fingers into his palms. "What kind of job are you looking for?" he asked, his voice rougher than he'd intended.

"You know me, I'm not picky." She lifted a hand to her hair and twisted a long strip of it around her finger. It was a nervous habit, one she'd had since they were kids.

It was about the only thing about her hair that never changed. The last time she'd been home it'd been chin-length and platinum blond. Now it poufed around her face, thick and wavy and back, mostly, to her natural dark blond.

That was how he liked her best.

Not that he'd tell her. He feared she'd notice that he paid too much attention to her, took note of the changes in her.

That she'd see what he desperately needed to keep hidden.

"What about your mom's store?" he asked. Irene had a high-end clothing boutique downtown.

Sadie let go of her hair, tucked it behind her ear. "Maybe," she hedged. Her relationship with her mother, he knew, was complicated. "Or maybe you could ask around? See if anyone has any openings?"

No. Hell, no. He didn't want to find her a job. Didn't want to continue being her crutch. He also didn't want to recommend her for a position knowing she'd only come home because she felt she had no other choice. And that after a few weeks or a month of licking her wounds and regrouping, she'd take off again, filled with big plans, a boatload of sunny thoughts and fantastical optimism about her next grand adventure. Leaving whoever hired her in a bind.

Leaving James to wonder what he had to do in order to make her stay.

"You don't have to," she added quickly, reading his silence correctly. "I know how busy you are. I'm sure I'll find something on my own."

She would. He had been honest when he'd told her she was capable. Bright. Quick to pick things up and eager to learn. She was also hard to say no to.

As he damn well knew.

"I'll ask around," he heard himself say. Some habits were impossible to break. "See what I can do."

She grinned, and his heart tripped, threatened to skip happily out his chest.

Christ, but he was a putz.

"Thanks, Jamie," she said. "It means a lot to me that I can always count on you."

Right. She could always count on him to come to her rescue. To be there for her, no matter how long she'd been away, no matter what mess she'd gotten herself into.

He would fix it for her.

Because they were friends. Because he was, by his own admission, a nice guy.

He would be there for her even though playing knight in shining armor no longer held much appeal. Even though part of him, a large, loud part, screamed at him to let her figure this out on her own. But he couldn't. She needed help. Needed someone to fix her latest problem. She needed him.

That used to be enough. Now he wanted more.

Elvis crossed over to them, sat next to the coffee table and laid his head on Sadie's lap.

Another Sadie Nixon conquest.

"What are your plans for him?" James asked.

She stroked Elvis's head. "I'm not sure. He doesn't have a collar or tags so I thought the first step would be to look in the paper and call the local animal shelters to see if anyone's reported him missing."

"If they didn't?"

"I'll worry about that when—if—it happens."

That was such a Sadie way of doing things, putting things off, never looking ahead or planning for the future. "You're not keeping him."

Sadie didn't keep things. She collected them—friends, strays, strangers. She loved having people around her. She gave them her time and attention and affection and then set them free.

No, she left. Set herself free so she could follow her next impulse, which, since they'd graduated high school fifteen years ago, included several stints in New York—and a memorable part in an off-Broadway production—and various jobs in at least a dozen cities around the United States.

"I'll make sure Elvis is healthy—and not missed by some family. If he's a true stray," she said, "we'll find a good home for him."

We. James shut his eyes. That was right. He'd

already agreed to help her find the dog's owners. How the hell did he get roped into these things?

He knew how. She was used to getting her way. Not that many people argued with her. Hard to disagree with someone who looked like a pixie, was as bright as the morning sun and as cheerful as a singing elf.

Tonight was the first time he remembered her not constantly smiling. Usually she let life's worries and problems roll off her back—whereas he took on those worries, carried those problems until he could find solutions.

But tonight she'd been different. More subdued. Almost cautious.

He hadn't liked how down she'd been about her latest venture not working out. Not when she had so much to offer. More than even she knew.

But he couldn't fault her for the caution. It was time he had more of it in his own life.

Time he put himself first, over his friendship with her, his feelings for her.

"Listen," he said, "I don't think it's a good idea for you to stay here after all."

Sadie froze, stared at him as if he'd sprouted two heads and told her he was considering taking on cannibalism as a hobby. "What? Why not?"

Because it was torture being so close to her, being around her. He shouldn't have to put himself through that just so she could avoid her mother and the issues between them.

He shot to his feet, agitated and antsy and too keyed up to sit still another moment. "I have a lot going on right now."

Not a lie. He always had a lot going on. Work and family commitments, his position on the Historical Architectural Review Board. And Eddie had asked if he'd be interested in helping him coach Max's basketball team this winter. He was a busy man. A busy, busy man who didn't have time to be a masochist.

"And it's not the best time for me to have a house-guest," he continued, crossing to stand in front of the windows. He glanced at her. "We'll still see each other." Only those visits would be on his terms and held in public venues where there were lots of lights and people, and Sadie was fully dressed.

"I'm really sorry we woke you up," Sadie said, sounding confused. "I promise, no more night wan-derings for either me or Elvis."

"That has nothing to do with it."

She tossed up her hands. "Well, obviously I've done something to make you mad."

"I'm not mad." Though he'd be hard-pressed to explain the roiling emotions inside him. Frustration. Bitterness. A sense of impatience, as if he had an opportunity to do…something with himself. With his life. That he was missing out.

"You're upset about something. What is it?"

He stared out the windows at the dark night, saw

her image in the reflection as she came up behind him. She laid her hand on his upper back. Her touch burned through his shirt, seared his skin.

"You can't hide it from me, Jamie," she said, her voice low and husky. Intimate. Too close for his comfort and peace of mind. His willpower. "I know you too well."

That was laughable. He didn't dare so much as crack a smile, though. Not if he wanted to keep his thoughts to himself. He may be open with most things, but his secrets were his own.

Sadie wouldn't agree. She thought that because they were friends they should share every thought that came into their heads. Which was how he knew more than he ever wanted about her thoughts on politics, religion and, worse, every aspect of her relationships with other men.

Even now she watched him with an open expression as if he should simply lay himself bare to her. Rip his soul open and let her see inside his heart.

He turned, his fingers twitching with the need to touch her, really touch her like a man touched a woman. Wishing he could.

Why can't you?

The thought, unbidden and irrational, slid through his mind like smoke.

Why couldn't he have the one thing he'd craved for as long as he could remember? Just a taste of all he'd been missing. She'd leave in a few weeks anyway. Since she wouldn't be staying here, he could control how often he saw her during those weeks.

And when she went, his life would return to normal.

She'd always left him feeling as if his emotions had been twisted and turned, his thoughts muddled until he couldn't think straight. Couldn't think of anything but her.

Always her.

His mother had once described him as a straight line, going from one point to the next without any fuss or muss.

He wanted to add some curves, some angles, to his route.

"I'm not upset," he said, stepping forward until their bare toes touched. He trailed his finger down the softness of her cheek, had the satisfaction of her eyes going wide with surprise and confusion. "I just think it's time for a change."

I JUST THINK it's time for a change.

Sadie frowned. Those were the words that had come out of James's mouth. She'd heard them with her own ears, saw his lips moving with her eyes, but she still couldn't process it. He hadn't sounded like himself. The sentiment was way off. Plus, it'd been sort of sexy the way his deep voice had gone all rumbly, had rubbed across her nerve endings like sandpaper.

Like a caress.

And the way he'd skimmed his finger down her cheek? Her skin still tingled.

She prayed like mad he didn't do it again.

Wished with all her might he would.

"But I…" Her voice cracked. She swallowed in an effort to work some moisture back into her mouth and tried again. "I don't want you to change."

"You love change," he pointed out reasonably, which was so much better, so much more like him that she relaxed fractionally.

"That's me, not you. You're steady. Reliable. Dependable. Like…like…"

"A lapdog?"

She frowned at the edge to his voice. He didn't usually get edgy, amped up, angry or overly excited. "Not a lapdog, no," she said. "More like the sun. Always up in the east, down in the west, burning bright no matter how many clouds are hiding it from view."

Besides her family, he was her one constant. She didn't want that to change. Ever.

"As poetic a description as that was," he said, "as steady, reliable and dependable as I am, I still want a change."

"I guess that's okay," she said grudgingly. "If it's not a big change."

One side of his mouth kicked up in a heart-stopping grin, and he slid his hand around to cup the back of her head. His thumb pressed lightly against the tender point on her throat.

"So," he asked in a rough murmur as he edged closer and closer until the soft material of his sweats brushed her thighs, his elbow grazed the side of her breast, "I have your permission?"

Her permission, she thought dumbly. To change?

No, she realized, her knees going weak. That wasn't what he was asking. What he was asking was bigger, so much bigger than him deciding to switch his morning workouts to evenings or giving up his beloved smart phone.

What he was asking had the possibility of shaking up their relationship, cracking its very foundation.

No. Absolutely, positively no.

She didn't want this. Didn't want anything shook up. Sure, she was usually all for the next adventure, had no trouble going into a situation blind, but she had a feeling this was one of those times when she needed to keep her eyes wide open. Think through her options, analyze each step before making even the slightest move.

What was at stake was too important to risk. To lose.

"Sadie?" he asked quietly. Patiently. Waiting for her answer. Waiting for her to make the choice.

He'd never push her, never expect more than she had to give. If she gave the slightest indication she wasn't interested, he'd let her go. Just like that. They could pretend none of this had ever happened. No hard feelings. No recriminations.

That's what she needed to do. Because if they

went any further, things between them would never be the same. But this was James. Nothing between them could ever be wrong. Could ruin what they had.

She laid her hands on his chest, felt the strong, steady beat of his heart, and it calmed her. Thrilled her. Nodding, the only answer she could form, she slid her hands up to his shoulders. His eyes darkened, his fingers tensing on the nape of her neck before tangling in her hair and tugging her head back.

Her lips parted on a soft gasp. But James didn't close the distance between them. Anticipation built as their breaths mingled, as he scanned her face, his gaze dropping to her mouth for one long breathless moment.

"Did you ever wonder?" he asked in that low, not-quite-James voice. "What it would be like between us?"

A denial would be useless. And a lie. But she couldn't make herself admit it. Of course she'd thought of it. She was human, wasn't she? Ever since adolescence, there had been a strong, physical attraction between them, one she'd been all too happy to ignore.

"I have," he said into the ensuing silence. He placed his other hand on her hip, dragged her flush against him as he leaned down and murmured, "I've thought about it a lot."

And he kissed her.

It was the faintest of touches, the brush of his

mouth against hers, as if he was worried she'd bolt, or worse, disappear. He eased back, held her gaze for a moment and then settled his mouth on hers again.

Her eyes fluttered closed. She hadn't known, had never imagined that his kiss would be so potent. That it would inflame her, have desire flicking along her veins like fire, burning hot and bright.

It was over all too soon. They stared at each other, both breathing hard from one simple kiss. And she knew all she had to do was drop her hands, step back and he'd let her go. That would be the end of it, the end of this—whatever it was. Whatever it could have been.

"Jamie?"

"Hmm?"

"I think…" She swept her tongue across her bottom lip, watched as his eyes narrowed. "I think I'm about to hit another of those bumps in the road."

He smiled, the easy smile she loved so much. "Mind if I tag along?"

She rose onto her toes, pressing fully against the hard lines of his body, and tangled her fingers in the silky hair at his nape. Stopped when their mouths were so close her lips brushed against his as she spoke, his mustache tickling her upper lip. "I'm counting on it."

His kiss was ferocious and so hungry she had no choice but to return it with equal fervor. The move of his mouth against hers, the light scratch of his whiskers and touch of his tongue, the taste of him all made it impossible to think, to consider the doubts and worries at the back of her mind. He stole it all, her words, her thoughts and her breath, with his slow, mind-drugging kisses, with the way his hand smoothed over her lower back, his other hand massaging her scalp.

Still kissing her, he lifted her in his arms. One of the dogs barked—once, twice—but even that sound seemed to come from far away. Sadie wrapped her legs around his waist, held on to his shoulders as he adjusted her weight, lifting her higher, his hands gripping her ass. He tore his mouth from hers and carried her into his bedroom, his strides long and determined.

He deposited her on the bed with enough force that she bounced once, then watched as he walked away. She was about to call him back, but he stopped at the door, jabbed a finger into the great room. "Out," he told the dogs. "Both of you."

Zoe went first, followed by Elvis.

Turning her head, Sadie watched his dark form as he shut the door then walked back toward her, flipping on the lamp next to the bed. The light brought with it a sense of reality, a vague hint of unease.

She was in James's bedroom, lying…no, more like sprawled…on his bed, her lips still tingling from his kisses, her skin heated from his touch. "Wait," she cried, holding her hand out when he approached her. "We need to…to set some limits. Some ground rules."

Yes, that's what they needed. He loved rules and regulations. Loved knowing what to expect. It would be better for both of them.

He climbed onto the bed, came toward her on his hands and knees, his movements slow and somehow predatory, his eyes glittering with intent. "No."

Her mouth dropped, and she scrambled back until her head and shoulders were pressed against the wooden headboard. "What?"

"I said no." He stopped, his knees on either side of her calves. "No rules. No limits. Not tonight. Tonight," he continued huskily, his narrow gaze on his finger as he traced the tip of it up her inner thigh, "I want to touch you. All of you." That finger crept higher. And higher until it slipped under the material of her shorts, his nail lightly scraping against the elastic of her panties. "Are you going to let me, Sadie?" He flicked his thumb over her center. She bit into her lower lip to stop from whimpering like a baby. "Are you going to let me do all the things I've dreamed of doing to you?"

Her breath shuddered out. Her fingers curled into the bedspread. Who was this man, this exciting, enticing man with the capable hands and heated kisses? She couldn't resist him.

Bracing himself with his hands on either side of her chest, he leaned down, his mouth hovering over her breast. A torment. A promise.

"Say it," he demanded softly. He exhaled heavily, his warm breath washing over her. Her nipple tightened and strained. He rubbed his chin over it, his beard scratching it through the material of her shirt. He lifted his head, pinned her with his hot gaze. "Say you want me."

Her breasts ached, her core grew damp. "I want you," she whispered, lightly touching his face, his familiar, dear face. "I want you, James."

His grin flashed, and he skimmed his hands under her shirt, tugging the material up past her rib cage. He brushed the undersides of her breasts with his knuckles and then lifted the shirt off, tossed it aside. He rubbed the pads of his thumbs across her nipples in the faintest of touches.

He kissed her again, kept his weight braced on his arms when all she wanted, more than her next breath, was that hard body against hers, pressing her into the mattress. She smoothed her hands over his shoulders, down his arms, across his broad chest. When she grabbed the waist of his sweats and tried to bring his hips down to her, he resisted, lifted his head.

He pressed hot, open-mouthed kisses along the curve of her jaw, down the line of her neck, his beard scratching her sensitive skin, bringing her senses alive. Lower and lower he went, his body sliding down hers, his lips firm and smooth as they glided across her collarbone, down the swell of her breasts. She gripped the hard muscles of his arms, her fingers digging into his skin. His right hand cupped her breast, held it like a gift, an offering to himself. And he feasted, sucking her into his mouth. She arched her back, stabbed her hands into his hair to hold his head there.

He trailed his fingers down her ribs, across her stomach. Moved his attention to her other breast, shifted, knees pressing against her outer thighs. His touch was almost reverent as he stroked her shoulders, her arms, slid her shorts and underwear down and lightly scraped his nails along her inner thighs. Heat pooled in her lower stomach, her muscles relaxed only to tense when he gently touched her center.

Squeezing her eyes shut, she bit back a moan. She didn't want to make any sounds, didn't want to see. This was a fantasy, a dream. A surreal moment out of time. If she spoke, if she opened her eyes, it would be too real.

It would mean too much.

So she kept her lids closed, focused on the feel of him under her hands, the sensations of her body as he touched her, his light strokes bringing her closer and closer to the edge. As if sensing how close she was, he stopped.

And eased down her body to replace his hand with his mouth.

Her eyes flew open as she gasped. Her breathing grew ragged as she watched James, his dark head between her thighs, his strong shoulders bunching and flexing as he pleasured her. Pressure built, became almost unbearable. She squirmed, raising her hips in supplication. In a plea.

With a low growl that seemed to reverberate through her core, he gripped her thighs, lifting her to him more fully. His mouth danced over her flesh, his beard scraped pleasantly, and when he flicked his tongue over the most sensitive part of her, she threw her head back on a long, low groan, fisted her hands in his hair and flew. Pleasure coursed through her, taking her higher and higher, kept her soaring until she was spent, her body humming with aftershocks.

James kissed her forehead, her cheek and finally her mouth. His erection nudged her thigh, hard. Hot. But he just lay next to her and pulled her into his arms. Brushed her hair from her face, his touch incredibly gentle.

She could end this, here and now. She somehow instinctively understood that he was giving her a chance to change her mind, to walk away.

She couldn't. It was going to change everything between them but, God help her, she couldn't.

JAMES COULDN'T CATCH his breath. He'd lost that ability the moment he first kissed Sadie. He had the feel of her now on his hands, the taste of her on his tongue. But if this went any further, it had to be her choice. Her move.

He didn't know what he'd do if she turned him away.

She rolled onto her side facing him, laid her hand on his cheek. He bit back a grimace. His chest ached. This was it. She was going to tell him they'd made a mistake.

He'd never seen her look so serious. Her eyes searched his and he opened himself for her, let her see everything he'd kept hidden, all of his secrets. What she meant to him, what she'd always meant to him, how much he cared about her. How badly he wanted her.

She kissed him, hesitantly at first, her lips warm and seeking. But she grew bolder, her hands sliding up and down his arms, her tongue flicking over his mouth. Though it cost him, he let her keep control. She tugged at the hem of his shirt and he leaned back so she could push the fabric up. He broke away long enough to shuck his shirt, then groaned into her mouth as she touched him.

Her hands were cool on his chest, her nails scraping lightly down his ribs. She pressed against him, her nipples brushing his skin, the incredibly soft skin on her belly against his lower stomach. His erection pulsed, leaped between them.

When her hands went to the waist of his pants, he helped her pull them down, kicked them off. Her gaze swept over him like a caress. Watching him, she skimmed a finger down the middle of his chest and across his stomach. His muscles contracted.

She shifted, those fingers going lower, lightly rubbing the narrowing path of dark hair leading from his belly button, following it to the base of his penis. Her eyes heavy with desire, the flush of her orgasm still staining her cheeks, she smiled—a small, feminine smile full of power and triumph.

And she stroked him. His hips lifted. His breath wheezed out. When she added her second hand to the mix, he grabbed her by the waist and rolled her onto her back. Reaching into the drawer of his bedside table, he took out a condom and covered himself.

Then he kissed her, settled his body on top of hers, where he'd always wanted it. Finally, those glorious curves and long, supple limbs, all that soft, sweet-smelling skin was his to touch and taste and pleasure.

He kissed her until they were both panting, their hands frantically moving over each other's body, their skin coated with sweat. Until he thought he'd go insane with want, with need.

Holding his weight on his elbows, he waited at her entrance until she opened her eyes. Held her gaze as he entered her, inch by slow inch. Her eyes widened as he stretched her. Filled her.

Loved her.

He'd always loved her. And now he was showing her how much. After all this time, all the years dreaming of her, wanting her, the moment had arrived. He was making love to Sadie. It was real. She was hot and tight and wet for him.

For him.

His body demanded he plunge into her again and again, that he find his release. But he wouldn't be rushed, wouldn't let this moment be just about heat and flash. Not when he'd waited so long for it. He'd make it last, make it be enough—just in case.

Except she grabbed his ass and rolled her hips in a move that left him cross-eyed and shaking with the effort to hold himself back.

He stilled her hips with his hands, held her immobile while he drove into her, again and again, his pace slow and steady. Tension built. Her nails digging into his back, she wrapped her legs around his waist, pressing her heels against the base of his spine. He moved faster, went even deeper until her body pulsated around him.

As she shuddered with her second orgasm, her eyes wide and dark with pleasure, she called his name.

And took him over the edge with her.

CHAPTER SIX

H<small>E WAS ALONE.</small>

James flopped onto his back, threw his arm over his eyes, let his other arm hang over the edge of the bed.

Shit.

It was barely nine o'clock and Sadie wasn't still in his bed. After they'd made love, she'd fallen asleep in his arms. He hadn't been able to sleep, had been too afraid she'd slip away from him, that the whole night had been nothing more than a dream. He'd finally drifted off only to wake up a few hours ago to find Sadie wrapped around him.

He'd made love to her again, slow, sleepy sex.

He could still hear the sounds she'd made when she'd come.

Zoe licked his fingers. Except when he reached for her head to give her a pat, it wasn't his dog's long, soft fur and pointy snout he felt. He sat up. Frowned at Elvis.

Goddamn it. She'd taken off, left him to deal with the dog on his own. He kicked off the sheet that'd tangled around his legs. Yanked his sweatpants on commando style and stormed out into the great room.

No Sadie. Just his own dog whining by the front door.

His mouth tight, he unlocked and opened the front door. Both dogs raced out. James stepped onto the cold, wet porch and shielded his eyes from the rising sun.

And noticed Sadie's Jeep still parked behind his truck.

His hand slowly dropped back to his side. Relief filled him, weakened his knees. She hadn't run off, her usual M.O. when faced with a potentially awkward situation, one she didn't want to deal with.

She was still here.

At the sound of footsteps, he went back inside, saw her coming down the stairs, her large suitcase in one hand, the blue bag he'd gotten out of the car for her at his mom's in the other. She had on another of her long, flowing skirts, a pastel pink this time with a creamy white tank top edged in lace. Her hair was pinned up on the sides but fell loose down her back.

She looked up and, noticing him watching her, waiting for her, froze.

"Good morning," he said, thankful his quiet tone was easy, that it didn't give away his fears.

"You're awake," Sadie said, her expression unreadable.

Good sign or bad? He wasn't sure. Was almost

afraid to find out. But he wasn't like her. He couldn't hide from something, even if it had the potential to cause him pain. Besides, he was optimistic enough to think, to hope, things would work out for the best.

That after what they'd shared last night, things would work out exactly how he wanted them to.

So he smiled, ignored how wary she seemed as she descended the stairs and set her bags by the door.

"You look pretty," he said, giving her the words he'd always wanted to share. The compliments he'd kept to himself for fear he'd give himself away. He dipped his head and sniffed the side of her neck, told himself not to take it personally when she stiffened. He straightened, kept that damn smile on his face. "Smell pretty, too."

"Thank you."

"You're welcome," he said, mimicking her solemn tone. That, at least, earned him a flicker of a smile. He'd take what he could get. When it came to Sadie, he had always taken what he could get. He'd always wanted more.

Was afraid he always would.

But last night, things had changed between them. He wouldn't let her uneasiness or nerves force them back to how it used to be between them.

"Why don't I get dressed?" he asked, ignoring the image of his to-do list that flashed in his mind. "We can go out, grab some breakfast."

"I'd better not." Her gaze met his then skipped

away. "I thought I'd stop by the store. See Mom about my staying with them."

"She's working? On a Sunday morning?"

"The store doesn't open until eleven on Sundays, but you know Irene. Always early."

"You don't have to go," he said, kicking himself for ever bringing it up last night. For sounding as if he was begging now. "Forget I said anything about it."

"No, no. You were right," she said, crossing her arms and staring out the narrow window next to the door. "About my not staying here. God, I never should've asked, I mean, what an imposition on you."

He went behind her, turned her to face him. "You're not an imposition," he murmured, sliding his hands up her arms. "You're a temptation."

Her mouth parted. He lowered his head.

And she leaped back as if he'd just set her hair on fire.

Shit.

His optimism and his stomach dropped. "Sadie—"

"Could we…" She shook her head. Inhaled deeply. "Jamie, we really need to talk."

"Mind if I make some coffee first?"

He needed the caffeine, and the few minutes it would give him to work out how to convince her not to say what happened between them had been a mistake. Because that's exactly what he saw on her face. Regret.

Without waiting for her to answer, he went into the kitchen. Kept his hands busy with the coffee preparation—fill the pot, measure out grounds, start the machine. While it brewed he grabbed two mugs, took the milk from the fridge, set the sugar on the island.

He sensed the moment she came into the room, felt the tension that thickened the air.

When he turned, she was still standing on the threshold between the kitchen and great room, looked ready to bolt at the slightest provocation. He handed her a full cup.

"Why don't we sit down?" he asked, indicating the stools.

She took the cup and looked as if she had no idea what to do with it. "I can't sit. I've got too much bottled up inside of me to be still. But you go ahead."

Sipping his coffee, he sat while she began to pace, her skirt whirling around her legs when she turned. She flitted from one corner of the kitchen to the next, mumbling under her breath. Finally, she nodded as if to herself, stopped and faced him. "Last night was...it was..." Part of him wanted to help her out, to be that nice guy, her good buddy by filling in the silence for her. But another part, a part he hadn't realized was so strong, so serious, refused to make this easier on her. So he waited, watched her carefully. She had dark circles under her eyes, and that gave him a pang of regret.

More than that, it hurt to know she obviously

didn't feel the same way about him, about what had happened between them.

She crossed to stand on the other side of the island, as if needing that barrier between them. "Last night," she repeated, sounding a bit crazed, "was good—"

"Good?"

She blushed. "Okay, it was…" She waved a hand through the air as if to wipe away everything they'd said so far. "Look, that's not the point. The point is that it can't happen again. Obviously."

"It's not obvious to me."

"It was a mistake, Jamie. We got…caught up in the moment."

"What do you want from me?" he asked calmly, despite the turmoil inside of him. "You want me to agree with you? To do…what? Pretend it never happened, that I don't want it to happen again? Because I can't do that. I won't."

"James, please. This is the sort of thing that tears friendships apart. Can't we just let it go? We don't have to pretend it never happened, but we both need to know it can't happen again. I don't want anything to change between us. I don't want to lose you as my friend."

He didn't want to lose her, either. But in order to keep her as his friend, keep her in his life, they would have to go back to the way they'd always been. He would have to forget he'd ever touched her, had her moving beneath him. He would have to continue to keep his feelings to himself, bottled up inside of him, letting them eat him alive.

He could do it. He could swallow it all down, had been doing it for years, for all his life it seemed. He'd kept his feelings hidden, pretended to be just her friend, listened to her problems, heard about her relationships with other men.

Watched her walk out of his life again and again without so much as a backward glance.

Yes, he could do it. But he wouldn't. He wouldn't live half a life, not even for her. Not anymore.

"What if I want it to change?" he asked, watching her intently. "The dynamics between us?"

"What?"

"What if I want us to be more than friends? We could make it work, Sadie. We're already good together, and last night proved there's something between us."

She began pacing again. "That's the problem. Don't you see? Last night is going to mess up what we've got going here."

"And what's that?"

She whirled on him, her hair fanning out before settling around her shoulders. "What's that? How about our friendship? We've been friends for twenty years. Do you really want to risk that? Lose it?"

"Maybe it's time to let our relationship take its natural evolution. Maybe I want it to."

"Why on earth would you want that?"

He looked at the counter then raised his head

and met her eyes. And told her the truth. "Because I want a family. A wife. And it just hit me that the reason I don't have one yet is because I never let another woman get close to me. But mostly," he admitted softly, "I'm tired. I'm tired of being alone. And I'm tired of pretending that all I feel for you is friendship."

SADIE WENT HOT then cold all over. Her thoughts spun, her stomach turned. She wanted to run, to escape from James's steady gaze and his patient voice. He was confused, she thought frantically, panic coating her throat, making it difficult to breathe. Hadn't she known sex would ruin things between them?

She should have resisted him last night. Should have been stronger. Instead, her weakness was costing her everything.

"Why are you doing this?" she asked hoarsely, hugging her arms around herself. "Why are you saying these things?"

He stood and walked toward her. She shook her head, held out her hands, but he kept coming. She backed up, but was trapped with the counter behind her, James—shirtless and barefoot—in front.

He wrapped his fingers around her upper arms, lifted her onto her toes, his heat burning her skin. She wanted to touch the smooth, golden skin covering his chest, to once again press her lips against the flat planes of his stomach just to feel his muscles quiver underneath her.

She curled her fingers into her palms, tightened them until her nails bit into her skin.

"I'm doing it," he said, his voice soft, his eyes searching, seeking something she wasn't sure she could give him, "because I'm in love with you."

She flinched. "Jamie, I—"

He let go of her so quickly she stumbled. "Christ, I tell you I love you and you go white. Do you have any idea how that makes me feel?"

"I'm sorry. I'm so sorry." She hated hurting him. Hated knowing she had the power to do so. "I'm—" Shocked. Scared to death. "God, you can't just... toss something like that out there and then expect me to know what to do."

He stared at her, calm and long-suffering. As if every day he threw an emotional grenade at somebody and then stood back to watch the fallout. She used to envy his ability to remain so centered and in control. But not today. Not when her feelings were so raw, her emotions ragged.

"Look," she said, "this is all just...residual...emotions from last night. You're confusing sex with love and—"

He laughed. He actually laughed.

So glad to see she could still amuse him.

"I'm a grown man. I think I know the difference between sex and love. This has nothing to do with last night. All that did was show me I needed to speak up. Before, when I thought I didn't have a chance, I kept my secret. But last night proved you have feelings for me, too."

This was too much. Too much pressure. There was too much at stake. "Of course I have feelings for you." Tears clogged her throat. She cleared them away. "You're my best friend. I love you."

"Don't." Though it was barely a whisper of sound, the force of the word, the vehemence, caused the hair on her arms to stand on end. "Don't give me some goddamn pat response like that. I'm in love with you. I always have been."

"What do you want from me? What do you want me to say to that?"

"I'm not asking you to give me words that aren't true or to make promises you can't keep. All I'm asking is for you to give me a chance, to give us a chance. To see if there's the possibility that you have more for me in your heart than you realize."

He asked for too much. Expected too much. She didn't have that much to give, not for him, not for any man.

For the first time, she wished she did.

But she refused to lead James on that way, letting him think they might have a chance at something down the road. How could they when she didn't plan on staying in Shady Grove? He wanted a family, to be settled, and settled was the very last thing she wanted to be. Ever. There were still so many things she wanted to do with her life, so many places she wanted to visit, so many things she hadn't explored yet.

She wouldn't give up her freedom. Not for anyone.

She couldn't love someone that much. If she did, she'd lose her independence. She'd lose herself.

"I can't," she said, her voice unsteady. "I'm sorry, but I can't."

It was worse, so much worse seeing the acceptance on his face. The pain. Pain she'd caused.

"Yeah," he said on a soft exhale. "I'm sorry, too."

Gripping the counter, he lowered his head. Her heart broke for him. And for herself.

She touched his back, to offer comfort, to let him know she still cared.

He recoiled, then straightened and walked out of the room.

She hurried after him, caught up to him as he let the dogs back inside. "James? Jamie, can we at least—"

"You need to leave."

She blinked and stopped in her tracks. Not because his voice had been harsh. James was never harsh. He was too kind, too tolerant. Too good for her.

He was also walking away from her. Again.

She followed him to his bedroom, stood in the doorway as he yanked on the shirt he'd been wearing last night. "I'll take Elvis to my mom's," she said. "I can come back in a few hours. Or we can go out—"

"No."

"Okay, we'll stay in. I could bring some groceries, make my famous fish tacos—"

"Sadie," he said, something final in his soft voice making her pause, her stomach to cramp. "I don't want you to give me a few hours by myself. I don't need time to gather my thoughts or get over this. What I need is for you to leave. And I don't want you to come back."

Her pulse pounded in her ears, dull and deafening. "You...you don't mean that."

He met her eyes. "I've never meant anything more in my life."

"Jamie, please. We can work through this—"

"You're right. We could."

"Then why—"

"We could," he repeated, towering over her, his jaw tight, his eyes so cold it was all she could do not to shiver. "All I'd have to do is agree that what happened last night was a mistake, that making love to you didn't mean anything to me. That my feelings toward you were strictly platonic. That I don't dream about you. That jealousy doesn't eat me alive every time you tell me about the latest man in your life. I could go on being your friend, Sadie. But the thing is, I don't want to."

It was like he'd punched her in the stomach. She

wanted to bend over from the pain, wanted to sob with it.

"And I don't think you have any goddamn right asking me to do so," he continued relentlessly. "I can't keep living my life wanting something I'm never going to have. I can't keep hoping you'll notice me, that someday you'll see me as something more than your good buddy. I'm done." His mouth was a thin line, his shoulders rigid. "*We* are done."

He turned from her as if that was it, as if it didn't matter what she wanted, how she felt.

"That's it?" she asked, storming into his room while he went into his walk-in closet. Who was this man? How could he treat her this way? He came back, a pair of running shoes in his hands. "How can you abandon our friendship after all these years?"

"Self-preservation." Sitting on the edge of the bed, the bed that was still unmade, where he'd touched her so gently just a few hours ago, he pulled the sneakers on, left them untied. "For once in my life, I'm thinking of myself." He stood, grabbed a sweatshirt off the chair under the window. "I'm taking Zoe for a run. If our friendship meant anything to you at all, you'll be gone before I get back."

And he called his dog and walked out, shutting the door quietly behind him, leaving Sadie standing in his bedroom that smelled of him, feeling as if she'd lost the most precious thing in her life.

Wondering if she'd ever be able to get it back.

"OH, SADIE," IRENE ELLISON said, her tone laced with equal amounts exasperation and love as Sadie walked into WISC, her mother's upscale clothing boutique, "what did you do now?"

Sadie stopped so suddenly, the door swung and hit her in the rear. Had her mom heard about her and James? That was taking the whole moms-know-all-and-see-all thing a little too far.

"What have you heard?" Sadie hedged.

Irene shook her head. "Let's not play word games, Sadie. You—" Her eyes widened as she looked behind Sadie. "Did you get a dog?" she asked, sounding as scandalized as if Sadie had brought a coyote pup home and begged to keep it.

Sadie entered the store fully, set her hand on Elvis's head. "He's only staying with me temporarily."

As if that was pushing her patience to the limit, Irene glanced at the heavens. "Well, can't you tie him up outside? I don't allow dogs in the store."

"I would, except I don't have a leash for him."

A leash. A collar. Food and water bowls. You know, all the essentials a person needed for the care and feeding of a dog. But first she'd have to borrow some money from her mom and stepfather.

So much for being a strong, self-sufficient woman.

"I'm heading to the mall to get him one," Sadie continued, "but wanted to stop and say hi, let you know I'm in town—"

"I already knew you were in town," Irene said. "Your sister told me."

Figured. Sadie loved her little sister, but she'd always been a tattletale.

"I got in late," Sadie said, Elvis following her as she wound her way around racks of designer clothes, Irene watching the dog as if ready to leap on his back if he so much as thought about leaving a dog hair on a precious silk blouse. She stopped in front of the checkout counter, across from her mom. "So…I'm in town, Mom. It sure is nice to see you."

Irene, still thin, blond and a stunner at fifty-four, smiled. Definitely stunning. "I'm sorry, dear." She hurried around the front counter, enveloped Sadie in a hug. "It's wonderful to see you."

Sadie held on tight. No matter what their problems—and she and Irene had more than their fair share—they both knew the other loved them unconditionally. She shut her eyes and breathed in her mother's perfume—Chanel No. 5, of course. Classy, elegant and timeless, just like Irene.

Being in her mother's arms was familiar. Safe. Sadie didn't want to let go.

Irene leaned back, her smile fading when she saw Sadie's face. "What's wrong?"

"Nothing." Sadie averted her gaze. Damn her mother and that ability to read Sadie's thoughts, to always know when she was hiding something and, worst of all, when she was lying through her teeth.

"Laura," Irene called to one of her three part-time employees, "I'll be in the back if you need me."

Laura, a cute blonde who looked to be at least

thirteen months pregnant, glanced over her shoulder from where she was working on a display of silver necklaces. Smiled. "Okay." She waved. "Hi, Sadie."

"Hi, Laura. Good to see you."

Sadie followed her mother toward the back of the store. On Sundays, WISC was open from ten until two, a nice little window, Irene had once explained to Sadie, for people to stop in after brunch or church, but closing early enough so that Irene still had the majority of the day free. As it was just past ten, and the store had only been open a few minutes, no customers milled about. But there would be people in there soon. Her mom ran the most successful clothing store in the area.

Everything her mother did was successful.

Well, everything except Sadie.

"Watch that tail, dog," Irene told Elvis, whose wagging tail came close to knocking a display of cocktail rings off a low table.

Elvis hung his head.

No one could dole out the reprimands like Irene. Luckily, she was equally good at dishing out the compliments. But only ones that'd been earned. When Irene said something nice about you, you knew she meant it.

Sadie snapped her fingers and Elvis sidled up next to her. They walked through a large stockroom into a kitchenette.

"Tea?" Irene asked.

"Sure." Sadie sat at the small table while her mom

put a kettle of water on, retrieved two cups and put a tea bag in each one.

Sitting across from Sadie, Irene folded her perfectly manicured hands on the table. "How have you been?"

"Good," Sadie said, matching her mother's polite tone. They were nothing if not polite to one another. Oh, they loved each other, but Sadie thought her mother was too concerned with appearances and what other people thought than in supporting her eldest daughter's decisions. Irene worried that Sadie was wasting her life and would end up alone.

A distinct possibility.

"How about you?" Sadie asked.

"Honey, I'm fine. Now, let's get back to you. What's wrong? And please, don't try to tell me 'nothing' again. I know you too well."

Sadie wasn't so sure about that.

Irritated, still reeling from her conversation with James, she shifted in her chair like a wayward two-year-old. "What makes you think something's wrong?"

Irene reached across the table to clasp Sadie's hand. Her eyes, the same light blue as Sadie's, were shrewd and saw way too much. "Because you're home."

For some crazy reason, Sadie found herself wanting to tell her mom everything. Admit to everything, all the decisions she'd made that had led her to this point, all the mistakes. She knew her mom would help her, but she wasn't in the mood for the whole disappointed, where-have-I-gone-wrong lecture that came along with that help.

The kettle whistled and Irene went to make their tea. Chewing the inside of her lower lip, Sadie rubbed Elvis's head, which was in her lap. But she hadn't confided in her mom in years. Oh, they didn't fight—Irene was too composed to resort to arguments. But she did set pretty high standards for her daughters, and if you didn't meet them, didn't fall into line with what she thought you should do, who she thought you should be, she let you know it.

But she was always there to help Sadie get back on her feet.

Sadie wished she could appreciate it more instead of just feeling like a huge failure. To come crawling back to her mommy was humiliating.

Somehow, some way, this was all James's fault.

Irene set the teacup in front of Sadie and placed a plate of fancy cookies in the center of the table. Sadie chose a sugar-dusted molasses cookie and bit into it. She groaned. "Delicious. Homemade?"

Irene made a humming sound as if Sadie should know better than to even ask if Irene Ellison would give anyone—even her prodigal daughter—store-bought cookies.

Sadie took another cookie, nibbled on the edge, then palmed it and slid it onto her lap. Kept her expression smooth as she lifted her hand so Elvis could eat it.

"Please don't feed your dog at the table," Irene said, not even glancing up from where she studied the plate of cookies before making her own choice—shortbread.

"You should really think of taking that whole ESP thing on the road."

With a secret smile, Irene lifted her cup for a sip. Sadie added two teaspoons of sugar to her tea and stirred it. Stirred and stirred and stirred while Irene calmly, patiently drank her own tea.

Waiting her out, Sadie knew. No one did that whole sit-and-wait-and-the-other-person-will-soon-crack tactic like Irene. She would have made a great cop.

"I need a place to stay," Sadie admitted.

"I see. Did something happen between you and James?"

Sadie stared at her tea. "Why do you ask?"

"Because you usually stay with him."

"Well, this time I'm not. I'd like to stay with you."

"That's a change."

Yes, it was. For as long as she could remember, Sadie had wanted to get out from under her mother and stepfather's roof. To live her own life free of their rules.

To live life like her father had.

Irene glanced at Elvis. "And does the dog that's staying with you temporarily need a place to stay as well?"

"He does. But only until I find his owners or someone to adopt him."

"Is he house-trained?"

"Yes."

"And up-to-date on his shots?"

"Definitely."

Probably. Maybe. She glanced at Elvis, but he didn't pull out an immunization record, so she'd just have to go with her gut. And hope she could slip this one little fib past the human lie detector.

She held her breath while her mom mulled it over. If she said no, Sadie didn't know what she'd do. She'd never been homeless, not really. But it was a distinct possibility now. She could ask Charlotte to let her bunk on the couch, but her sister would have to run it by her roommate first.

And honestly, it was lowering to ask your baby sister to get you out of a jam.

Especially when that baby sister was more accomplished, more responsible and way more mature than Sadie ever hoped to be.

But she couldn't leave Shady Grove. Without money, she had nowhere else to go. She also couldn't afford a hotel room, and while she had quite a few friends in town still, most of them were married with families, jobs and their own busy lives.

Her throat clogged. This was, without a doubt, the absolute worst morning of her life. And that was saying something. She'd left James's house in a daze, stunned that he'd thrown away a lifetime of friendship.

Hurt that he'd dismissed her that way because she couldn't give him what he wanted. Couldn't be who he wanted her to be.

"Mom," Sadie said, her voice thick with emotion. She cleared her throat. "Can I come home? Please?"

"Honey," Irene said, getting up and walking around the table to crouch next to Sadie. She wrapped her arm around her daughter's shoulders. "Of course you can. You're always welcome, you know that."

Sadie sniffed, fought the urge to throw herself into her mother's arms and bawl like a baby. "You don't think Will will mind?"

"Don't be silly. You know your father loves nothing more than having his girls home."

Willard Ellison wasn't her father, though. Yes, he loved her and had always treated her like his own daughter. But she'd never been able to think of him as her father. Not if she wanted to keep the memory of her own dad clear and strong in her mind.

Loving Will too much had felt like a betrayal to Victor.

Irene gave her one last squeeze and straightened. "But—"

Sadie groaned. "Why is there always a *but* with mothers?"

"All the better to annoy our children," Irene told

her. She rinsed her cup, set it in the sink. "Since you're bringing that dog, there need to be a few rules."

Of course. There were always rules at her mother's house. You couldn't outgrow it.

"You," Irene continued, "and only you, will be responsible for his care. I will not feed him, not once. Nor will I walk him or let him out to take care of his—" she wrinkled her nose "—business."

"Agreed." Sadie thought about adding a sharp salute, but had enough sense to resist.

Irene turned, faced her, her hands linked at her waist. "Now, I take it you have employment lined up while you're here?"

She usually picked up money tending bar at a local spot, but that wouldn't be enough to cover the cost for her to go to California. "I'm going to talk to Gordy this afternoon, see if I can take a couple of shifts at O'Riley's. But I'm also looking for something during the day."

"You could work here."

On a surprised laugh, Sadie dropped the cookie she'd been slipping to Elvis. It fell to the floor, but he didn't eat it, just looked at her.

It took her a moment to realize her mother was serious. "Thanks, but I don't think that's a good idea."

"Why not? You're great with customers. And you've always had an eye for color."

"It's just that this is your thing."

"My thing?"

Feeling as if she'd somehow hurt her mother's feelings, Sadie rose. "Your hobby." One bought and paid for by her husband, Dr. Ellison, a local ophthalmologist. "Besides, you know I've never been one to follow fads or trends."

And Lord knew her mother's store catered to those trends. And to the women who could afford to spend a couple hundred dollars on a pair of jeans just because they had someone else's name on the tag. It wasn't like they were stitched together with gold, people.

"It was just a suggestion," Irene said, but her voice sounded weird. Strained. "I guess I'd better get back to my little hobby now."

Uh-oh. Definitely hurt her feelings.

"Mom, I didn't mean—"

"Shall we expect you for dinner?" Irene asked.

"Sure," Sadie said slowly. "Is it all right if I drop my stuff off at the house?"

"Of course. Goodbye, dear."

"'Bye."

But her mother had already walked away.

CHAPTER SEVEN

"Just to let you know," Maddie said Tuesday afternoon as she helped James lay the floor in one of the bedrooms at Bradford House, "the workers are talking mutiny."

Using a mallet, he hit the plunger of the flooring nailer, nailing a board to the floor. Grunted.

She set her hands on her hips above her tool belt. "Did you *grunt* at me? Really? Just when I think having three brothers couldn't get more annoying, one of you proves me wrong."

He straightened. "What's your point?"

"My point is that you've been moody, grumpy and a general pain in the ass for the past two days. You yelled at Art and he's like…eighty years old."

"He's forty-seven."

Her brow wrinkled. "Well, he looks older. A good reason right there not to smoke."

James sighed. "Maddie…"

"Oh, right. Anyway, you're pissing off people left and right. Which isn't like you at all. What's going on?"

"Nothing."

"You don't want to talk about it? Fine. But you'd better do something. Get therapy or have someone help you pull your head out of your ass. But stop snapping at your coworkers before they decide working alongside someone as witty and awesome as me isn't worth putting up with you."

He didn't want or need advice, especially from his younger sister. He'd had a rough few days. He was entitled, wasn't he? Christ, he'd finally slept with the woman he'd been in love with since he'd been ten freaking years old only to cut her out of his life completely.

He deserved to be grumpy for a few days. Maybe even a week.

"Are you done?" he asked.

She narrowed her eyes. "Yes."

"Good." He picked up the next piece of flooring and set it in place. Grabbed the nailer. "Then we can get back to work."

"You're not still upset about Bree going to breakfast with Neil today are you? Because she's really looking forward to hanging out with you this weekend."

"I'm looking forward to it, too." Even if it meant getting used to his new position in his niece's life.

Even if it meant acknowledging that now that Bree had her father in her life more often, she didn't need James. Not like she used to.

Which proved he needed to focus on his own life. On moving forward.

It'd proved how right he was to finally let go of his crazy, stupid dreams regarding Sadie.

"Does this have anything to do with Sadie?" Maddie asked, watching him shrewdly.

He missed the plunger, hit his knee. He dropped both, straightened and hopped over to the wall for support and carefully straightened his leg. "Son of a bitch."

He glanced at Maddie, but instead of sympathy, his sister stood there looking as if he'd gotten what he deserved. "I take it that's a yes?"

Rubbing his knee, he glared at her.

Maddie, of course, wasn't intimidated in the least. "Because after work yesterday, I stopped by WISC looking for a dress to wear to some fundraiser Neil is taking me to when Bree and I fly out to Seattle in a few weeks, and Irene said Sadie was staying with her."

"Not interested." He crossed to the corner, grabbed a bottle of water from the cooler Maddie had brought. Drank deeply. He hadn't let himself wonder where Sadie had ended up. But if he had let his guard down enough to let her into his head, he would have thought she'd end up with Charlotte. Or one of her other friends. She'd always felt so stifled at her mom's place.

"Well, I was interested, seeing as how Sadie usually stays at your place. What's the deal?"

"Drop it, Maddie."

"Did you two kids have a fight?"

He finished the water, crushed the bottle. "Damn it, I said drop it."

Her eyes widened, and she crossed to him. "Oh, James. You did it, didn't you? You told her."

Foreboding touched the back of his neck, cold and clammy. "Told her what?"

Maddie rolled her eyes. "That you're in love with her."

"Aw, Christ."

"You did," she breathed. "What did she say?"

"What do you think she said? And how the hell did you know anyway?"

"I'm your sister, but more importantly, I'm a woman. And I know you. I see how you look at her when you don't think she'll notice." She removed her ball cap and hit it against the side of her thigh. "I figured once you finally stopped messing around and were honest with her, you two would…"

"Would what?" James asked, hating that his sister had seen what he'd tried so desperately to keep hidden. If Maddie had seen his feelings for Sadie, who else knew? It was demoralizing to realize he was an open book, and yet Sadie had been shocked when he'd admitted how he felt about her.

It was humiliating.

Maddie's expression softened. She felt sorry for him. Okay, it was worse than humiliating. It was pathetic.

"I thought you two would work out," Maddie said, her voice gentle. "That she'd stay in town, you'd get married and have a couple of incredibly adorable kids."

He lifted another piece of flooring. Realized he hadn't finished nailing in the previous piece so set it down. "Yeah? Well, Sadie isn't interested in any of that." Wasn't interested in him, not in the way he wanted her to be. The way he needed her to be in order to remain in her life. "It seems I'm not her type."

No, she preferred assholes who wore leather jackets and perpetual sneers. Men who were misunderstood, brooding and antiestablishment. Hell, James was the opposite, and he wasn't going to apologize for it. He didn't want to change who he was, not for anyone, not even Sadie.

Maddie hugged him, and he sighed. Patted her back.

"I'm sorry," she said. "I know how it feels, believe me."

She did, too. She'd loved Neil ever since she was a kid, had gotten pregnant when she'd been a teenager only to have Neil leave her and Bree.

But Neil had come back. James doubted Sadie would. Wasn't sure he wanted her to. Not when he was so pissed at her. Not when she'd hurt him so badly.

"I know you're probably not ready to hear this now," Maddie continued—she was like a damn dog with a bone, chewing it to death. "Maybe you don't even want to hear it, but this might actually be a good thing."

"You're right. I don't want to hear it."

Maddie ignored him. She excelled at ignoring anything and everything she didn't agree with. "The perfect woman for you is out there. And now you're free to find her. To let yourself fall for someone you can build a life with, someone you can have a future with."

She was killing him.

Death actually seemed preferable to finishing this conversation. "Could we please stop talking about it altogether before what's left of my manhood curls up in a corner and dies?"

"Men. So sensitive."

He'd gotten four more nails in when his coworker Heath stepped into the room. "There's a woman here to see you," he told James. He wiggled his eyebrows. "She's a pretty thing, too. And she brought you something."

James's first thought, the one that had everything inside of him stilling, was that it was Sadie. But Heath had worked for them for fifteen years and had met Sadie several times. If it was her, he would have just said so or simply sent her upstairs to James.

Not Sadie, come to beg him to take her back, to give her another chance. To forgive her.

He couldn't figure out if he was disappointed or relieved.

With a sigh, he leaned the flooring nailer against

the wall and went down the back staircase to the gutted kitchen, through the dining room and into the large reception hall. As he passed the fireplace— one of five on the first floor—he heard conversation coming from the living room, then the sound of feminine laughter.

"Char," he said, mildly surprised to find her chatting with Art. To find her there at all.

She smiled, had her dimple winking. "Hi," she said.

Art, on scaffolding eight feet above the ground, nailed crown molding in place. Heath joined him a moment later.

James took her elbow and led her into the reception hall then slid the pocket doors shut, muting the sound. "What's up?" he asked.

"I hope you don't mind, but I've been dying to see the inside of this place, and at your party I was talking to your mother and she said it would be all right if I stopped by sometime to look around."

She inhaled. Well, that had been a mouthful, one she'd said in a breathless rush.

He couldn't help but smile—the first since he'd kicked Sadie out of his life. Charlotte was cute as hell with her red hair, freckles and rapid-fire words. She was also smart and funny. Good company. But he had a million things to do, and while he didn't mind showing off their work, doing so would put him behind schedule.

"I brought a bribe," she added quickly, as if reading his thoughts. She peeled the lid off the square, plastic container she carried, her eyes—the same shape as her sister's but more green than blue—sparkling with warmth and humor. "In case you need convincing. Chocolate-chip cookies."

They smelled good. Really good. James took one, bit into it. They tasted even better.

"Sure," he said. Schedules could always be adjusted. And being with bright, lively Char would help keep his mind off Sadie. He hoped. "Come on, I'll give you the grand tour."

THIRTY MINUTES LATER, Charlotte preceded James into the kitchen, glanced back oh-so-casually as if admiring the loose brick of the dining room's fireplace. James, on the phone, was looking straight ahead.

She faced forward again, pursed her lips. Okay, not checking her out. A girl could hope, right? And, really, it wasn't as if she was dressed to kill. On the contrary, she'd chosen the faded jeans and loose, black T-shirt because they were casual. Had kept her makeup minimal—just a hint of color on her eyes and cheeks, a glossy pink on her lips. She'd braided her hair, leaving a few tendrils loose around her face to soften the look, some brushing against her nape to show off her long neck.

All in all, it was a look that cried out: *No need to fear. I'm not trying to impress, or heaven forbid, seduce anyone.*

She'd known getting James on board with her plans would take time—time, effort and perhaps more than the usual amount of persuasion. She had a few things against her, the biggest one being that he thought of her almost as a little sister. Even though he already had a little sister and certainly didn't need another one.

The other was the age difference. A man like James, someone decent and honorable and responsible, probably saw those ten years as a barrier, like a stone wall, keeping them apart. She would simply have to show him that they meant nothing to her. Convince him that it was okay for him to see her as a woman. A grown, intelligent woman. That it was more than okay for him to be attracted to her.

That she was worth climbing over that wall.

She stepped into the kitchen. It was empty. Finally. She hadn't realized how many people were working here or that every room she and James entered they would encounter someone else, carpenters or plumbers or electricians.

The kitchen was also completely gutted. No cupboards or appliances. There weren't even walls or a ceiling, just parallel boards and electrical wires, a few pipes. The floor had been ripped up, leaving large sheets of plywood.

As they'd toured the house, James had helpfully pointed out the changes and improvements they'd made—how they'd shored up the fireplace in the front parlor, had managed to save and refinish most of the original trim and installed all new windows. He'd explained what was on the agenda for the bedrooms and bathrooms upstairs.

She could listen to him talk forever. She loved how enthusiastic he was about his work. How much he obviously enjoyed what he did.

But for the most part, she'd had no idea what he was talking about. He'd explained what each room would look like when it was done, but all she could see was how they were now. And no way would she admit she had no idea what wainscoting was or exactly what a tongue-and-groove floor looked like—though she could guess.

Just because she wanted to be married to a carpenter didn't mean she had to learn everything there was to know about renovating an old house. She highly doubted he knew how to start an IV or read a 12-lead ECG.

It would give them more to talk about during the year they dated—casually for the first two months, then exclusively for another eight to twelve months before he proposed.

She already had the perfect engagement ring in mind.

"Sorry about that," he said, putting his phone away as he joined her.

"Please don't apologize. I'm the one who interrupted your day. I really appreciate you showing me around."

"My pleasure."

Did he mean that? She thought he did. Yes, she was sure of it.

Progress. Slow and steady, but they'd get where she wanted them to eventually.

She almost giggled. Wanted to give herself a nice pat on the back for a job well done. Okay, so maybe she'd had to stretch the truth a few times here and there. She didn't *really* feel guilty about taking him from his work. And she couldn't care less about this house. Yes, it was nice enough, and she was sure it would look great when it was done, but right now it was a mess.

Dangerous, with all those sharp power tools and loose boards, rusted nails. Unsanitary with the sawdust and plaster and possibly asbestos floating through the air.

So she'd stretched the truth a bit. All was fair in love and war. And James's mother *had* told her she could stop by to look around Bradford House. No, Rose hadn't specifically said James would give her a tour, but the only way to get what you wanted was to take chances.

Achieving goals, especially big ones, took careful consideration, planning and, most importantly, execution.

Such as giving him the cookies in a plastic container so he would either have to return it himself—the perfect scenario, just the two of them alone in her very cramped apartment—or she'd have to drop by to pick it up.

"Maybe next time I should come later in the day," Char said casually. "That way I won't take you away from your work. Oh," she continued, with a thoughtful frown, "then you'd be forced to stay later."

"You're welcome anytime. I'm here until seven most nights, but if you stop by and I'm not around, one of the guys can take you through," he said, dashing her dreams that he wanted her to return so he could have her all to himself. "Just don't ask Maddie. She doesn't give tours."

"Really? I would've thought she'd love showing this place off. It is Neil Pettit's, right? And they're back together?"

Plenty of people in Shady Grove were interested in the restoration of Bradford House, both because it was such a historical fixture in town and because Neil Pettit was such a big deal. That he'd bought it and was paying to have it renovated into a bed-and-breakfast for his sister to run only made the gears of the old rumor mill spin that much faster.

Especially after Fay Lindemuth had attempted suicide over a month ago when her husband left her and their two young sons to run off with some minimart clerk.

"It is Neil's house," James said, "and yes, he and Maddie are back together." He was such a good man. Too good to share idle gossip. "But she still hates being interrupted when she's working." He lowered his voice, leaned in close enough that Charlotte inhaled the spicy scent of his aftershave. "Or eating. Makes her grumpy."

Then he grinned.

She went warm all over. Oh, goodness.

"Speaking of eating," Char said, her voice unsteady, her heart racing. "Uh…I was thinking on Friday, after we look at the house, we could stop at Salvatores? I've been craving pasta." Plus, the Italian restaurant was perfect—delicious food, great atmosphere, but casual enough that it wouldn't freak him out or make him uncomfortable. "I could make reservations, just in case they're busy."

"You don't need to do that. I'm sure you have better things to do on a Friday night than hang out with me."

"Don't be silly. Besides, you're doing me a favor by looking at this house. The least I can do is make sure you have a decent meal after." A thought occurred to her, a terrible, horrible thought. "Unless… unless you already have plans. A date."

She was watching him so carefully she didn't miss the way his jaw tightened as if he was clenching his teeth. What did that mean? Was he seeing someone?

"No," he said. "No date."

Relief made her light-headed. Or maybe that sensation was from standing so close to him.

"Great." Though she had nowhere to be and not a damn thing to do other than a load of laundry, she glanced at her watch. "I'd better get going." Always leave them wanting more, her mother advised. Her mom was one smart lady. "Thanks again for the tour. The house is really, really great."

Testing them both, she gave him a hug, kept the contact light, just a quick, friendly squeeze. One he returned without resistance.

Yes!

"I'll see you Friday," she said, stepping back.

Unable to stop the self-satisfied smile she knew was lighting her face, she slipped out the door, walked around the house, stepping carefully across the uneven yard. She had things to do after all. First on the agenda, buy the perfect outfit for Friday night, one guaranteed to finally get a few second looks from James Montesano.

STANDING ON THE brand-new porch of Bradford House, Sadie opened the front door only enough to stick her head in. Noise hit her: country music, the buzz and whine of power tools, the pounding of hammers and the occasional male laugh or good-natured shout.

She stepped back and closed the door.

Her heart raced, her palms were damp. She shifted the bakery box to her other hand. Though it only held two dozen cupcakes, it felt like it weighed twenty pounds.

She was nervous. She rolled her eyes. Please. Nervous? She was scared out of her mind.

What if James was still angry with her?

No. He couldn't be. James didn't stay mad. He'd been embarrassed the other day. Understandable. But they were friends; they could get past this. They'd made a mistake by sleeping together, had let the physical attraction that had always simmered underneath their friendship take over. She was partly to blame, she realized. She'd been upset about having to return to town and feeling low about herself.

And, yes, maybe she had wondered what it would be like, the two of them together.

But knowing wasn't worth losing James over.

He'd confused his feelings for her, that's all. Now that he'd had a few days to think about it, to calm down, he'd realize that. He'd realize it and he'd want her back in his life. He had to.

She missed him.

She always missed him, of course. When she was away, she thought about him often and fondly, but being in Shady Grove somehow made it worse. Knowing he was within reach, literally, but didn't want to be around her, didn't want to see her, hurt. It hurt a lot. The idea of never repairing their relationship, of losing him for good?

Unfathomable.

She had to get him back.

It might not be as easy as she'd like, not when she couldn't stop thinking about their night together, how it'd felt to have him touch her. Kiss her. Make love to her.

She frowned. He didn't have to be so damned

good at it, did he? If he'd been boring in bed or fumbling and bumbling, she wouldn't keep reliving it. Wouldn't still want him. But that was just physical. Sexual. It had no bearing on why she was here or why she wanted him to forgive her. She couldn't have romantic feelings for him, couldn't let this physical attraction to him overtake her senses.

Sex had only complicated things between them. Threatened to ruin the best thing that had ever happened to her.

She opened the door and forced herself to step inside. Blinked. Wow. She'd seen the outside of Bradford House, of course, had driven or walked past it hundreds of times over the years, had always liked the look of it with its pitched roofs and narrow windows. There was history here, and the Montesanos were obviously trying to preserve it, to bring the house into the twenty-first century while keeping its integrity and charm.

There was still a long way to go, but she could see the care that had gone into the place so far. Ornate moldings along the ceiling and wall, wooden floors, arched doorways. And she could clearly imagine what it would look like with furnishings, paint and wallpaper designs. Could envision what was needed to bring the house alive, to give it warmth and charm and make people want to stay here, to come back.

She did a quick tour, stopping to chat with Art and Heath, who were used to her coming and going on James's job sites. He must not have told them they'd had a disagreement because the guys greeted her with grins and jokes. Pointed to the stairs when she'd asked where James was.

The top of the stairs ended in a wide hallway. She followed the sound of power tools and voices to the left, glanced into a bathroom, almost getting run over by someone—a plumber?—in white coveralls carrying a huge wrench. She'd just passed a large, empty room when she heard it. James, the deep rumble of his voice, low and familiar.

It brought a long, warm tug to her belly.

Happiness to hear him again, she assured herself. Nothing else.

Pasting on a smile, she knocked on the door frame and then walked in. "Here you…are," she said lamely because, obviously he was here, standing tall and broad in front of the window, the afternoon sun reflecting off his dark hair.

She kept that damn smile in place when James frowned and averted his gaze.

Maybe this wasn't going to be as easy as she'd hoped. Too bad. She really did so much better when things came to her easily.

But James was worth a bit of work.

"Hi, Maddie," she managed to say, stepping toward her, intending to give her a hug. Maddie crossed her arms and Sadie stumbled to a stop. "Uh…how…how's Bree?"

"She's fine. What are you doing here?"

Ouch. There wasn't a trace of warmth or welcoming in Maddie's voice. Sadie had considered the other woman a friend. They usually got together when Sadie was in town, went out for dinner or a drink.

She glanced at James. He'd told his sister what had happened. He met her gaze equally, as if he had any and all right to share the personal facts of their relationship with anyone he damned well pleased.

Okay, so he did, she thought grudgingly. But not if it meant getting people mad at Sadie.

People didn't get mad at her. They didn't dislike her. She was Sadie Nixon, for God's sake. A ray of freaking sunshine. Just ask anyone.

Well, anyone other than these two. And perhaps their mother.

Sadie tucked her hair behind her ear with an unsteady hand. "I, uh…wanted to see the house. James had said I could stop by whenever I wanted, so…"

He'd told her that at his party, before they'd had sex and he'd dropped the bombshell about his feelings on her, blowing her mind and their friendship to bits.

"It looks great," she said into the silence. Who knew a Montesano could remain quiet for so long? The only naturally quiet one was Eddie—and even he spoke when he was around his family—so having James and Maddie just watching her, waiting for her to crumble like a cookie, was nerve-racking.

Damn them.

"The house," she blurted. "It's great. Really

great," she finished weakly. Realizing she still held the bakery box, she raised it. "I brought cupcakes. White and German chocolate."

"We've already had chocolate-chip cookies," Maddie said, cold enough to cause frostbite. "Charlotte dropped them off an hour or so ago."

Sadie frowned. "Charlotte was here?" Her entire family was friends with the Montesanos, but she hadn't realized Maddie and Charlotte were close, as Lottie was a few years younger than Maddie. And, as Maddie had a preteen daughter, at very different stages of their lives.

"We're working," James said, not sounding angry, more like polite. Removed. As if she was some stranger off the street who'd walked in and interrupted his day.

"Oh." It came out barely above a whisper, the best she could squeeze out around the tightness in her throat. She sent James a pleading glance, but he was unmoved. "I guess I'll just—"

"For God's sake," Maddie muttered, tossing up her hands. "It's like kicking a puppy," she said to James.

He shrugged. "She's always been good at getting people to feel sorry for her."

"I'm standing right here," Sadie pointed out, irritation growing. She did *not* make people feel sorry for her. God. "I'd like to talk to you," she told James tightly. She sent Maddie a pointed look. "Alone."

At first, she thought Maddie was going to argue,

but then she looked at her shrewdly, glanced over at James and seemed to change her mind. "I do have to call Bree, see how her day went. But I'll be back in ten minutes."

While Maddie walked out, Sadie set the cupcakes on a sawhorse, then faced James. "I can't believe you told her what happened between us," she said in a harsh whisper, unable to hide the hurt in her voice.

"I didn't tell her," James said, wrapping up an extension cord. "She guessed. Seems I haven't done such a hot job of hiding my feelings for you."

He didn't sound too happy about it.

Welcome to the club, buddy.

He kept working, cleaning up the room, which had a new floor. She didn't know how to approach him when he was so distant. It was like talking to a stranger, which she usually didn't have trouble with, so it was doubly weird and frustrating.

"The house really does look amazing," she said, injecting some lightness in her voice. The best way to do this, she decided, was to act as if nothing had happened. "Have you hired someone to do the interior design yet?"

"Fay's supposed to handle all that."

"You don't sound like that's such a good idea."

"She's fragile. I'm not sure taking on a project this size is the best thing for her."

"How's she doing?" When James sent her a questioning look, Sadie continued, "Mom mentioned she was in the hospital last month." The only delicate way she could think of to put Fay's situation.

"We don't see much of her around here." James crouched in the corner, neatly setting tools into a metal box. He snapped the box shut, straightened. "Was there something you wanted, Sadie?"

And that wasn't quite back to normal. Looked as if that part would take a little while longer.

"I wanted to see you. I miss you."

Nothing. No expression change, not even a flicker of emotion crossed those dark eyes.

"I got a job," she blurted. "Tending bar at O'Riley's a few nights a week. Did you know Gordon sold it to some ex-army guy? Says he wants to move to Brazil—Gordon, not the army guy—"

"Guess you didn't need my help after all. You managed to gain employment all on your own. Congratulations," he said, not sounding as if he really meant it.

She hadn't known he could be so cold. She couldn't say she liked it much. "It's only part-time. It'll take me a while before I make enough to...to..."

"To run off to California?"

"Yes," she said, lifting her chin despite the blush warming her cheeks. Why should she be embarrassed for wanting to get out of Shady Grove? For wanting more than an ordinary existence, more than her mother's life?

"If you're in a hurry to leave, why not ask Will for the money? I'm sure he'd loan it to you."

"I'd rather earn my own way." It was something she'd learned how to do despite being spoiled as a kid and teenager. It wasn't always easy, but having that independence and not being beholden to anyone else was so worth all the hard work, long hours and crappy-paying jobs she'd had.

Her failures, her successes, were her own.

"Besides," she continued breezily, "I'm not in a hurry. I still have to find Elvis's family, and who knows how long that'll take. I contacted the paper, put an ad in with his picture and I called all the animal shelters in a fifty-mile radius, but so far, no one's reported him missing or contacted me."

"You could always drop him off at the local ASPCA."

"Put him in dog jail? Abandon him?" She shook her head, hardly believing he was even suggesting such a horrible thing. "No. No way. If no one claims him, I'll find him a good family."

And though she'd asked him to help her with that, she was perfectly capable of doing so on her own.

He picked up a metal toolbox. "Good luck."

"Wait," she cried as he headed toward the door.

He turned, sighed as if she was just too much to deal with when he was the one making this so difficult. Raised his eyebrows in question.

"Jamie, I...I'm sorry. I'm so sorry I hurt you."

"So you said."

"I said it, but obviously you don't believe it."

His expression softened, making him look like

her old friend, the person she could always go to, the one person who'd always fully accepted her. "I know you mean it, Sadie. That's not what this is about."

"What is it then? Punishment?"

"No," he said, sounding appalled. "You know me better than that."

"I thought I did, but what am I supposed to think when you're standing there, obviously still mad at me?"

"I'm not." The way he said it made it seem as if he was surprised by that fact. "I'm not."

Relief and hope bloomed inside of her. "So you forgive me? We can forget the other night, the other morning, ever happened and go back to how we were before?"

They could. She knew they could. Hadn't she known he'd never stay angry with her for long, that they'd be able to work things out?

"I forgive you," he said slowly. "I have to—not for you, for me. But, no, we can't go back to how we were."

His voice was incredibly gentle, and she even detected a hint of regret there. But not enough to overcome the resolve in his eyes.

"I don't understand," she said, unsure of which emotion to focus on, which was the right thing to feel. Sadness, yes, but also frustration. Anger. "If you forgive me, then why does anything have to change between us?"

"I forgive you because we have a history, a past

that means a lot to me. Because, no matter what, no matter how much I may not want to, I still care about you. I'll always care about you." He lowered his voice, stepped closer and her heart picked up speed. "But I can't be your friend anymore, Sadie. I can't be your friend because I'm in love with you."

"Do you have to keep saying that? God! You are not in love with me," she said, her voice rising despite realizing at any second someone could come into the room. "You're confused. If you'd just give it some time—"

"I know my own heart," he said, not sounding angry, just as if he was stating a simple fact. "I've been in love with you for most of my life, and it's not going away. It may never go away, but that doesn't mean I have to torture myself by being your friend. It's not enough for me. Not anymore. And it's not fair of you to ask me to pretend it is."

Her blood went cold. He was right. He was absolutely right. But doing the right thing for him meant she'd lose him. "I don't know if I can let you go," she whispered.

"You have to. You don't have a choice. You're going to have to find someone else to take care of your problems, to hold your hand when your life turns upside down, because I can't do it. Not anymore."

CHAPTER EIGHT

"ALL I'M SAYING is that most men don't have two beautiful women bringing them cookies and cupcakes." Sitting on James's deck railing, Leo grinned, bit into a cupcake. "I mean, I do. Women go crazy over us firefighters. But mere mortals like you?" He shook his head. "Not normal."

"Don't you have a fire truck to wash?" James asked.

"Nah. We let the rookies wash 'em. Makes them feel useful."

James sighed and tipped back on the rear two legs of his chair, sipped his beer. He'd told Eddie he was grilling steaks if he and Max wanted to come out to his house, but when they'd arrived, they'd had Leo in tow.

Which usually wouldn't be a problem except he hadn't stopped ragging on James about Sadie and Charlotte.

Out in the yard, Max threw the tennis ball over and over again for Zoe. Neither one of them ever seemed to tire of the game.

"You're in denial," Leo said, polishing off the

cupcake and reaching for another one. "He's in denial," he said to Eddie, who came out through the glass door from the kitchen.

Eddie took three cookies, settled into the seat next to James. "About what?"

"This idiot," James said before Leo could finish chewing and open his big mouth again, "thinks Charlotte Ellison has some grand designs on me, that her bringing those cookies you're eating was a scheme to..." He looked at Leo.

Leo swallowed the mouthful he'd been chewing. "Lure you into her bed. Though why she'd need cookies is beyond me. She's a goddess, and I've heard redheads are real firecrackers in the sack."

"Shut it," James and Eddie said at the same time.

"What? Like you two haven't noticed how sexy she is."

"She's too young for you," James said.

"Age is just a number, my friend."

"For you," Eddie said, "it's a guideline. How old was that brunette you were with a few months ago?"

"Twenty-two is legal in every state in this great country of ours."

"Just make sure Charlotte isn't anywhere in your future," James said. "She's Sadie's sister and therefore off-limits. You hear me?"

"I can't make any promises. If she starts coming by the fire station bearing cookies, I can't be held responsible for what may develop between us."

"Don't pound on him in front of Max," Eddie

said, calmly sipping his beer as James started getting out of his seat to do just that. "I don't want him getting into any fights during recess this year. And convincing him it's better to use his words instead of his fists is hard enough without explaining how it's okay for you to do it and not him."

James sat back reluctantly. He could always beat on his smug brother later.

"Is Sadie coming?" Eddie asked. "I thought she'd be here."

"Yeah," Leo added. "She's the only reason I agreed to this dinner invitation—"

"You weren't invited." But he could sniff out a free meal from a mile away. "She's staying with her mother," James continued.

Eddie frowned. "I thought she and her mother didn't get along."

"They get along fine."

But it was easier for them if they weren't together so much. Irene had no problem letting Sadie know she wished her daughter would make different choices with her life, find a place to settle down. And Sadie was too eager to prove she was some free spirit, going wherever the wind took her. She took great pride in taking after her father, who'd died when she was nine.

From what Sadie said about the guy, he was as close to perfect as a parent could get, though James wasn't sure Irene would agree. Not when Sadie said they moved several times a year so that her old man could chase his dreams.

Sounded familiar.

"How come she's not staying here?" Leo asked.

"Because she's staying at her mother's," James growled.

He stared out at his yard. The sun was setting, crickets were chirping. Zoe barked and jumped and Max laughed, a deep, rolling belly laugh that had James's lips curving. That was what he wanted. A couple of kids running around his yard, racing through his house. A wife to share it with.

What the hell was wrong with that?

"I slept with her," he said.

He could feel both of his brothers' shocked stares.

"Holy shit," Leo breathed, sliding to his feet. "You slept with Sadie's mother?"

"Okay," Eddie said with a decisive head nod. "I'll keep Max's attention occupied while you beat the shit out of dumb ass here."

"Not her mother." James ground out the words. "Sadie. I slept with Sadie."

The relief on Leo's face would have been comical had they been discussing something else. "That does make more sense. Details. And don't go too fast. Eddie doesn't have the ability to picture a story in his head the way I do."

Eddie and James exchanged a look. "Hey, Max," Eddie called as he stood. "Look, it's a hawk."

He pointed in the air and when his son turned

his back to check it out, Eddie slapped Leo upside the head.

"Where?" Max asked, head still tilted up. "I don't see it, Dad."

"Huh," Eddie said while Leo grumbled about cheap shots and how his brother should sleep with one eye open because paybacks were a bitch. "Must've flown off."

James slouched in his seat, wished he'd kept his mouth shut.

Leo nudged James's knee with his beer bottle. "Don't look so glum, chum. Sleeping with a knockout like Sadie is cause for celebration. And after all these years of you jonesing for her—"

"What?" James sat up so fast, he spilled his beer. "What?"

"It's not a secret, is it? Hell, you've had a thing for her since…forever. I say, about time you did something about it instead of mooning over her."

James stood, fisted his hands, the back of his neck heating up. "What am I, wearing a goddamn sign?"

"Might as well have been," Leo said cheerfully.

"I'm going to have to kill him," James told Eddie. "So if you don't want your son to witness a murder and you be charged as an accomplice, I suggest you get going now."

Eddie slapped James's shoulder. "I've got this. Max," he called again.

"I'm not looking for any more hawks, Dad," Max

said, shaking his shaggy brown hair out of his eyes. "You just want to hit Uncle Leo again."

"Kid is too damn observant," Eddie muttered.

"I heard that," Max yelled, throwing the ball for Zoe.

"Remember what we talked about on the way out here? That thing with the thing?"

"The thing with the thing?" James repeated.

Eddie ignored him.

"Really?" Max asked, his face lit up. He raced over, his left sneaker untied, his T-shirt sporting both steak sauce and ketchup stains, his knees scabbed over. "I'm allowed and I won't get into trouble?" he asked in a whisper, glancing at Leo.

Eddie laid his hand on his son's head. "You'd be doing the world a favor."

Max laughed. Looked at Leo again. Laughed louder. "Okay!"

He ran off, legs and arms pumping, Zoe giving chase.

"What's going on?" Leo asked suspiciously.

"Nothing you need to worry about," Eddie assured him.

Leo turned to see what Max was up to and Eddie caught James's eye, inclined his head toward the door. James followed him inside and was shutting the door when Leo turned. Scowled. "Hey, what—"

The rest of his words were drowned out. Literally. Max, wielding James's hose, sprayed his uncle right in the face. "Good aim," James said, locking the door as Leo reached for the handle.

"He goes for the weak spot and he's relentless," Eddie said as his son kept up a steady stream of water against Leo's face. Leo, trying to block the spray with his arms, swore viciously while Zoe raced around him, getting into the spray.

Water hit the glass directly in front of James's face, cascaded down. "Now I'm going to have a wet, stinky dog."

"Life's a bitch that way. You get the bedroom, I'll get the front door."

By the time James made sure there was no way Leo could get into his house and walked into the kitchen, Leo was chasing Max around the yard.

"How long until he catches him?" James asked, joining Eddie at the window.

"Not long. Max is fast, but he's better in a sprint. Not enough endurance for the long race. Plus, he's cocky."

The word was no sooner out of Eddie's mouth when Max whirled around and shot Leo right in the crotch, soaking his khaki cargo shorts.

Still squirting, Max laughed like a hyena. Leo feinted left then lunged right. Even in the house, they winced at the volume and pitch of Max's squeal when Leo wrestled the hose from him. Before Max could escape, Leo grabbed the back of his shorts, tossed him over his shoulder in a firefighter's hold and doused him.

"That should keep them both busy for a while," Eddie said, grabbing two bottles of water from the fridge. He tossed one to James, who caught it one-handed. "You okay?"

"Pissed at myself," he admitted, knowing he'd never be able to tell anyone else but Eddie that. "I told her I loved her and she shot me down. Hard. Not the first woman to do so, but this…this was different. She's different."

"You took a chance. They don't always work out the way we want. If they did, I'd still be married and Max would have a mother in his life. Instead he's stuck with us and dealing with the fact that his mom decided she wasn't cut out for motherhood."

Eddie's short-lived marriage had soured him toward women and marriage in general.

"You ever regret it?" James asked. "The marriage?"

"I got Max out of it," Eddie said simply. "So, it didn't work out with Sadie," he continued in his take-no-prisoners way. "What did you think she was going to do? Completely change who she is, what she wants out of life because you told her you love her?"

"I thought she'd at least consider the possibility of being with me."

"But you know her. You've known her practically your entire life. People don't change. You're looking for something in a relationship, and you're not going to get it with Sadie. Why not look elsewhere? The only way to get what you want out of life is to grab it."

"You're right," James said. Looked like he was about to take another chance, several, actually. Not with Sadie. He wasn't going to make a fool over himself over her again. Not over any woman.

But it was past time he shook things up.

THURSDAY WAS SPAGHETTI night.

Every. Thursday.

Sadie set a stack of dirty dinner plates on the counter. "Don't you ever want to do something different?" she asked Charlotte, who was loading the dishwasher.

"You want to wash and I'll dry?"

"No, not that. Although, yeah, I would rather wash than dry. Washing dishes has a point, but drying them? Why not just let them sit in the drainer? They'll dry overnight."

"It only takes a few minutes to dry them," Irene said, her supersharp hearing in tip-top shape as she came into the kitchen carrying the leftover sauce and meatballs. "And I'd rather they be put away and the entire kitchen clean then wake up knowing I have to finish cleaning the kitchen every morning."

"I'm not saying leave dirty dishes in the sink until the next day." Although Sadie had done that plenty of times in her life. It was easier to wash them if you let them soak for a day. Or two. "Just a few items that need to be hand washed."

Irene sent her an unreadable look. "I prefer my kitchen to be spotless after dinner."

She preferred every room to be spotless all the time. Her house, while not exactly ostentatious, didn't exactly shy away from showing how much wealth they had. Set at the end of a cul-de-sac, the two-story Cape Cod had four bedrooms, four baths and a gourmet kitchen complete with two ovens and a six-burner range.

Her mother's knack with color and decorating made the space feel warm and inviting instead of showy. But every time Sadie was there, she was reminded of how close she'd come to turning into a pampered princess who was more concerned about making other people happy by living up to their standards than living her own life.

And wouldn't her father have hated that?

He would have hated everything about this house and Shady Grove. Would have hated the life Irene had chosen after he'd died.

"What did you think of the meatballs?" Irene asked as she put the Parmesan cheese in the stainless-steel fridge. "I used a new recipe."

"They were good," Charlotte said. She nudged Sadie with an elbow.

Sadie opened her mouth to say they were fine, that they tasted like the same meatballs Irene made every Thursday, but what came out was, "Don't you get tired of eating the same things week after week?"

"Really?" Charlotte asked under her breath. "This is something you feel the need to bring up?"

"What do you mean?" Irene asked Sadie with a confused frown.

"It's just so…boring. Meat loaf or steaks or roast beef on Mondays. Chicken on Tuesdays. Pork on Wednesdays. Thursday night is spaghetti, Friday you go out to Horseshoe Manor with the Longs and Kelleys. I bet you order the broiled tilapia every week, too."

How could her mother stand living that way? Where was the spontaneity? The fun and excitement. Life was too short and too precious to be so mundane and scheduled.

Not that Sadie had ever been able to convince Irene of that. She was too stubborn to listen to reason, was always so completely certain she was right, that her way was the one and only way to do something.

"I like knowing what I'm going to be cooking each day," Irene said slowly, as if Sadie was the one who had the issue here. "And for your information, we ate at the Wooden Nickel and I had the salmon."

For some reason, that tickled Sadie. Her lips quirked. "I stand corrected."

Irene ran a hand down the side of her already perfectly smooth hair. "I should hope so." But she didn't sound amused or even angry. Worse, much worse, she sounded hurt. "I'll just bring in the rest of the dishes."

"Do you have to antagonize her?" Charlotte asked as soon as they were alone. "It's like you purposely pick fights just to tick her off."

"All I did was ask a simple question."

"You asked a question guaranteed to get a rise out of her."

That wasn't true.

Was it? God, she didn't even know anymore. She was upset about James, worried about the direction her life was taking and, she realized, guilt making her sick to her stomach, had taken all of that out on her mom.

"I just don't understand how she can live this way," Sadie mumbled. "I wish you could've seen her before we moved here. She was so much fun."

Sadie remembered those days, moving from town to town, all the wonderful adventures she'd had with her parents. They'd lived all over the country by the time Sadie was nine—New York and Dallas and New Orleans. Every day had been an adventure.

"She'd been so carefree," Sadie told her sister, picturing Irene as a young mother, her hair long and loose, her clothes fun and funky. "She used to dance around the living room, throw together dinner out of whatever was in the cupboard, make up endless games. When we moved here, she changed. It's like she turned into some Stepford wife."

And every time Sadie came home, every time she was in Shady Grove, it only reminded her of all she'd lost. Her beloved father, who'd been the light of her life.

And the woman her mother used to be.

"Mom's still plenty fun," Charlotte insisted, her movements jerky as she shut the dishwasher door, turned the machine on. "But we can't all live our lives as carefree as you."

Sadie's eyes narrowed. "What's that supposed to mean?"

"Some of us have jobs," Charlotte said, stressing the word. "Responsibilities. People who depend on us."

When had Charlotte grown up? Gotten so damned smart and reasonable? Sadie couldn't argue with a reasonable person. They always tripped up her logic.

"All I'm saying is that it wouldn't kill her to be spontaneous now and again," Sadie said. "A person can still have a job—" she mimicked her sister's tone and how she'd drawn out the word "—responsibilities and all that other stuff and still live a happy life filled with plenty of surprises and carefree moments."

"Well, all *I'm* saying is that it wouldn't kill you to give Mom a chance. You're so judgmental."

Sadie about choked on her own spit. "Me? I'm judgmental?"

"Did I stutter? Shall I say it again, this time with a little bit of spontaneity and drama? You," Charlotte continued, her voice deep and booming as she pointed at Sadie, "are so very judgmental. Emphasis on the mental."

"Ha-ha. They teach you that tired joke in college?"

Charlotte's lips twitched. "I thought of it all on my own."

"I wouldn't brag about it." And she was not judgmental. Nor was she the problem here. The problem was her mom always looking down her nose at Sadie and the choices she made.

"Look," Charlotte said on a sigh, always the one to give in first, to make concessions, "let's not fight, okay? We obviously have different opinions on this, but that doesn't make either of us wrong." She waited a beat. "Except you."

"Except you," Sadie said at the same time.

They both grinned.

"No more fighting," Sadie agreed. "And as a show of good faith, I'll even promise that I will do my best not to antagonize, provoke or poke at our mother during the remainder of my stay in Shady Grove."

"It's a spaghetti-day miracle."

"Amen," Sadie said. "Hey, tomorrow's my first night at O'Riley's. If you're not working, stop by. It'd be nice to see a friendly face."

"I'm sure you'll see plenty of friendly faces, many that you know. Besides, tomorrow I'm looking at a house."

"What do you mean?"

"I mean, I'm buying a house."

"What?" Sadie asked. How could her sister buy a house? She was only twenty-four. Was that even legal? "A whole house?"

"No, part of a house," Char said drily. "I thought I'd start with just the bedroom and bathroom and see how I like it."

"I'm just…you're so young. You've got your whole life ahead of you. Are you sure you want that kind of commitment?"

But the thought of it, the idea of a house to maintain, of a mortgage and taxes and yard work and being stuck in the same place year after year after year didn't give Sadie the creeps the way it used to. It actually sounded sort of…nice.

Too bad the house she pictured as her own was a log home filled with brown furniture. Too bad it already belonged to James.

And she wasn't going to think about him. Not after he'd blown her off, had tossed aside their friendship not once, but twice.

"I want a home of my own," Charlotte said firmly. "And I found a great place by the river. It's not too big, not too small, and it has the best kitchen and a yard."

"Before you put any money down on it, even one cent, have a building inspector look at it."

Charlotte leaned back against the counter, rubbed at a spot on her shorts. "Actually, I'm doing better than that. James said he'd look at it for me."

"James is helping you?" Sadie asked. "My James?"

Charlotte sent her an amused look. "Yes, your friend James. We're going there tomorrow evening."

So that was why Charlotte had been at Bradford House the other day bearing cookies. Not to see Maddie—which hadn't made sense to Sadie anyway—but to bribe James into helping her.

Not that she'd needed the bribe. James was a good guy, a sweet one, always ready and willing to lend someone a hand.

And he was spending Friday evening with her sister. Helping Charlotte.

When he couldn't even stand to be in the same room as Sadie.

Her stomach burned. Her throat hurt. She averted her gaze, pretended great interest in looking around the kitchen. "Have you seen Elvis?"

"I believe he's left the building." Char smiled widely at her own lame joke. "Dad took him out back."

"I'd better go check on them."

She kept her movements unhurried as she went into the family room and out through the sliding glass doors to the covered porch. The sun reflected off the crystal water of the inground pool, the deep green of the professionally manicured lawn. Shielding her eyes, she crossed the yard toward the spot where her stepfather stood.

Will still had his work clothes on—black pants and a short-sleeved white button-down shirt— though he'd removed his tie. He had a ring of dark auburn hair around the crown of his head, like a halo that had fallen and gotten stuck there. The top was shiny and smooth and bald as a baby's bottom.

He whipped a thick, braided rope in the air. Elvis, sitting by Will's feet, watched it fly and land near her mother's garden shed.

Will looked down at the dog. "I think you're missing the whole point."

Elvis licked himself.

"Ah, well. I guess I don't blame you," he said, taking something from his shirt pocket. "I throw the rope. You bring it back. I throw it again. It does seem like a fruitless endeavor."

He unwrapped a chocolate bar and bit into it.

Grinning, Sadie crept up behind him, her bare feet sinking into the cool grass. "Busted," she whispered into Will's ear.

He whirled around, his green eyes wide behind his glasses. Looked at her then the candy then her again. Held his hands up. "It's not mine," he said solemnly. "I'm just holding it for a friend."

"Oh, I believe you. But if you plan on fooling Mom, you'll need to wipe that spot of chocolate from the corner of your mouth."

Using the pad of his thumb, he wiped both corners of his mouth. Smiled and gave a sheepish shrug, his tall frame still thin thanks to his thrice-weekly tennis game. "She'll know anyway. Your mother always knows."

"True. So true."

Even though his physician had put him on a strict diet to try to get his cholesterol levels under control, Will was having a hard time giving up sweets. Irene had stopped baking desserts for every meal and had stocked the fridge and pantry with healthy options.

When she found out he'd snuck candy into the house—or, in this case, onto the property—she'd pick what hair he had left off his head.

"You're a brave man," Sadie told him. "Risking the wrath of Irene."

He handed her a piece of chocolate, saluted her with the bar. "A man only lives once."

"I'll eat to that."

The rich, dark chocolate melted on her tongue. Part of her wanted to snatch the candy from Will, and not just because it was good, but to keep him safe. Healthy.

She didn't want to lose another father.

Not that she'd ever let Will know how much he meant to her, how much she appreciated him treating her like his own daughter. She couldn't. To do so seemed disrespectful to Victor's memory.

Still, there were a few things she could thank him for.

"I really appreciate you letting Elvis and me stay here."

"My pleasure." He winked at her. "Taking a daily antihistamine is a small price to pay for having you home."

He was such a nice man. Kind and patient. He reminded her a lot of James.

And damn it, she wasn't going to think about James anymore. Not after losing sleep over him again last night. Not after she'd finally drifted off around four that morning only to dream of him— hot, sweaty dreams of the way he'd touched her. Kissed her. Dreams she should not be having about someone who was just a friend.

"How's the search going for Elvis's family?" Will asked.

"Not so well. His picture's been in the paper for three days and no one's called yet."

"Why don't you let me pay to have his picture put into a few papers in some of the surrounding towns and Pittsburgh?"

"I couldn't ask you to do that."

"You didn't."

She thought of the cost. Money she could ill afford to spend. She hated borrowing money from her mom and Will, had already had to do so to buy supplies for Elvis.

She couldn't even take care of herself. It was beyond embarrassing. This wasn't the first time she'd been down on her luck and flat broke, but it was the first time she'd had to ask for someone else's assistance in getting back up.

It was the first time she wondered if she'd be able to get back up at all.

But for Elvis, she'd lower herself to asking for

help. For a handout. She had to do whatever she could to help him find his family. To help him get back what he'd lost.

"Thanks," she said to Will, "I'll pay you back. Every penny."

"Sadie, I don't expect you to—"

"I'll pay you back." Luckily she was working at O'Riley's over the weekend. It wouldn't be much, but it would help put a dent in what she owed.

And she could start saving to leave.

"I heard there's going to be an opening for a receptionist at the medical building," Will said. "If you're interested."

"I am." At this point she was interested in pretty much anything except maybe pole dancing and animal husbandry.

And she'd consider the animal husbandry if the pay was good.

"It won't be available for two weeks, but you could get your application in now."

Two weeks? Crap. Well, beggars couldn't be choosers. Especially when it was the first job opening she'd heard about that she was qualified for.

"I'll stop by tomorrow, first thing in the morning," she said as the sliding doors opened and Irene came outside walking toward them, the house phone in her hand.

Sadie stood in front of Will with her hand behind her back. He tucked the candy wrapper in her palm, stepped smoothly to the side.

"Is that for me?" he asked.

"Actually, it's for Sadie." She held out the phone. "It's Frank Montesano."

Frank was calling? For her?

Sadie took the phone, turned her back to her parents. "Hello?"

"Sadie," he said, his voice booming over the phone. "It's Frank. I didn't catch you at a bad time, did I?"

"Not at all. Is everything all right?" Had something happened to James?

"Everything's fine. I was wondering if I could possibly interest you in a job."

FRIDAY MORNING, JAMES strolled across the parking lot toward the shop as he checked the local forecast on his phone. Years ago, when his father had started the company, he'd built a shop behind his house. The original building—two stories and large enough to hold two semi trucks—had gone through several changes, most notably the addition of an office where Rose worked as office manager.

His agenda clear in his mind, what he had to get done already prioritized, James switched over to his messages, catching up on a few he'd missed. He had the day's schedule both on his phone and in his hand on paper. After assigning the workers to their jobs, he needed to stop by the Carlisles', check on the progress of their foundation. He also needed to drop off the Websters' estimate and order the lumber for Mrs. Kline's cupboards.

Inside the shop was where Eddie—the best at finish work—made one-of-a-kind built-ins, entertainment centers and bookcases, cabinets, vanities and occasionally even furniture. It was also where James, Maddie and their father built stair treads and measured and cut countertops. Across the paved lot, a two-story warehouse housed lumber, doors and windows and all supplies kept on hand. Next to it was an oversize garage that held three flatbed trucks used for hauling that lumber or supplies to and from jobs.

It was, James had to admit, a very nice setup for a thriving business like this one. One his father had built—ha-ha—from the ground up, starting with a workshop in the basement of his and Rose's first house.

James often wondered how he'd gotten to be a part of it, how he'd gotten to take on so much responsibility. Without planning to, he'd ended up an integral part of Montesano Construction. Now, for better or worse, it was his life. Or at least a big chunk of it.

He wasn't sure how the hell he felt about that.

He inserted his key into the lock on the door only to discover the handle turned easily. Frowning, he stepped inside. The lights were off, the interior dim and cool. It smelled of stale air and sawdust, a light coating of which covered the concrete floor, machines and workstations.

He squeezed the key in his hand until the edges bit into his skin. He was going to kill Eddie for not locking up. Swear to God, if so much as one board was missing, he was kicking his brother's ass.

Not that anything seemed out of place, and with the shop being behind his parents' house, they would have noticed if anyone had come and gone—especially if that person was carting machines or supplies. Relaxing his grip, James pocketed the keys. And noted the scent of coffee.

What the hell?

He wound his way around the machines toward the rear of the building, turned the corner to the addition where the office, a small bathroom and kitchenette were and found the lights on.

And Elvis lying on the floor next to the metal desk.

He hated to repeat himself but...

What. The. Hell.

He heard a sound to his right, turned and gaped at Sadie as she came out of the kitchenette, his favorite mug in one hand, a scone in the other.

"Morning, Jamie," she said, as chirpy as a freaking bird. "Coffee?"

CHAPTER NINE

JAMES LOOKED AT Sadie, then to Elvis, who'd gotten to his feet and come over to have his ears scratched, then back to Sadie. She looked real enough in a red floral skirt that ended well above the knee, a red checked top with puffy sleeves, ankle socks and silver high heels with an open toe.

No one threw together an outfit like Sadie.

And, unfortunately, he couldn't dream up that getup on his own. Besides, most of his dreams of her started off with her clothed, but then quickly progressed so that those clothes magically disappeared. And ever since their night together, ever since he'd felt her skin, tasted her, those dreams had become frequent, more torturous and way more erotic.

This was real. Sadie was real and so beautiful it hurt just to look at her.

"Your Jeep's not here," James said.

She stared at him as if he was the one who'd lost his mind. "It's at the shop getting that dent fixed. Will dropped me off."

"How did you get in here?" he asked, the only question he could think of.

She went behind the desk and sat, putting the scone onto a napkin. "My key, of course."

"You don't have a key."

"Yes, I do."

He opened his mouth, realized he was about to say, "No, you don't," and snapped it shut again. Inhaled deeply. Unfortunately, all he could smell was the coffee and her damned perfume, which only made him crave them both.

"Why do you have a key?" he asked, once again in control.

"That's easy. Because your dad gave me one."

As if sensing James was at the end of his rope, and ready to use it to strangle the sexy blonde in front of him, Elvis slunk over to sit by Sadie's chair.

"Why—" James ground the words out "—did my father give you a key?"

But before she even could swallow her mouthful, he knew what his father had done.

"Because he hired me as your new office manager."

The words, the truth he saw before his very eyes, rang in his head. "Like hell he did."

She broke off another piece of scone. "Wait a minute…he didn't tell you?"

"No."

If his father had run this by James first, Sadie wouldn't be sitting here.

Blushing clear to the roots of her hair, she stood,

wiped her fingers on that skirt. "Jamie, I'm sorry. I thought you knew."

"Yeah, well, I didn't." And he didn't care that he sounded like an ass. Didn't care that she seemed sincere and almost as upset about this as he was. Hearing the shop door open, he jabbed a finger at her. "Don't move."

"Can I at least sit down?"

"No." He didn't want her to sit. He wanted her gone.

"Sadie," Frank said as he walked into the office. "You're here bright and early."

Sadie slid James an anxious look then circled the desk to give his father a hug. "Just eager to get started, I guess. Or at least, I was."

Frank sniffed the air appreciatively. "Is that coffee I smell? And—" another sniff as if he was a blood-hound, able to discern between jelly and cream-filled "—doughnuts?"

She began twirling her hair around her finger. "I…uh…stopped at the bakery on my way here."

"Looks like we got ourselves a real find, huh, James?" Frank asked.

"Yeah. She's a peach."

At his flat tone, Sadie flinched. Shit. James pinched the bridge of his nose. He hadn't meant to hurt her.

Didn't you?

No, he told his snide inner voice. He just wanted

her gone. Out of his life for good. It was the only way he'd ever get over her.

"Let me get you some coffee," Sadie said, practically running into the kitchenette.

While she poured, Frank took his time searching through the two glossy white bakery boxes for the perfect doughnut.

"Can I speak with you?" James asked his dad when Frank had a cup of coffee in one hand, a doughnut in the other. James jerked his head toward the shop. "Alone?"

Without waiting for an answer, James walked into the shop, crossed to the far end by the windows.

"Is there a problem?" Frank asked, breaking his cake doughnut in half so he could dunk it in his coffee.

"Fire her."

Frank raised his bushy eyebrows. "Excuse me?"

"I want you to fire Sadie. Tell her you made a mistake, that she can't work here."

"Why would I do that?"

Because it was bad enough knowing she was in town, a mere few miles away, without talking to her, without seeing her. When she was half a country away, he could put her out of his mind, pretend she wasn't always in his heart. But seeing her every day?

It would be pure hell.

But he didn't want to tell his father that, couldn't admit how deep in over his head he'd always been for her. Though his father probably knew—everyone else seemed to.

"Why the hell did you hire her in the first place?" James asked. "We don't need her."

"I hired her so your mother could cut back her hours, concentrate on her classes." He looked confused. And implacable. "I hadn't realized it would be a problem."

"It is. Sadie won't stay," James said as the door opened and Maddie came in. "She'll take off, leaving us in a bind. It might be next week or next month, but she will leave."

Frank finished off his doughnut then sipped his coffee. James grimaced, thinking of all those crumbs in there. "She already told me she'd only be able to fill in temporarily, which works out for all of us. Now we can take our time, find the perfect person to take over the job from your mother."

"Does Mom even know about this?"

"Not yet. I wanted it to be a surprise."

"It's a surprise, all right."

"What is?" Maddie asked, joining them.

"Dad hired Sadie to be our new temporary office manager so Mom can focus on her classes."

"Oh, Dad, you didn't. How could you?"

"Sadie mentioned you and she had a falling-out," Frank told James. "But that's no reason to let a lifetime of friendship go. Think of it this way, not only does this help your mother out, but it also gives you and Sadie a chance to work through your differences."

"I don't want to work through our differences. I want her gone." Out of his shop, out of Shady Grove, out of his life for good. "Fire her. Now."

Frank bristled. "I think you've forgotten who you're talking to, son." His voice was deadly soft. "This is my company. I make the decisions. Not you." He nodded as if that was the end of it. "Sadie's hired and she's staying hired."

As Frank walked away, fury colored James's vision, vibrated through his body. He wanted to rail, to punch the wall, grab his dad and shake him. Curse him out for doing this to him, for not giving him a say in the matter.

His father's company. His father's decisions. James was just another employee.

"He didn't mean that the way it came out," Maddie said quietly. "You know how he gets when he thinks someone is questioning his authority. You push him, he pushes back to let you know he's still in charge—as our father and our boss. That's all it was."

But James wasn't so sure. "You ever think about what you're doing here?"

Her eyebrows drew together. "Here as in the shop?"

"Here as in working for Dad. Being stuck in the same place you've been—the same place we've both been—since we graduated high school."

"We're not stuck, James. This is our job."

"Yeah? Well, maybe I'm tired of my job." Tired of busting his ass every day, of keeping the company running smoothly. Of his thoughts, his feelings being brushed aside.

"What are you going to do?" Maddie asked sardonically. "Quit?"

He could.

The realization shot through him like an electric bolt, had the tips of his fingers tingling, the hair at the nape of his neck standing on end.

He could quit. Nothing was forcing him to stay. He'd never thought of it before, had never considered the possibilities that were out there. But now that he had...

Since it wasn't his company, his business, he didn't have to take on all the stress and responsibilities, the endless customer complaints or employee frustrations. There was no need for him to work twelve-hour days and spend his weekends putting out fires or trying to get ahead of the game, to stay on top of the jobs. Trying to make Montesano Construction an even bigger success.

He could walk away.

The breath left his lungs on a soft whoosh. *He could walk away.*

Holy shit.

"James," Maddie prompted, "I was kidding."

"I know," he murmured distractedly.

But now that the idea had taken hold, he couldn't

shake it. Didn't want to. He wanted to explore it, turn it over in his head and weigh all of his options.

And then, after careful deliberation, after he'd listed the pros and the cons, he'd decide if he wanted to stay with his father's company.

Or start one of his own.

WELL, SO FAR her first day on the job had completely and totally sucked.

Sadie glanced at the clock on the computer. And she'd only been working for Montesano Construction for twenty minutes. Twenty minutes of Maddie glaring at her hard enough to incinerate her on the spot. Of Eddie barely speaking to her and, the worst, James not even glancing her way, as if he couldn't stand to look at her.

Finally, thankfully, their little meeting broke up. Sadie stood as the carpenters started filing out, James having given them their work orders for the day.

"James," she called from the office doorway, not meaning to sound quite so...desperate. She toned it down and tried again. "Could I speak with you?"

Everyone—Frank, Eddie, Maddie and their six employees, every last damn one—stopped in mid-stride.

Everyone, that was, except James, who kept right on walking toward the door. "I'm busy."

Sadie's face flamed, got so hot she was surprised steam didn't rise up and cause her hair to curl. "Jamie," she managed to say through the mortification tightening her throat. "Please."

He stopped, his shoulders ramrod straight. She could practically see his internal debate, sensed how much he wanted to ignore her. To brush her aside when he'd never, not once before, treated her with anything less than the utmost respect.

She'd lost his respect, his kindness. Her own fault, yes, she thought as irritation rose, but surely he carried some of the blame.

The workers left, the last one—a super slow-moving Maddie—hesitating at the door while James crossed the shop to Sadie. "Yes?"

She opened her mouth. Shut it. Okay, so he wasn't going to apologize for embarrassing her. That was fine. She could handle this new James.

But, man, she hoped the old James came back soon.

"I'm sorry," she said.

"What for this time?"

That flicker of irritation grew, threatened to become a full flame. She smothered it. "I thought you knew your father had hired me."

"You expect me to believe that?"

She narrowed her eyes. "It's the truth."

He smirked—James Montesano actually smirked at her. She wished it wasn't so damned sexy on him.

"And you always tell the truth, don't you, Sadie?" His voice was a low, husky purr, a tone she'd never heard from James. Intimate. Knowing.

Arrogant.

"I do when it's important."

He nodded. Grudging acceptance. If that was the best she could get, she'd take it.

"I thought you knew," she repeated. "In fact I'd hoped…"

"What?"

She met his eyes. "I'd hoped it was your idea. That you wanted me here."

A stupid assumption on her part. But she'd been so excited about the job that she hadn't asked too many questions. She never would have guessed that Frank would make a decision like this without getting James's input first.

"Look," she continued, "I don't want to make things difficult for you, and I certainly don't want to be the cause of any trouble between you and Frank—"

"Who said there was trouble between us?"

"Voices carry in here, James. I heard you two arguing."

I don't want to work through our differences. I want her gone.

She wiped her damp palms down the sides of her skirt. "I think it'd be better, for everyone, if I just quit."

His phone buzzed. He checked it, read whatever the text message said.

And answered it.

She wanted to slap the stupid thing out of his

hand. Or better yet, shove it down his throat. There she was, willing to give up a job that was the answer to her prayers, and he couldn't give her his full attention.

Whirling around, she stormed over to the desk, all high indignation, and grabbed her purse. "Come on, Elvis."

"Don't bother with the theatrics or going through with this grand gesture," James said, putting his phone in his pocket as he stepped farther into the office. "They're not necessary."

"You want me to stay?" she asked, raising her eyebrows.

His mouth thinned. "It's recently come to my attention that what I want doesn't matter, so you might as well keep the job. Besides, the sooner you earn enough money, the sooner you can take off to California."

"Well," she breathed. "Ouch."

He dropped his gaze. Sighed. "Go. Or stay. It's up to you."

"And I suppose if I stay, I'll have to deal with the new you—"

"New me?"

"This—" she waved vaguely at him "—new... different...version of you. Who, by the way, is sort of an ass."

"Sort of?"

"Keep working on it," she muttered. "I'm sure you'll be a whole ass in no time."

His eyes gleamed, but she wasn't sure if it was from humor or anger. She couldn't read him, not anymore. She used to think she knew him better than anyone.

Now she wondered if she'd known the real him at all.

"If you stay," he said, as if they were discussing what type of dry dog food was best, as if their entire friendship ending didn't bother him in the least, "I'll do my best to keep any and all versions of myself out of your way. I'd appreciate it if you'd do the same for me."

She carefully set her purse on the desk—instead of winging it at his stubborn head. "Believe me, I will."

Jerk. And that was one thing she'd never, ever thought she'd call James.

Yes, she'd hurt him, but she hadn't meant to. Didn't that count for anything? Did it give him an excuse to treat her this way? To stay so angry?

He was the one who'd kept a secret from her. He'd made the choice to hide his feelings for her all these years. She may not have handled it well when he'd admitted those feelings to her, but he had his share in the blame for this.

Didn't he?

"If we're done here," James said, "I need to get to work."

"Please," she said from behind a fake, toothy smile, "don't let me stop you."

He turned, only to stop and face her again. "If you do decide to keep the job, you might want to leave the dog at home."

She checked on Elvis to make sure he wasn't chewing—or peeing on—anything, but he was sound asleep next to the wall. "I don't like to leave him by himself."

"You're getting pretty attached to him."

Did he have to sound so shocked?

You're not keeping him. James had sounded so certain of that, as if the idea of her taking care of Elvis—long-term care, forever and ever, amen— was implausible. "Elvis gets anxious when I leave him. Whether he ran away, got lost or was left on the side of the road somewhere, his entire life changed," she said, her voice shaking. "Everything he knew and understood and liked—loved—suddenly just… disappeared. It's frightening."

"Was that how you felt when you moved here?" James asked after a moment. "Afraid?"

Her mouth wobbled. She firmed it. He shouldn't be able to read her thoughts, to see her so clearly when he'd completely cut himself off from her.

"The situations aren't quite the same." But she couldn't meet his eyes. She had been afraid. She'd been terrified. Not because they'd moved, but because they'd stayed.

And the longer they stayed in Shady Grove, the more they got sucked into a provincial, pedestrian life. The more it seemed as if they'd lost her dad all over again.

"It's a lot to process. For Elvis," she stressed, in case James wanted to try to psychoanalyze her. "Besides, your dad said I could bring him along."

Yes, she sounded like a bratty ten-year-old, but that was only because he was bringing out the worst in her.

James frowned, almost as if he was disappointed she hadn't opened up to him, as if he hadn't been the one to put up these new barriers between them. Barriers she could be thankful for in this instance.

"If Elvis is anything like Zoe," James said, "he'll go nuts when the machines run, and Eddie's going to be starting the kitchen cabinets for Bradford House on Monday."

"Oh." She hadn't thought of that. Elvis hadn't seemed bothered by the thunder the night she'd found him, but that may have been only because he'd been so traumatized from being wet and cold and lost. "I'll see how he does. If it bothers him, I'll take him home."

He shrugged and glanced at the clock on his phone. He had work to do, as did she. His mom would be here any minute to show her how to do the payroll, give her a list of her responsibilities as office manager. Sadie needed to let James go. He was still angry with her.

He might not ever forgive her.

But she couldn't do anything that upset him,

even when he treated her with such coldness, such...
indifference.

That indifference was the absolute worst. She
wasn't sure she could face it day in and day out.
Wasn't sure she could be around him, even for a
few minutes each day when her feelings were so
conflicted. So confused.

"I want this job," she blurted. "I do. But I don't
want it if it means making you unhappy."

Didn't want it if it meant losing him for good.

"Again, that's your choice. But it's not one I'll
make for you. Know this, though," he said, leaning forward, so close she could pick out the sun-
lightened strands woven through his dark hair, could
smell the minty scent of his toothpaste, "it doesn't
matter to me what you decide."

Her gaze fell to his mouth, to that full bottom lip.
Remembered how it'd felt against her own mouth,
on her breast. Her core. She swallowed. Raised her
eyes to meet his. "James..."

It came out a question. An entreaty.

Shaking his head, he straightened. "Nothing you
do matters to me. Not anymore."

CHARLOTTE OPENED THE door to O'Riley's, stepped
inside and hid a flash of annoyance. It was packed
and noisy—the jukebox playing some ancient rock
song that battled with the crowd. Wasn't nine-thirty
on a Friday too early for a bar to be this busy? Then
again, O'Riley's always had been one of the more

popular bars in town. Guess having a new owner hadn't changed that.

Still, she'd been hoping for a little privacy. Had imagined her and James spending an hour or so cuddled together in a dimly lit booth, deep in conversation, lost in each other's eyes.

She scanned the room. All the booths lining the walls were filled.

"We could sit at the bar," James said from behind her.

A couple entered behind them, pushing James forward until his chest pressed against Char's back, solid and warm. She waited one long moment before edging away. They couldn't sit at the bar. If they did, there'd be no reason to linger over the drink she'd suggested they have after their dinner ended.

She rose onto her toes and spied two twenty-something women vacating a table near the back. "I see a spot," she said.

He followed her as she wove her way across the room, touched her lower back as they stepped up to the table and then held out her chair for her.

She smiled up at him, giddy at that faint brush of his hand, that he'd finally made a move. Even if it was just a friendly, could-be-construed-as-only-being-polite move.

"Thank you," she murmured, pitching her voice low, but instead of sounding sexy, it came out as more of a croak.

But other than her brief froggy imitation and

a few slow moments in their conversation, it was going well. Really, really well, she assured herself as a short, middle-aged man and his shorter wife stopped to talk with James.

Char pushed aside a lipstick-stained glass. Wiped her fingers on her jeans. Okay, so maybe it wasn't going well, exactly. But it wasn't a total disaster, either.

That had to count for something.

She needed to pick up her game, that was all. If only she had more experience with this sort of thing, the whole...dating...thing. Not that she was a social leper. She'd had dates. Just not as many as most women her age.

A late bloomer, her mother had called her fondly. As if knowing something better might possibly be coming made it easier to deal with being a flat-chested, gangly, clumsy teenager with bright red, unmanageable hair and a face full of freckles.

It hadn't. It had sucked, especially when her mother was petite and graceful and classically beautiful, her sister a pretty blonde who embraced her own sense of style and lit up any room.

Then, during college, it had happened. Char *had* bloomed. Thank God.

Even before that, though, she'd had a champion who'd assured her that though it seemed as if she was the only sixteen-year-old without a boyfriend, someday the boys would be lining up for her. And whomever she chose would be the luckiest guy of them all.

They weren't exactly lining up, she thought wryly, but more than a few had been interested. James had been right. More importantly, he'd been sweet to her, his best friend's little sister.

That was all it took, a casual comment made during her mother's annual Memorial Day picnic—one of the few Sadie had attended since leaving home, one she'd invited James to—and Char had fallen and fallen hard. That bright, sunny day that everything became clear.

James Montesano was the man of her dreams. The only man for her.

"Sorry about that," he said as he sat across from her.

She straightened. "No problem." He was so handsome—though she preferred him without the mustache and goatee he'd grown about a year ago. Maybe, after they were officially dating, she could drop a few hints about him shaving it off.

A harried-looking waitress with a neck tattoo and asymmetrical, black hair stopped, grabbed the dirty glasses. "I'll be with you guys in a minute."

"No hurry," Char said, but the waitress had already left. She smiled at James. "Busy place."

He nodded. Linked his hands together on top of the table. "So…work's going well?"

They'd already discussed both their jobs during dinner but, hey, she'd go with it. "It is. It really is."

She racked her brain for a topic of conversation, something witty and interesting. They'd been fine while they'd been at the house, as he'd inspected it, he'd explained what he was doing, what he was looking for...cracks in the walls or ceilings, warped floorboards, something about moisture and condensation. Honestly, she'd zoned out a few times, but she didn't think he'd noticed.

During dinner they'd exhausted local topics, had moved on to asking how each other's parents were doing, then had ended up on the weather before the check arrived.

Conversation shouldn't be this hard.

"I don't think our waitress is coming back anytime soon," Char said. "I'll just go up to the bar and order our drinks."

"I can get them," he said, starting to stand.

She gestured for him to sit, then grabbed some cash from her purse and stuffed it into her pocket. "You got dinner." Had insisted on paying. "I'll get the drinks. What'll it be?"

"Whatever they have on tap is good."

She smiled, hoped it didn't come across as strained as it felt. "I'll be right back."

Halfway up to the bar, she glanced back, hoping against hope that he was watching her. He wasn't. He was talking to a man around his age, laughing at something the guy said.

This was obviously a mistake. Not being with him, of course. But suggesting they stop here for a drink. It would have been better, much better, if they were alone.

Yes, that would work, and the more she thought about it, the better it seemed. Reaching the end of the bar, she squeezed between the wall and a brawny woman in jeans and leather vest. Char leaned forward, raised her hand, but the bartender's back was to her.

She fell back to her heels. They'd have a drink, then she'd ask James to her apartment to...to what? Check for intruders? Fix the toilet?

She studied James. She needed an excuse, that much was clear. Oh, he liked her well enough and they'd had a decent time so far this evening, but he wasn't falling all over himself. He hadn't even flirted, and she'd turned up her flirting skills by several degrees.

Men. Why did they have to be so difficult?

James was perfect for her. They would be perfect together. She knew it. And she was rarely wrong.

"Get you something?"

She tore her eyes off James and turned to face the bartender. Her scalp prickled, her mouth dried when she met his eyes, a cool green framed by dark blond lashes. The rest of him matched that deep, husky voice: a sharply planed face, tousled, golden hair, scruffy facial hair that made James's seem downright conservative. His white T-shirt clung to his broad shoulders and his well-defined biceps, where she caught the edge of indecipherable tattoos on both arms.

Bad boy, she thought dismissively. Trying too hard to keep those muscles, that edgy, dangerous mystique so many women found appealing. Not her, of course.

But he was still so pretty, so…potent…she had to clear her throat before she spoke. "Two drafts. Please."

He eyed her, his gaze steady and unreadable. "You got some ID there, Red?"

"Seriously?" she asked, fisting her hands so she wouldn't reach up and touch her hair, make sure it was as in control as when she'd left the house.

"I never joke about possibly being cited for serving minors."

"I'm not a minor." Damn her freckles. And double damn the blush heating her cheeks. She probably looked like a tomato.

"I don't care if you are. But if you want a drink, you'll have to prove that."

She could, easily. Except her purse was at the table. She glanced over her shoulder. And she didn't want to go over and admit to James that she looked so young, rebel-without-a-cause here wouldn't serve her. The age difference was already between them—and staring her in the eye every time she tried to think of a new subject for them to discuss.

She turned to the bartender, but he'd already moved on.

Asshole.

She waited, tapping her fingers on the sticky bar top. Because he wouldn't look her way again—she'd bet he was doing it on purpose—she had to resort to standing on the rail and lifting her hand, then waving it to get his attention.

"Find that ID?" he asked when he returned.

Realizing her hand was still in the air like a grade-schooler, she lowered it. "I'm twenty-four. Promise."

"I don't need promises, Red. Just proof." His gaze flicked over to James. "Maybe your date over there can run you home, let you get your license."

Her date. At least someone realized what was going on between her and James, as James didn't seem to have a clue.

"Hey," Sadie said as she came up behind the bartender.

Charlotte smiled. Saved by her sister. She'd forgotten Sadie had told her she started work tonight. "Hey. How's your first night going?"

"Actually, I just got here." Sadie nudged the bartender aside with her hip. "Give me an hour or two and I'm sure boss man here will realize he can't run the place without me."

"You're late," he said.

"Five minutes isn't late," Sadie told him. Her gaze bounced between him and Charlotte. "Did you two meet?"

"No," Char said, making it clear she had no interest in knowing this guy.

Sadie obviously didn't get it—though, if the smirk on her boss's face was any indication, he did.

"Lottie," Sadie said, "meet the new owner of O'Riley's and my boss, Kane Bartasavich. Kane, this is my baby sister, Charlotte."

"Baby sister who is of legal age to drink?" Kane of the complicated last name asked.

"Twenty-four this past May."

He nodded. "You take care of her then."

"This place'll close down in two months with that guy running things," Charlotte muttered after he'd left to wait on another customer.

Sadie grinned. "Oh, I'm not sure about that. He has a certain charm. And he's so easy on the eyes that the women of Shady Grove will be filling the place no matter what. Now, what can I get you?"

Char repeated her order and Sadie grabbed two clean glasses from under the counter. "How'd it go with the house?" she asked as she pulled the first beer. "Did James say it was okay to buy?"

"He thinks it's a very good investment." Char had already known that or else she wouldn't have had her real-estate agent put in an offer last week. "I think I have a good shot at getting it."

"Congrats." Sadie opened a bottle of water and tapped it against Charlotte's glass. They both drank, then Sadie pulled the second beer. "I take it you're here with someone."

For some reason the question irritated her. "I'm here with James."

Sadie stilled and almost had beer overflowing the glass. She shut off the tap in time, but when she set the full glass down, foam sloshed over the rim. "What do you mean you're here with James?"

"Just what I said." Charlotte turned, lifted a hand, noticed James's hesitation before he returned her wave. She held up a finger to indicate she'd be just a minute, then faced her sister again. "After we looked at the house, we grabbed dinner and since he insisted on buying, I thought the least I could do was buy him an after-dinner drink."

"Dinner? Drinks? As a thank-you, right? Not like a...like a...date."

Charlotte lifted a shoulder. Well, it was pretty damn close to being a date, even if James wasn't quite aware of it. What else would you call it when a man and woman had dinner followed by drinks?

"I'd say it's a little bit of both," Charlotte said, trying to be coy, but sounding more proud than anything.

"Whoa. Whoa," Sadie repeated, looking at Char as if she'd admitted she'd fallen madly in love with Elvis—the dog, not the man. "You are not dating James."

Charlotte narrowed her eyes. She'd known when she and James got together there would be initial resistance from certain segments, people who wouldn't be able to see how perfect they were for each other.

"Why shouldn't I?" she asked. "He's single. I'm single."

Sadie leaned forward so that she was practically draped across the bar. "Because he's mine. My best friend," she amended quickly. "God, he's...he's too old for you. You barely know him and you don't even have anything in common."

Was that why their dinner conversation had been like pulling teeth? Char brushed that thought aside. Didn't matter. They'd find common ground. She was sure of it.

"We'll get to know each other. That's why people date. And we have plenty in common. We're both two mature, responsible adults who love Shady Grove and want the same things out of life. God, he may be your best friend, but he and I are more alike than you and he are.

"And for the record," Char added, rage and indignation battling inside her, making her voice shake, "I can and will date whomever I choose. I choose James. You don't have a say in it." She slammed a twenty onto the bar between them, grabbed the beers. "Thanks for the drinks."

Her head high, she made her way to the man she wholly planned on making fall in love with her. No matter what Sadie thought about it.

CHAPTER TEN

"WHAT DO YOU think you're doing?"

Shit.

James stiffened, but didn't even glance at Sadie. He'd come to this end of the bar specifically because it was the one the new owner was working, leaving Sadie to handle the other end.

She slammed her hands onto the bar. "Damn it, James, don't you dare ignore me."

Several patrons glanced their way.

"Problem?" the new owner asked as he joined them.

"No," James said. "Two drafts."

"Yes," Sadie said. She glanced at her boss. "I'm taking a break."

"Your break's not for another hour."

"So fire me." She jabbed a finger at James. "You. Don't. Move."

He couldn't help but watch her walk away, her strides long and angry, her hips swinging. She'd changed out of the skirt she'd had on earlier at the office and into a swinging T-shirt with a huge rose on it and a pair of tiny black shorts she'd paired with black stockings and super high-heeled, strappy black sandals.

She was killing him.

He stared at the bar, silently urged the owner to hurry up. How long could it take to pour a couple of beers? James had known Sadie was working here, but he hadn't really thought she'd be here tonight. If he had, he never would have agreed to have a drink with Charlotte.

And he was nothing but a goddamned liar.

He'd considered the possibility that Sadie would be here, but had talked himself into showing up anyway. He wasn't going to let her dictate where he went or what he did. Wasn't going to let his life or choices revolve around whether or not there would be a chance he'd run into Sadie Nixon.

Especially since, thanks to his dad, James was going to see her every morning, five days a week.

She'd gotten to him this morning. He'd let her get to him. He'd been pissed—was still pissed—that his father had blown him off that way. Hurt that he didn't have more of a say in his father's company.

But it was good, he assured himself, that he found out now. Before he continued thinking he was somehow a bigger part, a more important part of Montesano Construction than he was. Before he wasted any more time there. He had some planning to do, some soul-searching. He'd take his time—no sense rushing something this big. And when he was sure, certain of his next steps, he'd take them.

Even if it meant stepping away from his family.

Until he made his decision, he'd keep doing what he always did. And if that meant dealing with Sadie until she took off, then fine.

She'd offered to quit and he'd wanted, more than anything, to take her up on it, but his pride had kicked in. Better late than never. Bad enough everyone seemed to know what a fool he'd been over her, he'd had to go and prove it by tossing out demands like a spoiled two-year-old because she didn't return his feelings.

No more. What he'd told Sadie that morning was the truth. Whatever she did, whatever choices she made, didn't matter to him. He wouldn't let her matter to him.

He paid for the beer and picked up the glasses only to turn and come face-to-face with Sadie. She grabbed the beers, spilling some onto his jeans and shoes, and set them on the counter. More people stopped talking to look at them.

"Come on," she said, taking hold of his wrist and pulling him down a dimly lit hallway.

The only reason he didn't stop her was because he didn't want to make more of a scene. But by the time she pushed open a door marked Emergency Exit and dragged him into the alley, he'd had enough. He was tired and all he wanted was to go home and go to bed. He was taking Bree into Pittsburgh tomorrow to the Carnegie Science Center.

But when he'd finished his beer and Charlotte had

asked him if he had time for another one, he hadn't been able to say no.

Look where being nice got him. Dragged out into an alley by a blonde obviously ready to do him bodily harm.

He stopped, just simply stopped letting Sadie drag him along like some spineless puppy, desperate for a scrap of attention from her. She jerked, stumbled on those heels of hers, her ankle twisting, forcing him to reach out and steady her.

"You okay?" he asked reluctantly, the warmth of her skin burning his fingers.

She yanked free. "No. I'm not okay. I am so mad at you I can't even see straight. I knew you were upset with me. But I never, not once, thought you'd stoop this low."

He wanted to grab her again. Shake her. Pull her to him and hold her close. "What are you talking about?"

"I'm talking about you dating my sister to get back at me!"

SADIE HAD TO give him credit, James looked thoroughly confused, as if he had no idea what she was talking about. As if she was the one in the wrong.

When had he gotten so sneaky? So cruel?

"You've lost your mind," he said before turning to head inside.

She hurried to block him, a sharp pain shooting up from her ankle. "You're out with my sister."

She glanced behind her. Knowing her rotten luck, Charlotte would come sauntering out here any moment. If she heard Sadie ripping into James, she'd never forgive her.

"We're having a couple of drinks," he said, as if speaking to someone of lesser intelligence. "She asked me to look at a house she's interested in buying."

"Yes, she asked you to look at a house and now, what…five hours later…you're here with her."

"She suggested we get something to eat."

Sadie crossed her arms. "Uh-huh. And it didn't cross your mind to refuse?"

"No."

"And who paid for the meal?"

He flushed, but Sadie couldn't tell if it was from embarrassment or anger. "I couldn't very well let her pay, could I?"

No, he would never let Charlotte pay for dinner, Sadie thought snidely. Not a good guy like James. That probably went against his very strict moral code.

"Well, that still doesn't explain what you're doing having drinks with her, looking all cozy at that little table."

"Since I paid for dinner," he said, his voice calm and patient, making her seem more out of control and crazy, "which was supposed to be her way of thanking me for looking at the house, she suggested buying me a beer. I figured it was cheaper than a meal and wouldn't make her feel as if she owed me anything."

"She made you cookies."

He frowned. Looked at her as if she'd lost her ever-loving mind. Who knew? Maybe she had.

"What?"

"Cookies," Sadie snapped. "Cookies! Remember? A few days ago when she dropped by Bradford House for a tour?"

"So she brought cookies. They weren't just for me. They were for the whole crew. You brought cupcakes."

"This isn't about me." But she had a feeling, a terrible, sinking feeling, that it was. That the real reason she was so upset, so horrified by the idea of Charlotte and James being out together, was because she didn't want him with anyone else. But that wasn't right. She wasn't what he needed, couldn't give him what he wanted. She had no right to hold him back.

"What is it about then?"

A siren sounded as a police car drove by. Sadie waited until the sound had faded. "It's about… about…" She held up her hand, mortification threatening to overwhelm her. "You and Charlotte—"

"There is no me and Charlotte. I told you. She asked me to look at the house—"

"And she asked you to dinner?"

"As a way to thank me."

It was all becoming clear. "And after dinner,"

Sadie said, "Charlotte was the one who suggested you come here for a drink? She did, not you?"

"I already told you—"

"Yeah, yeah, you told me. One more question. Did you invite Charlotte to look at Bradford House? Tell her to stop by and see you at work?"

"She said she was interested in seeing the progress and that Mom told her she could drop by anytime for a tour. Which is true. As long as Neil doesn't have a problem with people stopping by—"

"God, you don't even see it, do you?" How he could be so blind was beyond her. Unless he was deliberately fooling himself. "Charlotte has a...a thing for you."

He laughed, but as if the truth was sinking in, it died in his throat. "That's crazy."

"Oh, I don't think it is. Let's look at the facts. She approached you about looking at a house she wanted to buy, then about dinner and now drinks. She stopped by with cookies." Sadie tossed her hands up. "Cookies, for God's sake."

"She was just being nice," he said, but he didn't sound convinced.

"She is nice. She's also beautiful and fun and smart." Smarter than Sadie. More accomplished already. Closer to the type of woman James really wanted. Someone happy to stay in Shady Grove, to live the kind of life he'd always envisioned for himself. "She's also twenty-four."

"She's an adult and capable of making her own

decisions. As am I. We're two friends who had dinner and drinks. Drop it."

But she couldn't. "It's obvious Char's doing everything in her power to try to get you interested. She has her eye on you and when she wants something, she goes after it like a woman possessed. The question is, do you want her, too?"

Sadie held her breath, waiting for him to deny it. To laugh it off. To assure her that he didn't think of her sister as anything other than an extension of his friendship with her.

A friendship that no longer was.

"That," he said softly, looking hard and untouchable, "is none of your business."

It was like being kicked in the stomach, the loss of breath. The shocking pain. "If you're doing this to hurt me," she whispered hoarsely, "it's working."

A muscle worked in his jaw, but his eyes remained cool. "This has nothing to do with you. You don't figure into my thoughts, my decisions or my actions. Not anymore."

She wrapped her arms around her middle, holding herself together. "Just...be careful with Charlotte, with her feelings. Don't break her heart because you want to get back at me."

His eyes flashed, his mouth stayed a grim line. "You know me better than that."

She'd thought she had. A week ago she never would have even considered the possibility that James would be capable of being so cold. So unfeeling. Never would have thought he'd kick her out of his life because she refused to fall in line with his plans.

"I thought I did. I thought I knew you better than anyone." She shook her head. "But I don't know you at all."

SADIE HAD BEEN working for Montesano's for a week now and so far, James had to admit, it hadn't been bad. Sure, seeing her every morning after she'd ripped his heart out and drop-kicked it through the window wasn't exactly the way he wanted to start his day, but he'd kept to himself at the shop, getting in and out with minimal fuss. If he did have to talk to her—something he'd had to do only twice now—he kept the topic of conversation strictly professional.

She had, too. Which wasn't that surprising given their last conversation.

I thought I knew you better than anyone. But I don't know you at all.

He wiped at the sweat on his forehead with the back of his hand as he walked across the ramp from Bradford House's kitchen door onto the back of the flatbed truck. He bent at the knees, lifted another box of floor tiles, the sun warming his neck, his forearms.

Sadie thought he would lead Charlotte on, do something to hurt her feelings.

Then again, that was the impression he'd given

her, he thought, twisting his mouth. The impression he'd wanted her to have.

So much for not letting thoughts of Sadie color his actions.

He set down the tiles, turned for the return trip. He'd simply stay away from Charlotte. She was so young, Christ, he hadn't realized how young until he'd spent the entire evening with her. It hadn't been painful, exactly. She was charming and funny, but they didn't have much in common, and he'd had to work to think of conversation topics that wouldn't die a slow and painful death.

After he'd returned to Charlotte that night, two fresh beers in hand, he'd kept Sadie's words in mind. Hard not to think about what she'd said. He'd spent the rest of the night trying to interpret every word Charlotte said, every look or casual touch, and he'd come up with one conclusion.

Sadie was right.

He'd been an idiot not to see it earlier.

He'd finished his beer as quickly as possible, had gently and politely explained that he had an early morning the next day and had gotten the hell out of there. No harm done to anyone.

Now that he knew what was going on with Charlotte, he'd avoid her, wait until this…crush, or whatever it was she had for him, disappeared.

That should make Sadie happy. Or, at the least, help her realize he wasn't quite the dick he'd pretended to be.

That she obviously now thought he was.

Still, Sadie was working out okay as an office manager. She, with the help of his mom, had gotten the payroll done on time Friday, and she seemed to have no problem with their new computer program. She'd fielded calls from several customers, had charmed every one of them, even hard-to-please Meg Simpson.

She was good at the job, he had to admit.

He just wasn't about to admit it to anyone but himself. Because she wouldn't stay.

For the first time, he couldn't wait until she left.

From the corner of his eye, he caught sight of her walking toward him over the uneven backyard, the sun glinting off her hair, her eyes hidden behind a pair of huge black sunglasses, her mouth unsmiling.

He missed her smiles. Missed talking with her. Hearing her stories about life in some faraway city. He even missed her damned humming.

"Hi," she said, not sounding happy to run in to him. The breeze blew her long skirt around her legs, molded it to the curves of her hips and thighs. She held up a folder. "Your dad said I should bring these contracts over here for him to sign."

James lifted another box of tiles, grunting with the effort. "He's not here."

Sadie's mouth pulled down. She looked put out and irritated. "He specifically told me to meet him here at five-thirty." She waved the papers. "It's five-thirty."

"That it is," James said, walking toward the kitchen, though why his father would say that when he'd left over an hour ago was beyond him. He put the tiles down, turned only to find her standing in the kitchen. "But he's already gone."

She slapped the folder against her thigh. He brushed past her. When he returned with more tiles, she was still doing the slapping thing. *Slap. Slap. Slap.*

"Where is everyone?" she asked.

Slap. Slap. Slap.

He grabbed the folder, tossed it onto a sawhorse. "Workday ends at four-thirty."

She crossed her arms. "Then why are you still here?"

He wanted to take those glasses off her face, see her eyes. But trouble lay that way. Anything concerning touching her in any way, shape or form, of letting things get back to how they used to be between them, led directly to trouble.

"Working," he said simply. And he got back to it.

"Is Maddie here?" Sadie asked when he returned.

He shoved the box in place, straightened. "Plumber's finished two of the bathrooms. She's taking a video of them to send to Neil."

Sadie shifted, finally pushed her sunglasses to the top of her head. "Since you're still here, do you mind if I check out the progress that was done this week?"

She sounded sullen, as if daring him to say no. He shrugged. "Suit yourself."

He walked away. By the time he'd unloaded the truck, Maddie had her laptop on the makeshift table they'd formed out of plywood and sawhorses in the dining room.

"What'd he think?" James asked, twisting the lid off his water.

Maddie clicked a button. "I'm sending the videos now. I thought it'd be easier for him to see them on his laptop than just through his phone. It'll be a while, though, since he has a late practice today and is three hours behind our time."

James tipped his water up, drank deeply as Sadie entered the room. Kept his gaze somewhere over her head as she approached.

"Something we can do for you?" Maddie asked.

"Not a thing," Sadie said, her tone as bright and cheerful as Maddie's was cool. Purposely, James had no doubt. "The bathrooms are wonderful. The whole house is. It's just…"

James finished his water, crumpled the bottle in his hand. "Spit it out, Sadie."

"Where are the living quarters?"

"It's a B and B," Maddie said. "No living. Just visiting."

Sadie's smile was snide. "The guests visit. Oftentimes, the innkeeper or proprietor lives on-site."

Maddie cocked a hip. "Is that so? And you know this how?"

"She worked for a bed-and-breakfast inn outside

of Savannah a few years back," James said, watching Sadie carefully. "For what...a year?"

"A year and a half."

"What happened?" Maddie asked with a sneer. "Get fired?"

"She quit," James said. "They wanted to promote her to innkeeper, but she moved on to...Miami?"

"Atlanta." Pink stained Sadie's cheeks, but she met his eyes steadily. "You know me. I hate to be fenced in. Trapped like an animal in a cage."

"Yes," Maddie said drily. "You're like a wild mustang busting to be free. But, in case you haven't noticed, we're almost done with this job and there's no room for living quarters."

Sadie shrugged as if it didn't matter to her one way or the other. "It was just a thought. And I figured with everything that happened with Fay—"

"You don't know anything about Fay," Maddie said, stalking over to Sadie, all pissed off and aggressive, her work boots adding two inches to her already tall height.

Sadie, though, didn't back down. It was one of the things James had always admired about her, how she stood up for what she believed in. Even if he didn't agree with those beliefs.

"I know she went through a...rough time a few months ago," Sadie said, holding Maddie's gaze. "That her husband left her and their kids."

A rough time didn't even begin to describe what Fay, Maddie's best friend since grade school, had gone through. She and her husband, Shane, had been having problems ever since Shane had been discharged from the Marines this past spring.

Maddie had admitted to James how Neil, worried about his sister's emotional state, had bought Bradford House to give Fay financial security for her and her sons. He'd also hoped that by making her responsible for not only running the B and B when it was finished, but also having her involved in the decision making during the renovations, would give her confidence and a purpose other than holding on to her husband.

Unfortunately, it hadn't worked. Fay had been so distraught over her husband's desertion she'd swallowed a half bottle of prescription pills in an attempt to take her own life. Thankfully, Bree had been spending the night there with her young cousins and had called 911 when she'd realized what her aunt had done.

Now, over a month later, Fay was recovering, but she still seemed to have no interest in the renovations. Neil had postponed the opening until at least the new year, giving Fay plenty of time to get well, and to learn about the ins and outs of running a B and B.

"It's not a bad idea," James heard himself say.

Maddie whirled on him. "You can't be serious."

He felt Sadie's gaze on him, sensed her surprise. Her pleasure that he'd agreed with her.

"Neither you nor I know anything about running

a B and B, but think about it," he said to his sister. "Neil plans on Fay being a full-time innkeeper, right?"

Crossing her arms, Maddie nodded.

"It makes sense for Fay and the boys to live here instead of across town."

"I guess," Maddie conceded. "But it's a little late in the game to be deciding this now. They're going to need at least two bedrooms and a bathroom."

"It'd be preferable if they had their own kitchen and living space, too," Sadie said.

"Thank you," Maddie said icily. "You've been a huge help so far."

"No, no," James agreed, digging through the pile of blueprints on the table. "If we had to, we could do a suite in the basement instead of the game room and theater—"

"Have them live in a basement?" Sadie asked, sounding as if he'd suggested the small family live in an underground bunker. She looked over his shoulder at the blueprints, her breasts pressed against his back.

He edged forward. Studied the plans. "We could put an addition on the rear of the house," he said, leaning down, Maddie on one side, Sadie on the other. He tapped his finger on the kitchen door. "Move this to the west wall—"

"Yeah," Maddie said, "but that means pouring a foundation and a huge added cost—which Neil won't mind, but to maintain the integrity of the design of the house, we'll have to make it the full three stories."

Three stories…

"I have an idea," he murmured. "Follow me."

He rolled up the prints, and they walked into the kitchen and up the back staircase to the second floor, then over to the main stairway up to the third floor.

"Are you sure about this?" Maddie asked.

Bare bulbs hanging from the rafters along with the evening sun streaming through the dozen windows illuminated the attic space, making it bright and cheerful. It was huge, one large room that ran the length and width of the main stories. Empty space, since Neil had hired a cleaning crew to haul out the dozens of boxes that had been left up here when the previous owners moved. They'd discussed the possibility of converting the space into even more guest rooms in the future, but this…this was an even better idea.

"It's perfect," Sadie said.

And she smiled at him.

The air locked in his lungs and he looked away.

Just once he'd like to be able to breathe freely when she was around.

"It could work," Maddie said hesitantly, walking farther into the space, her steps echoing in the emptiness. She tipped her head up. "The ceiling's high enough, and there's plenty of natural light…." She turned to James. "What are you thinking?"

He slowly walked around the entire space, checked the view from every window. "Keep it simple. Open floor plan to maximize the space. Family room… here," he said, standing in front of the stairs, "opening into an eat-in kitchen on the right." He moved to the left of the stairs, stood in front of the window on the far side of the wall at the front of the house. "A bedroom here for the boys with a bathroom between it and the kitchen. Fay's bedroom on the other wall, her bathroom in between the bedrooms."

"What about a launderette off the kitchen," Sadie said, "along this windowless wall? That way Fay won't have to haul her laundry downstairs."

He could picture it. "That'll work."

"It's not a bad idea," Maddie said.

"Do you think Neil will go for it?" James asked.

"He'll do anything for Fay. And, as much as I hate to admit it, this makes sense. Fay would be close to the guests, but she and the boys would have their own personal space. His main concern when he bought the house was to get it finished as quickly as possible to give her a purpose. But her psychiatrist thinks it's best if she has more time to adjust to her life without Shane now that he's filed for divorce. She's worried that too much stress or change will stall Fay's recovery. So…" Maddie exhaled. "Yeah. I think he'll agree."

"What about Fay?" James asked. "Will she have any problem with moving?"

"I'm not sure. Ever since the—" she glanced at Sadie "—incident…Elijah's been having nightmares. Fay might be glad to get out of that house, live somewhere new where there aren't so many memories."

"Plus, if Fay decides running the B and B isn't for her, a third-floor suite would be an enticement to bring in another innkeeper," Sadie offered.

"Not everyone switches jobs at the drop of a hat," James said.

She shrugged. "It's nice to have options."

Options. That was what she wanted, what was important to her. The option of walking away whenever she was bored or failed at something.

"I'll draw up some sketches," he told Maddie, "so you can give Neil and Fay an idea of what we're talking about."

"Sounds good."

They walked down the stairs, Maddie in the lead.

In the hallway on the second floor, Sadie leaned close to James. "Thank you."

He didn't have to ask what she was thanking him for. He knew. She was grateful he'd heard her out, had taken her suggestion seriously and not blown her off because he was pissed with her.

He'd wanted to, he realized. He'd wanted to ignore what had been a reasonable, workable suggestion because it came from her. That was also the reason he hadn't been able to. Because it was Sadie. The girl who'd had his heart since he was ten years old.

The woman he was afraid had it still.

CHAPTER ELEVEN

"IT'S A GOOD idea," James said gruffly, standing close to Sadie. He smelled of fresh air and clean sweat, the combination intoxicating to her.

She backed up, bumping into the wall with a dull thud. "I sense a *but* in there," she said, inwardly cursing how breathless she sounded.

"But...as Maddie and I mentioned, we still have to get Neil and Fay's okay." His mouth flattened. "And run it by Dad."

She raised her eyebrows. "Is that a problem? It is his company, after all."

James's glance was so hot, so angry, she was surprised it didn't fry her on the spot. "That's right. His company. His say. On everything."

He brushed past her to walk down the stairs.

She followed. Stepping into the kitchen, she heard the sound of Maddie's truck engine start and the vehicle pull away. Sadie glanced outside, but didn't see James. She went through the dining room, found him in the reception hall.

"Are you still mad about your father hiring me?"

He checked that the front door was locked, not even bothering to face her. "No."

"Are you sure? Because things have seemed awful...tense...between you two at the shop in the mornings this week," she said, hurrying after him as he retraced the way they'd come.

She was sure she wasn't the only one who'd noticed it, either. Not if the exchanged glances between Maddie and Eddie and their coworkers were any indication. James only spoke to Frank when absolutely necessary, didn't offer any input on any of his father's suggestions, concerns or questions and had even been late, not once, but twice. Leaving Frank to assign the workers to their jobs.

"I don't want to be the cause of problems between you two," she said firmly.

"Believe it or not," he said, stopping in the dining room to roll up the blueprints, "not everything I do, say or think has to do with you."

"Good." It was better than good, it was exactly what she wanted. She could go on her way with a clear conscience. His issues were just that: his. They weren't friends anymore. She didn't have any reason to be concerned about what was bothering him. No reason to want to try to help him get through it.

She picked up the folder of papers she'd brought for Frank. "I guess I'll run these over to your parents' house. Leave them there for your dad."

"I'll take them," he said, holding out his hand.

"Since I'll have to talk to him about renovating the attic anyway."

"That's probably for the best," she said, handing him the folder as they walked into the kitchen. "Seeing as how your mother hates me and all."

She winced, wished the words back, but it was too late. They were out there, floating in the air, making James scowl.

"What are you talking about?"

She shrugged, tried to brush it off. "It's no big deal. And it won't affect my work performance," she assured him.

Sadie had tried to ignore it—after all, it was hard to believe—but she couldn't dispute the facts. Well, she could, and often did, but not when they were laid out so clearly in front of her, big as life and screaming at her.

Rose Montesano did not like her.

James stared at her as if she'd said the Pope had declared her persona non grata. "I thought everyone liked you."

She nodded solemnly. "Me, too. I am a ray of sunshine after all."

Nothing. Not the slightest hint of humor entered his eyes.

"You're imagining things," he said. "You have to be."

"Maybe," she said as he went out to put the blueprints and folder in the truck.

But she doubted it. She'd suspected something

before now, especially when Rose had been so cold toward her at James's party, and this past week, Rose had made it clear that, though she'd put up with Sadie temporarily working for Montesano Construction, she wasn't happy about it. Even though it meant freeing up more time for Rose.

Oh, she showed Sadie how the computer program worked, taught her how to do the payroll, but she was standoffish, short and, at times, downright snide. Luckily, Sadie had quickly gotten the hang of how she ran the office so they wouldn't have to deal with each other too much more.

"Did you tell her?" Sadie blurted when he came back. "About…you know. What happened between us?"

"Yes, Sadie. I always tell my mother when I have sex with a woman. Because that's perfectly normal and not weird at all."

"I was just asking. Maybe Maddie said something—"

"She wouldn't."

"Oh." Which meant Rose simply didn't like her. How fun.

In the doorway, he picked up the end of the plywood ramp, his faded jeans molding to his firm ass, the muscles of his thighs. She blinked, her mouth falling open as he straightened, the work gloves in his back pocket flopping. He lifted the ramp and pushed it onto the back of the flatbed, the muscles in his upper back and arms contracting and flexing. His hair was mussed, the tendrils at his nape damp and curling, the skin of his neck a deep golden brown.

She wanted to press her nose there, against that sun-warmed skin, breathe in his scent, taste the salt of his sweat. Swallowing, she lifted a hand to her throat, felt the erratic pounding of her pulse. Awareness flowed through her, tugged low in her belly, settled there, warm and insistence. Demanding.

She exhaled shakily. And met his dark eyes, his gaze heated and so hungry she had to look away.

Oh, God.

When she looked up again, he was walking toward her, his stride easy, his expression clear, as if the moment had never been.

And for some stupid reason, that made her want to cry.

"You need anything else?" he asked, his voice rough. Impatient. "Because I have stuff to do."

Irritation spiked, fast and furious. It was so much better, made so much more sense than those damn tears, that she grabbed on to it with both hands. Held on tight.

"In a hurry to get away from me?" she asked, walking out so he could lock up. "Oh, wait. I forgot. Not every thought, et cetera, et cetera, has to do with me. I'm sure you're just busy. What're your Friday night plans? Washing your hair? Giving the dog a bath?"

Pocketing the key, James studied her, inscrutable. Implacable. "I have a date."

Sadie went deaf for a moment. It was if all the sound in the world ceased to exist only to come rushing back with a roar. She shook her head, but her ears still rang. "What did you say?"

"I have a date."

"A date. You have a date. With a woman?"

"Seemed like the logical choice given my species and sexual orientation."

"Who...who..." She couldn't even complete the sentence. "Not Charlotte?"

Oh, please, God, don't let it be with Charlotte.

His expression darkened. "No. Anne."

"Anne."

"Yes. Anne. She works for Kloss Painting."

Sadie knew who Anne was. Hadn't she met Anne the other day when she'd come in for a work order? Hadn't Sadie smiled and been superpolite to the tall, gorgeous brunette even after she'd recognized her as the woman James had walked to her car at his party? The one who'd flirted with him and given him her number?

Now Sadie wished she'd gone with her first instinct and ripped every last gorgeous strand of that hair out of the woman's head. "You're going on a date with Anne the painter," she said, following him to the flatbed.

"You keep repeating everything I say." He opened

the truck door and climbed in behind the wheel. "Are you having a seizure?"

A seizure? Was that was this was, this feeling of being unable to catch her breath, her thoughts spinning, her stomach sick? Funny, it seemed more like jealousy than any medical condition.

And that was unacceptable.

"I…" She had to stop and clear her throat, wrapped her hand around the door so he wouldn't shut it. "I hadn't realized you and…and Anne—" tall, beautiful Anne, damn her "—were seeing each other."

"We're not. This is our first date."

"Do you…do you think it's wise to mix business with pleasure?"

"Guess we'll find out." He grabbed the door handle. "Sadie," he said quietly, his husky voice wrapping around her name like a caress.

She looked up, held her breath. "Yes?"

"Let go of the door."

Her face flaming, she peeled her fingers from the frame and stepped back. He slammed the door shut, turned on the truck and, just like that, drove away.

He left her.

She had to stop herself from calling him back. From asking him not to go.

Elvis barked, reminding her that she had things to think about, to concentrate on other than James Montesano and his social life.

This was what she'd wanted, she reminded herself

as she made her way toward her Jeep. For him to move on. She hadn't expected him to do it quite so…quickly.

Especially after he'd declared his lifelong love for her not two weeks ago.

I want a family, he'd told her after that declaration. *A wife. I'm tired of being alone.*

Obviously he'd decided to go find that wife. To get the life he wanted.

Sadie had no doubt he'd succeed. He'd meet a woman who would love him back the way he deserved to be loved. Who would move into his house and talk him into adding splashes of color to offset all that brown, who would be content to go there night after night, year after year.

Who wouldn't balk at being told how he felt about her or get antsy to move on after a few weeks. A woman who would have his babies and spend the rest of her life by his side. Happy. Content, knowing she had a man like James Montesano as her partner. Her lover.

Her best friend.

A damn lucky woman.

Sadie hated her.

"I THOUGHT YOU were going out to dinner," Rose said, entering the kitchen in answer to James's greeting when he'd walked into his parents' house.

He nodded at her red-and-black, short-sleeved dress. "Looks like I'm not the only one."

"Your father and I are going to Pittsburgh with the Pettits. Dinner and a show. I don't think they've had so much as a break since Fay...since she..."

"Maddie says she's doing better," he reminded his mother gently.

"I know and thank God for that. I just...it breaks my heart to think of her hurting that much. And even though Gerry and Carl are more than happy to take care of her, your father and I thought it would be nice to give them a break. At least for an evening."

Though Fay and her boys were back in their own house, they still spent quite a bit of time with Gerry and Carl Pettit, Fay and Neil's adoptive parents.

"Where are you taking Anne?" Rose asked, digging through her purse before pulling out a small mirror. "I hope it's someplace nice."

"I thought we'd start off with burgers and fries at Mickey D's—I might even let her order off the regular menu and not just the dollar one. Then we can head over to the Bronze Hawk for a couple of shots—I hear Friday nights it's two-for-one. There's a good chance one of us will even get a clean glass."

"I am forever astounded by how witty my children are," she said drily as she twisted up a tube of red lipstick.

Frank came into the kitchen in a pair of pressed dress pants and a crisp white shirt, his hair slicked back. "James," he said with a nod, his smile warm and welcoming, as if he didn't realize James was still pissed at him. "I hope you didn't stop by for din—"

"I didn't."

"He has a date," Rose said, obviously sensing the tension coming from her son.

"You don't have to sound so proud," James said. "I have had dates before."

"Yes, but you might not get a second one with Anne if you show up in your work clothes. And it wouldn't kill you to take a shower."

"I'm heading home to get cleaned up and changed," he assured her.

Cleaned up and changed for a date he wasn't the least bit looking forward to. But he'd promised himself he would move on, and this was the first step. He didn't really believe he'd find true love with Anne tonight, or possibly ever. But if he wanted to meet his future wife, he had to start searching.

Had to stop thinking he'd found her when he was ten years old.

"I stopped by to drop this off," he said, tossing the folder onto the table. "Sadie showed up at Bradford House. Said you were expecting her and those papers."

The papers his father didn't so much as glance at.

A suspicion formed, niggled at the back of his brain then—looking at his father's smug grin—formed fully. Son of a bitch.

"I can't help but wonder," James continued, "why

you'd tell her to meet you there at five-thirty when you knew damned well you were leaving an hour earlier."

Frank sat to put on his shoes. Winked. "Because I knew you'd still be there. No need to thank me," he said.

"No chance of that," James said softly.

Frank's expression slid from self-satisfied to confused. "I thought you'd appreciate an excuse to talk to Sadie alone."

"Frank," Rose said admonishingly, "why on earth would you do that?"

"Because he's been moping around all week like some lovelorn teenager. Listen," he said to James, "whatever problems you two had, I'm sure you can work them out. Relationships are complicated and a hell of a lot of work. They require give-and-take and you stomping around the shop every morning, growling at everyone, is helping no one." He looked at his wife. "Tell him."

"You want me to tell our son how to reconcile with the woman who has caused him nothing but disappointment and heartache?" Rose asked, her eyes wide. "I don't think so."

Frank slashed his hand through the air as if brushing Rose's words aside. "So they've had some ups and downs. What couple hasn't?"

"We're not a couple," James managed to say through gritted teeth. He stood so rigidly, his muscles ached. "We were never a couple. We were friends."

Rose shook her head at her husband. "Bad enough you had to go and hire her behind my back—"

"Not this again. I hired her as a surprise for you. To help you out."

"The last thing I need is help from Sadie Nixon. She's flighty. Selfish. And she's brought James nothing but disappointment and heartache."

James stabbed a hand through his hair. "Just shoot me now," he muttered.

Guess Sadie's assessment of his mother's feelings about her were on the money. Sadie always had been able to read people.

"It was a lovely surprise," Rose told Frank, relenting with a sigh, "and I appreciate you thinking of me, of giving me that extra time for my studies, but you went about it the wrong way."

"It was my decision," Frank insisted, as stubborn as always.

"That's the problem," James said quietly. "It's all about what you want. Your choices. You're not the only one who has a stake in Montesano Construction. The only one who puts your heart and soul into that company day in and day out."

Frank stood. "I'm the one who started it. Who made it what it is today."

Rose groaned. "Oh, Frank."

"Yes, you started it," James agreed. "Yes, you built it up from nothing. But for the past sixteen years, I've busted my ass helping to keep it a success. Eddie and Maddie and I have done everything in our power to help Montesano Construction grow. Because it's important to us. Because it means something to us—it's our past and present, but obviously not our future."

"What is that supposed to mean?" his dad asked.

"It means that you've never, not once, so much as brought up the idea of taking us on as partners—full partners. We've never discussed what your plans are for when you retire."

"When I retire, you and Eddie and Maddie can take over, but until then, I run Montesano Construction." Frank's face was red, his voice unsteady. "I've seen what happens when families go into business together. It tears them apart. I won't let that happen to us."

"I think you're too late for that," James said, needing space to get his thoughts together, some breathing room.

He kissed his mother's cheek, shook his head at her soft plea for him to stay. There was no reasoning with his father when he got like this, no way to find equal ground.

"We're not done discussing this," Frank said, his voice brooking no argument. James kept going, had opened the door when his father's voice, a mixture of hurt and anger, stopped him. "I am your father. I deserve your respect."

James turned. "You're my father, and I love you. More than that, I've looked up to you. My whole life all I ever wanted was to be like you.

I've given you respect. Always. And now it's time you gave me some in return."

IT WAS ALL James's fault.

Sadie was sure of it. Everything that sucked in the world—global warming, the crappy economy, her bad mood and ruined dinner and the fact that she'd inhaled a half dozen of her mother's really excellent oatmeal-raisin cookies in a ten-minute time period.

James's fault. All of it.

She pulled into O'Riley's lot, her tires squealing, found a spot near the far corner and parked. If the number of vehicles was anything to go by, it was another busy night. There was a good chance that if she walked in, Kane would want her behind the bar even though it was her night off. That thought, and that thought alone, had her pausing, had her considering taking her money and her dangerous mood somewhere else.

It was the thought of James and Anne wrapped around each other by the end of the night that had her moving once again.

She glanced at her phone as she stepped into the building. Seven o'clock. They were probably at the restaurant right now. A twenty-something guy smiled, started her way—her quick sneer had him doing an about-face.

Though she'd come dressed for it, she wasn't here to troll for a man. She had every right to wear her favorite black skirt, the high-waisted one covered with faux feathers. The one short enough, tight enough, to guarantee she'd garner plenty of second—and third—looks. She'd topped it off with a sedate cream-colored tank and long beaded necklace that swung when she strode across the room to the far end of the bar.

She had every damn right to look her best. For herself.

And, well, if James just happened to stop by here like he had with Charlotte, if he just *happened* to see Sadie looking truly excellent, that was okay, too.

Not that he would. He probably took Anne into Pittsburgh to some fancy restaurant. Somewhere cozy with dim lighting and classy food, one of those places where they served small portions, barely enough to fill a real live person. After, he'd take her to a show or, better yet, dancing. James was an excellent dancer and he wasn't afraid, embarrassed or too shy to get out on the dance floor. To be the first person out there if necessary.

He had moves, Sadie thought, sliding onto an empty stool next to the wall. She remembered him at their school dances, at weddings here or there and the few times they'd gone out as friends to a club or to hear a local band play.

Yeah, she thought bitterly, he had moves. Hadn't he used them on her two weeks ago? Shocked her with his words, tempted her with his touch. Seduced her with his kiss.

He had moves and tonight he'd be putting them on the long-legged Anne.

Tears stung, but she blinked them back. She'd cried over men before, had shed buckets of tears, had her heart broken plenty of times.

She'd never, not once, thought that James would make her cry. Would make her feel so sad, so lost.

Kane noticed her, headed her way.

"I'm not working," she said when he was close enough to hear her over Rush's "Fly by Night" blaring from the jukebox behind her, "so don't even ask."

"I don't need you to work," he said, wiping the already-spotless bar. He inclined his head toward the two female bartenders. "Julie started tonight, remember?"

He'd hired Julie, a law student, to help cover the weekend shifts. "Good, because tonight I'm here as a patron." She set her purse on the bar, crossed her legs. "Don Julio Blanco," she said, ordering her favorite tequila. "Neat."

"Drowning your sorrows?" Kane asked, his cool green eyes assessing.

"I will be once you get my drink."

He flicked his gaze over her. "You sure you don't want that mixed with some fruit and crushed ice? I'm not sure you can handle a grown-up drink."

With a laugh, she leaned forward. "I've tended bar from here to Seattle and back again. I can not only handle it, I could drink you under the table."

"That's what they all say. Until they puke all over my clean floor."

"No puking." She held up her hand. "I promise."

Kane poured her drink and set it in front of her. She picked up the glass in both hands, inhaled the notes of lemon and spice.

And downed it.

It was smooth and warm as it hit the back of her throat.

"That's a sipping tequila," Kane said.

Resting her elbows on the bar, she held her chin in her hands and smiled. "Then I'll be sure to sip the next one." When he didn't move, she waved her fingers at him. "Go on. Shoo."

His eyes narrowed to slits. "Did you just shoo me?"

In answer, she gave him another finger wave then turned, leaning back against the bar, her legs crossed, her foot swinging.

Another song started. "Simple Man" by Lynyrd Skynyrd. Not her favorite, but if she was there spending money instead of making it, she sure as hell wasn't going to put so much as a quarter in the jukebox. She swiveled slightly, brushed her hair off her shoulder. Most of the tables were full, the long bar crowded. Both pool tables were in use, as was the dartboard.

She could go over, find someone to play, hustle them out of a few bucks or more, but she didn't want to be sociable. Didn't want to chat or be delightful.

She wanted to sit here in the corner and sulk. Drink until her vision blurred and her thoughts grew fuzzy.

That, most of all, was James's fault.

The song changed. She watched a group of pretty twenty-somethings laugh brightly and send flirtatious glances at a couple of guys two tables over. But they only reminded her of Charlotte, of how her sister hadn't spoken to her in a week. After a few minutes, another song played.

Sadie turned, but Kane was nowhere in sight. Where was he? More importantly, where was her drink?

Finally she spotted him as he came out through the swinging doors from the kitchen. He laid a plate in front of her.

"What's this?" she asked, frowning at a burger the size of her head and a pile of thick-cut fries.

"You want to drink here? You'll eat first. Unless you're going to tell me you already had a full meal...."

She would have, except she'd burned the scrambled eggs she'd made for dinner. Who the hell burned scrambled eggs? They were in a nonstick pan, for God's sake.

The nonstick pan that had accompanied the eggs into the trash.

"Do six cookies count as a full meal?" she asked.

"Six cookies is a snack. A full dozen equals a meal."

"Ha." She picked up the burger. Lord, but the

thing was huge. And smelled really, really good. "There's that hidden charm. I knew it was in there somewhere."

"That so?"

Nodding, she bit into the burger. Chewed and swallowed then wiped her mouth with a cocktail napkin. "Anyone who looks like you has charm. It might not be polished, but it's there. This is good," she said around a second bite. "Really good."

"I'll pass your compliments on to the chef."

"We have a chef?" That was new.

He pulled a draft beer. "There's no *we* in this equation. Me boss. You lowly employee."

She snorted, held up her empty glass and wiggled it. "Tonight me thirsty customer."

"You eat at least half of that and I'll get you another drink."

She wanted to complain. Worse, she wanted to pout. But she wouldn't stoop that low.

Besides, now that she had food in front of her, she found she was hungrier than she would have thought.

She dipped a fry into some sort of ketchup–ranch dressing sauce. "So, *boss,* what's your policy on sleeping with employees?"

If the question shocked him, he hid it well. "Considering that out of the five female employees I have, one is old enough to be my mother, two are married, one is a lesbian and one is you, I didn't think I needed a policy."

She narrowed her eyes. Sat up straighter. "What's wrong with me?"

"Nothing. But you're not interested."

"I could be," she said, though that was such a lie, she was surprised her nose didn't shoot out and knock the bottle of gin from his hand. "I should be. After all, you're perfect for me. Just my type."

"That so?"

"You bet."

He gave a woman in a sundress her gin and tonic then wiped his hand on a rag he kept in his back pocket. "What's your type?"

"You. Haven't you been paying attention? Oh," she said, picking up the burger for another bite. "You mean specifically. Well, let's see…brooding, rebellious, cranky, smoldering with repressed emotions…you know, your typical bad boy. In other words—" she took a huge bite, chewed and swallowed "—you."

He lifted one golden eyebrow. "Smoldering?"

"Blazing, baby."

"And that's your type."

"From the top of your artfully mussed hair to the tips of your scuffed biker boots." She sighed. "You're just the kind of guy I usually go for. Emotionally unavailable with a mysterious past and dozens of ex-lovers—"

"More like legions," he said so soberly she wasn't sure if he was kidding or not.

"Legions. That's even better. I'll fall hard and fast

and convince myself I can fix all that's broken inside of you, and you'll steal my credit cards, sleep with a few of my friends and break my heart."

"The great sex might just be worth it," he said, sliding another drink in front of her.

She looked down, surprised to find she'd finished most of the burger. And felt better for it. "It might be."

She thought of James, out with some other woman, charming her with his easy laugh, his slow, sexy grin.

She raised her glass in a toast. "Before the night's over, maybe we'll find out for sure."

CHAPTER TWELVE

ZOE BARKED. And barked. And barked some more.

With a groan, James rolled over and read the clock on the bedside table.

Three-forty.

His dog kept up with the histrionics, yapping and racing around. "All right, all right," he muttered, tossing the covers off and swinging his legs over the side of the bed. "But if this is your way of telling me there are deer in the backyard, I will kill you."

It wasn't until he stepped into the great room that he realized why his dog was in such a frenzy.

Someone was knocking on the door. Pounding, actually, like they'd break it down if he didn't answer soon enough.

Flipping on the porch light, he opened the door.

And almost slammed it shut again.

It was Sadie, pretty as a picture in a fuzzy black skirt, her loose hair blowing in the cool, night breeze, a small smile on her pink lips.

Or, at least she would have made a pretty picture if her hair wasn't frizzing, her body wasn't swaying and her smile wasn't that of someone who'd had too much to drink.

If she'd been alone instead of leaning heavily on the tall blond man beside her.

"Hi, Jamie," she said, cheerily drunk. "I'm home."

James squeezed the door handle so hard, he was surprised it didn't snap off in his hand. "You're not staying here." He looked at Kane. "She's not staying here."

"I don't care where she stays," the bar owner said. "But as of now, I'm off the clock. I've babysat her long enough."

Sadie tipped her head back and sent Kane a quizzical look—almost toppling over in the process. "We're not going to have sex?" she asked.

He righted her. "Not tonight."

"That's probably for the best." She patted his cheek. "I'd only ruin you for other women. I'm pretty darn amazing in bed. Isn't that right, Jamie?"

James held Kane's gaze. Wasn't sure which one of them he wanted to strangle more—her or him. "I'll give you five hundred dollars to take her with you."

"Not if you tripled that amount," Kane said, shoving her at James.

She staggered, so he wrapped his arm around her waist. She curled into him, sent him a sloppy grin.

Shit.

"Since I doubted she'd be able to stay on the back of my bike," Kane said, "and I wasn't sure she'd even be able to get on in that outfit, I drove her Jeep out here. She can pick it up at the bar. I live upstairs."

Without looking back, he walked away.

Leaving James with a drunk blonde plastered against his side.

He sighed. Looked at his dog, but she was no help. "Come on," he said, leading Sadie into his house.

"Where are we going?"

"Inside so I can get my truck keys. I'll take you home."

She pushed away, stumbling a bit before regaining her balance. Her long necklace swung then settled back in the valley between her breasts. "I don't want to go home. That's why I had sexy Kane bring me here."

Sexy Kane.

Son of a bitch.

She stepped up to James, bringing her warm, curvy body way too close to his. "Let's have a drink."

"It's late...."

But she'd already turned and walked away.

Leaving him to stare after her and wonder how she could even stay upright in those chunky heels. And wondering why she had on what appeared to be leg warmers when it was warm outside and not 1985.

What had he done to deserve this fresh bit of hell?

He found her in the kitchen, searching through his cupboards. "What are you doing?"

She slammed one door shut. Opened another. "Where do you keep the liquor?"

"Liquor? What are you, a gunslinger from the Wild West?"

She turned, her long, smooth legs crossing, her hair fanning out. Setting a hand on the counter to steady herself, she shook her head as if to clear it. "I'd like a drink."

"It's the middle of the night."

And she was already drunk. Had arrived in this condition on his doorstep on the arm of another man.

She resumed her search. "Don't be such a drag, James. Surely it's not too late to have one little drink with an old friend. Ah...here we go." She pulled out a bottle of whiskey, swung it so that the liquid sloshed back and forth, catching the moonlight coming in through the window. "Now, you can either have a drink with me or you can watch while I drink alone."

He stepped forward as she grabbed two glasses, but there was something dangerous about her tonight, something ill at ease, and he stopped before he got too close. "I think you've already had enough."

She laughed. "Do you? Well, I'll take that into consideration. Yes, I certainly will." She poured a generous shot into a glass. "Why, if James Montesano thinks I've had enough, then I probably have. And I should listen, right? I should do exactly what the great, oh, so very responsible and superior James

Montesano wants me to do, think what he wants me to think, be who he wants me to be."

Holding his gaze, she tossed back the drink, not batting an eye as it went down.

He wasn't sure whether to be impressed or scared shitless.

She poured more whiskey, set the bottle next to the sink then sashayed up to him, the swell of her breasts spilling out of her top, her bare legs gleaming, her eyes overly bright and determined.

Scared shitless it was.

"Is she here?" she asked in what she probably considered a whisper, but was more like a shout.

"Who?"

"Your date."

"Anne's at home."

"Well? How was it?"

"Huh?"

How was he supposed to think when all he could see was her face? When she was close enough that he felt her warmth, could smell the sweetness of alcohol on her breath?

"The big date. How'd it go? Is Anne 'The One'? The future mother of your children, the perfect woman for you to make your tidy, perfect life with? Tell your old pal all about it." She tossed back the drink, raised the glass and almost clipped him on the chin. "Were there sparks? Fireworks?" She frowned. "Or maybe those aren't a necessary requirement for you?"

He plucked the glass from her to save them both pain and embarrassment. "Why don't we—"

"Did you kiss her? Did you kiss her the way you kissed me? Did you take her home, touch her, make love to her the way you did me?" She kept getting closer—which was weird because he kept backing up. "Did you tell her how much you love her, how you've always loved her? Oh, wait. That's me. Your great love. The only woman you've ever loved, and yet, tonight you were out with her. With...Anne," she said, practically spitting out the name.

And it hit him. She was pissed. At him. Jealous. Un-freaking-believable.

"You were the one who said you couldn't be with me that way," he reminded her, his temper growing. "Your choice."

"Right. My choice. Well, aren't you the noble one, letting it all be my choice. My choice whether I could suddenly stop being myself and somehow morph into the person you want me to be. My choice whether we remain friends—but only if I change everything about myself."

How could she think he wanted her to change when he'd always, always loved her for who she was?

When all he'd ever wanted was for her to love him back.

"Hey," he said softly, taking hold of her upper arms, bending at the knees so he could look into her eyes. "I don't want you to change—"

"You don't want me to do anything *but* change. Well, guess what, James? You win."

He had no idea what she was talking about. It sure as hell didn't feel like he'd won.

Until she kissed him.

SADIE FELT THE sharp intake of James's breath, could taste his surprise. Tension emanated from him, tension and that patience and control she'd always found so fascinating, so frustrating. Under her hands, his shoulders were rigid, his bare chest hot and solid against her breasts.

She might have been a little tipsy—and those last two drinks hadn't helped, though Kane had cut her off well over an hour ago—but she wasn't so drunk she couldn't tell that James was reacting to her kiss, to her body plastered against his. His arousal, hard and hot, pressed against her lower belly; his breathing was ragged. His grip on her upper arms almost painful.

But she also couldn't miss one vital fact.

He wasn't kissing her back.

She lowered to her heels, the movement causing her head to spin. "What's the matter, James?" she asked, her voice harsh, her words only slurring slightly. "Isn't this what you wanted?" She spread her arms out. "Well, here I am. Come on, what are you waiting for?" she continued when he just watched her warily, like he didn't even know her, like he hadn't been an important part of her life, her world, for the past twenty years.

"Let's sit down," he said in that annoyingly reasonable tone of his. "I'll make some coffee—"

She wrenched away from him, slapped his hands when he tried to steady her. She didn't need his help. She'd stay on her own two feet, would find her balance herself.

"I don't want coffee," she said, some distant, sober part of her brain realizing she sounded like a bratty toddler. Thankfully the rest of her brain didn't care. "You had no right to change the rules like this. It's not fair."

The more she thought about it, the more it bugged her. The feelings, her frustrations and anger that had been building inside of her ever since he'd kicked her out of his life, threatened to explode inside of her. The longer he stood there all quietly imposing and sanctimonious and sober, the more out of control she felt.

"You can't just…throw something like that at me," she continued, her voice ragged. "You can't just say you love me and then toss me aside when I don't fall in line with your plans." She held her hair back from her face because it kept getting in her way. "Damn you, Jamie. Damn you! How dare you change everything between us?"

"I had to do what was right for me," he said. "This isn't easy for me, either. I've loved you my entire life—"

"You say that and yet, all those years, you never, not once, let me know that you felt anything other than friendship for me and then, when you do decide to spring it on me, you get pissed off when I don't react how you want. Well, guess what? I'm pissed, too." She shoved his chest. He barely moved, which only made her angrier. She growled low in her throat. "You changed everything between us! How could you do that?" Her words were choked, her vision blurred. "Why would you do that?"

Her eyes welled. Too much alcohol, she assured herself. She hugged her arms around herself. She was chilled and not feeling all that well.

He grasped her hands, his touch incredibly gentle, his voice low. "Sadie, I never meant to hurt you."

She forced herself to meet his eyes, held that gaze even when he blurred at the edges. "Didn't you?" she asked softly.

He flinched. Dropped her hands. "I don't know. Maybe."

Her stomach roiled. "I..." She wiped her forehead, her fingers coming away damp with sweat. "I..." A wave of nausea rose. She swallowed it, but another followed. "I'm sorry," she whispered, unsure why she was apologizing when he was the one in the wrong.

But she didn't have time to worry about it, not when her stomach rebelled. She raced into the bathroom, fell to her knees in front of the toilet.

And cursed herself for those last two drinks.

A SHAFT OF sunlight speared Sadie's eyes, seemed to penetrate her skull and set her head on fire. She groaned and rolled over, but that had her stomach turning. Oh, God. Her mouth was dry. Her tongue felt swollen and fuzzy. Her entire body hurt.

All letting her know she wasn't dead.

Yippee.

The events of last night rushed into her mind— her anger and frustration, the burger and her conversation with her boss, the few guys who'd come up to her during the course of the evening wanting to buy her a drink, wanting to dance with her, wanting to take her home to bed. She'd refused each and every offer because she hadn't wanted any other man, no matter what she'd told Kane about them getting together. Not when the only man she could think about was James.

But he'd been out with someone else.

So what did she do? Brilliant mind that she was, when Kane asked for directions to where she lived, she'd led him straight to James's place, where she'd capped off the night by yelling at him and then puking for an hour.

At least it had been a memorable evening.

Now it was time to face the music—and that damn bright light.

Peeling her eyes open, she blinked, trying to get used to the glare, but that only made her dizzier, so she shut them again. Keeping them shut, she pushed up onto her elbows slowly, let her head acclimate to the change in altitude, then sat all the way up and opened her eyes again. She stared at the painting of a river James had hanging on the wall, done by a local artist. Waited until the room stopped spinning and her stomach settled.

Finally, she stood. At some point last night, James had helped her out of her clothes and had pulled one of his T-shirts over her head. Reaching only midthigh, it was incredibly soft and smelled of him.

She wasn't giving it back.

She made her way to the bathroom, her steps slow and measured. Washing her hands in the sink, she caught her reflection in the mirror. And groaned again. Her hair was a mess, tangled and frizzy around her pale face, her makeup smudged, dried mascara and eyeliner rimming her bloodshot eyes.

She gargled with some mouthwash, washed her face. It was an improvement, getting that old makeup off, but there was nothing she could do about her hair, not when every pull of James's hairbrush was pure agony. Pale and resembling a zombie—minus the craving for human brains—she forced herself to leave the sanctity of his bedroom.

Worst walk of shame ever.

And she hadn't even had sex.

She headed to the kitchen, but stopped when she saw him out on the deck, the morning paper spread out in front of him. With a deep, fortifying breath and a prayer, she went into the bedroom and opened the door leading outside, stepped onto the cool wood.

He lifted his head, his gaze hooded. "You're up."

"Am I?" Her voice was a painful croak. She squinted against the rising sun, but the cool, fresh air felt good on her skin, in her lungs. "You sure I'm not dead?"

"Pretty sure." He stood, guided her to a seat. "How about some toast?"

Though she would have sworn there was nothing left in her stomach, bile rose in her throat.

"Now you're just torturing me," she whispered, hoping he'd follow suit and stop all that yelling.

"It'll help. Trust me."

Before she could tell him she planned to never, ever, eat again, he went inside.

Zoe whined, watched Sadie with her head tipped to the side.

"Don't judge me," Sadie told the dog.

The breeze ruffled the edges of the paper, the sun felt warm on her face and she shut her eyes, slid down in the chair. She must have dozed off because it seemed like in the next breath, James was back. He set a plate of two slices of dry toast, neatly cut in halves, in front of her.

"I didn't think you'd be up for coffee," he said. "So I got you some ginger ale."

She took the glass, sipped from it. The tiny bubbles exploding in her mouth were like rockets, but it did soothe her dry throat, calmed her stomach. "Thank you."

Because he was watching, she forced herself to pick up one of the toast slices, nibbled on it until she'd finished it and its other half.

"Better?" he asked.

"A little."

He looked as if he wanted to say more, but only nodded. "Come on. I'll take you to pick up your Jeep."

That was it. No recriminations. No lecture.

It was a reprieve. One she was weak enough to take.

"Yeah. Okay."

They drove to town in silence. Though she sat close enough to touch him, she'd never felt such distance between her and another person. She clutched her purse in her lap—hoped he couldn't tell she'd stuffed his T-shirt in there after she'd changed into her own clothes.

He pulled into O'Riley's and drove around back, where steps led to the second-floor apartment, and parked next to her Jeep. Kane's motorcycle was there, a machine as sexy and dangerous looking as its owner.

"You all right to drive home?" James asked.

"I'll be fine." She unbuckled her seat belt and reached for the door handle, but couldn't make herself open it.

And she really, really wanted to open it. To escape.

Instead, she sat back and cleared her throat. "James, about last night…"

What could she say? *Thanks for holding my hair while I repeatedly threw up? Thanks for washing my face with a cool cloth, for helping to steady a glass of water so I could rinse my mouth out? Thanks for undressing me so carefully, so gently and then tucking me into your bed?*

As he stared out the windshield, his hands gripped the steering wheel, his knuckles white. "How much do you remember?"

This was her out. She could claim she didn't remember much, could make a joke out of it, laugh it off. He might let her. The old him certainly would. That James would never humiliate her by telling her what she'd done, what she'd said.

She had no idea what this new James would do.

But there seemed to be a new Sadie, too. One who didn't want to take the coward's way. Who wanted to give him the truth. As much as she could admit to.

"Unfortunately, I remember everything."

She felt, more than saw, him glance at her. "Everything?"

She met his eyes. "Every last thing." She twisted her fingers together. "Jamie, I… God, I'm sorry. I'm so sorry I showed up your house drunk and made a complete idiot of myself. For yelling at you and getting sick and kicking you out of your own bed." Humiliation swept through her, heated her face. "I was jealous. I was so jealous you took another woman out I couldn't even see straight and I know," she continued when he opened his mouth, "I know I have no right to be, but I can't help how I feel."

His jaw was tight, his mouth a grim line. "Is that all?"

"No." She licked her lips, turned in her seat to face him fully. "I am sorry about all of that, for how I acted, but I…I'm not sorry for what I said. I'm so angry with you. I am absolutely furious with you for changing the dynamics between us. I hate that we're not friends anymore, that you made that choice for both of us."

He remained silent. Unmoving. Unapproachable.

Her heart heavy, her eyes blurry, she fumbled for the door handle, managed to wrench it open and practically fell out of the truck. Leaning in, she reached for her shoes on the floor, straightened and moved to shut the door.

"Last night," he said, stopping her, "after you passed out, I had plenty of time to think about what you said. About what happened between us, how we got here. For years, I kept my feelings from you, went out of my way to keep them hidden so nothing would change. Maybe that was wrong. Maybe it wasn't fair of me to make the decision to end our friendship, to change the dynamics between us." He tipped his head against the seat. Shut his eyes. "I don't know. All I know is that I can't go back."

Rolling his head to the side, he met her eyes, his voice quiet. "I don't want to go back to how we used to be."

"I know. And that hurts." More than that, it scared her.

Because lately she wondered if going back was the best thing for them. If it might be better if they went forward. Except she wasn't sure what that meant, what she wanted it to mean. It was too complicated. Too frightening.

She picked at the material of the truck seat. "I know what it looked like…last night…with me and Kane. But I…I wasn't going to sleep with him. I just…I wanted you to know that," she finished lamely.

She'd needed him to know it. To believe it.

James went so still she began to wonder if he was even still breathing. "No?"

"No. I mean, even if he was interested—which I highly doubt, especially now—I wouldn't. I wouldn't," she repeated. "I'm not interested in him. Not that way."

James sat up, put the truck in Reverse. "None of my business."

"And I think," she continued stubbornly, "the reason I'm not—interested in him, that is—is because I…" She stopped. Swallowed. "I can't stop thinking about you. And I don't know what to do about it. I don't know how to stop it."

His hands opened and closed on the steering

wheel. Opened and closed. Opened and closed. His chest rose and fell rapidly. But he didn't look at her. So she did the only thing she could. She shut the door and walked away.

CHAPTER THIRTEEN

IT WASN'T STALKING, Charlotte assured herself. Just because James had happened to mention during their date how he picked up coffee for himself, his brother, sister and father for a weekly Saturday-morning business meeting, and just because Char happened to be at the same coffee shop at the same time didn't mean she was lying in wait for him. For goodness' sake, it wasn't as if she was some crazed, obsessed person. Sometimes a woman had to make it clear to a man that she was interested, that was all.

James didn't seem to be getting her hints.

It had been over a week since they'd had dinner and drinks. She'd waited patiently for him to make the next move, to call her. She'd wanted him to, had hoped he would.

Not that he needed to chase her, but it would be nice if he put in a little effort.

Their almost date might not have been perfect, but it had gone well. Smoothly. Char appreciated smooth. No, he hadn't tried to kiss her good-night, but he had hugged her.

After she'd initiated said hug.

He just needed a push, she told herself as she slouched down in her seat when she spied his truck pulling into the coffee shop's parking lot. A gentle nudge in the right direction.

She was an excellent nudger.

He walked past her car, tall and handsome even in jeans and a T-shirt, his hair disheveled. She waited until he'd gone inside, then sat up and checked her reflection in the rearview mirror, applied a fresh coat of lip gloss and finger-fluffed her hair before getting out. As soon as she stepped into the coffee shop, she glanced around, spotted him in line at the order counter. She slipped to the side behind a display of ceramic coffee cups, pretended to check them out while sneaking glances at him.

This wasn't weird or creepy, she assured herself as she held up a mug to hide her face. It was cute. After they got engaged she'd tell him how she'd planned this. Later, they'd tell their kids and then their grandkids how she'd had to chase after him because he was too honorable, too decent to take advantage of her, what with her being so much younger and his good friend's little sister.

But in the end, he'd say to those adorable kids, he couldn't resist her.

He paid for his coffee, picked up one of those carriers that held four large cups. The cashier handed him his change, then a bulky, white paper bag filled, Charlotte guessed, with some of the treats the shop was known for: muffins or doughnuts or Danishes.

He didn't return the clerk's smile, just took his items and stuffed a few bills in the barista's tip jar as he headed toward the door.

Pretending to study the types of bagged coffee, Char stepped directly in front of him.

"Oh," she said, looking up with feigned surprise, "I'm sor— James!" She laughed brightly and, she hoped, with sparkling eyes. "Hi. How are you?"

"Charlotte." He stepped back, looking grim and… unhappy. "I'm fine."

But he wasn't acting fine. He was acting brusque and semirude, which was so unlike him.

She'd simply have to cheer him up.

"I'm glad I ran into you," she said. "I've been meaning to call you, but I've been so busy—" So busy she hadn't been sitting around waiting for him to get in contact with her. Mostly because she'd taken extra shifts to keep her mind off of him and the lack of progress they were making in their relationship. "I wanted to let you know it's official. I got the house."

"That's great." He nodded at a couple when they waved. "Congratulations."

And he headed toward the door.

Her mouth dropped. She snapped it shut, plastered a smile on her face and hurried after him.

"Thanks," she said, hoping she sounded breathless and not irritated. "I was hoping you'd be able to look at it again, maybe give me an estimate for adding a mudroom?"

Mudroom, bedrooms for their future children. Whatever.

"An estimate?"

What was up with the strangled voice? The dark expression? "Yes. I'd love to possibly even schedule the work for before winter. That is, if you're not too busy."

He glanced at the door a few feet away. If she didn't know him better, she'd say that look was almost…longing. As if he didn't want to be standing there. Didn't want to be talking with her. "We're booked solid for the next eight months."

Her eyes wanted to squint. Her mouth wanted to tighten. Wide-eyed, she kept right on smiling. "Then I guess I'd better get on the schedule as soon as possible. If we're talking next summer, I might as well redo the master bathroom, too. You saw how outdated it is. It'd be great if you could stop by sometime after work. Say…Thursday?"

Her night off.

She held her breath, kept grinning, an innocent, friendly grin meant to put him at ease. But really, waiting for the man to show some interest was getting on her last nerve.

"Thursday?" He frowned. "I'm not sure if that'll work for me. Maybe Eddie or Dad can drop by."

Eddie? His dad?

It hit her. Why he was acting so strangely, why he couldn't wait to get away from her and his horrible mood—that honestly, she didn't care for in the least.

Sadie must have warned him off.

Charlotte was going to kill her.

"You're busy," she said, her voice coming out tight and embarrassed to match the blush staining her cheeks. "And here I am, taking advantage of our friendship, asking you to give up one of your evenings to help me out after everything you've already done, looking at the house for me, taking me to dinner. I'm sorry. It was incredibly selfish of me to ask you, to put you on the spot like this."

"That's not it. And I'm not on the spot."

"You're sweet, but I've obviously made you uncomfortable. Made you feel as if you can't say no. I...God, I'm so embarrassed." She laid both of her hands on her cheeks, just about burned her palms. "I'm just going to go."

She made it out onto the sidewalk and halfway to her car before he caught up with her.

"Charlotte," he called, exasperated. "Wait."

She stopped, kept her back to him, her arms crossed.

"I can come over," he said, his tone reluctant, his expression closed. "Work up an estimate for you."

She lifted her chin. "It's really not nec—"

"Thursday, right? I'll stop by around seven-thirty."

He walked away, leaving her gawking at his back.

Char shook her head. What just happened? She must have stepped into an alternate universe where up was down, black was white and James Montesano was an ass.

He'd had a bad morning, that was all. She headed into the coffee shop. Everyone had them, was entitled to them once in a while.

She hoped he didn't plan on making a habit of it, though.

She ordered a caramel macchiato, adding whipped cream and a chocolate-chunk biscotti to her order on a whim. It may not have been pretty, but she had scored another victory today.

And the hard-earned ones deserved celebrating the most.

I CAN'T STOP THINKING about you.

James's fingers tensed, dented the takeout cup of coffee he held. He shifted on his chair, straightened his legs as Maddie explained to their dad and Eddie the ideas they'd come up with for renovating Bradford House's attic. But his family's voices faded, became murmurs of sound. Only one voice was clear in his head. Crystal clear.

I can't stop thinking about you.

What the hell did Sadie think would happen when she said that? That he'd forgive her? What for? Their friendship was over. Or maybe she was throwing him a bone, like that kiss last night.

Isn't this what you wanted? she'd asked, offering herself to him like some goddamn sacrifice.

He had wanted her. How could he not when she'd had on that skirt, that clinging top?

He'd wanted, but he'd resisted. Had proved he could. And he'd go right on resisting.

"James?"

James jerked his head up, frowned at his father. "What?"

Frank's eyes narrowed, reminding James of the few times he'd been disciplined as a teen for being mouthy. "I asked how far behind we'll be with the attic renovation."

He shrugged irritably. "A month. At the least."

"So we shuffle a few things," Maddie said with a wave of her hand. "Jobs can be pushed back. Schedules can be reworked."

James glared. Slouched in his seat. "You only say that because you're not the one reworking them."

Yeah, he sounded grumpy. Hell, he was grumpy. He'd had a crappy morning. First Sadie and her declaration, and then Charlotte. All he'd wanted was to put some distance between him and Sadie's sister.

Instead he'd treated her badly. It'd been like kicking a cute little kitten. And in his guilt, he'd agreed to spend another evening with her, albeit in a professional capacity.

But as much as his morning had sucked, it was nothing compared to last night. After getting Sadie cleaned up and tucked into bed—into *his* bed—

he'd lain wide-awake on the couch, wanting nothing more than to slip into his room, to sleep with her. To just...hold her.

He really was a complete patsy over her.

"I could rework the schedule," Maddie insisted. "But there's no way I could come even close to your anal tendencies. Stick with your strengths, I always say. And I think we'd all rather do the reno while we're there instead of coming back. I know Neil would prefer to have it done before it opens to guests."

"We'll make it work," Frank said, snapping shut his briefcase. "Eddie, let me know what the distributor says about those damaged doors. Maddie, do up the estimate for the added work at Bradford House. James," he continued as he headed toward the door, his voice going frigid, "84 Lumber is dropping off a delivery today at eleven. Please wait here for them."

"Jeez," Maddie said after Frank left. "What did you do to Dad?"

James looked around, realized she was talking to him. Thought about denying it, but that was pretty useless as the tension between them was obvious.

"He's pissed because I told him he needed to consider making me—making all three of us—full partners."

His brother and sister both gaped at him, but Maddie recovered first. "You *what?*"

"Relax. I told him he needed to consider it. I didn't forcibly conscript you into service."

"What'd he say?" Eddie asked, taking the seat behind the desk.

"What do you think he said? He said no. That when he retired, if the three of us wanted to take over Montesano Construction together, that was fine by him, but until then, he's not giving up the reins."

"Bitter much?" Maddie sat on the edge of the desk, her leg swinging. "Dad's worried if we're all equal, it'll break up the family."

"How did you know that?"

"He told me when we were finishing the basement at the Todds' a few years ago. Mr. Todd brought both his sons in as partners in the grocery store. A year later, things were so bad he had to buy back their shares. The brothers haven't spoken since. It really tore the parents up. Tore their whole family apart."

"I remember that," Eddie said. "The younger one...what was his name? Brandon?"

"Brayden," James corrected, having been a few years behind him in school.

"Right. He was a real hothead."

"Didn't he 'borrow'—" Maddie added air quotes to the word "—money from the store's account to pay his gambling debts?" She gave an exaggerated shudder. "Talk about a cautionary tale about mixing business and family."

"An extreme case," James said dismissively. "You ask me, Dad just doesn't want to give up control."

"Would you?" Eddie asked.

"Would I bring my children in? You bet your ass."

"Eddie has a point," Maddie said. More often than not, those two thought alike. Maddie was just more vocal about those thoughts. "Think about it. Dad's been his own boss close to thirty-five years. He's made all the decisions—good or bad. Mistakes or successes, they've all been on him. Now you expect him to give that up and do things by committee? It'd be a big change for anyone. A scary one."

That was just it. James didn't want to be afraid of change. Not anymore.

"What if the four of us were partners," she continued, her heel thumping lightly against the desk. "What if two of us want to purchase a new company truck and the other two don't. How do we decide— what's the tie breaker? Or if one of us wants to fire an employee, but the other three want to keep him on. There'd be hurt feelings. Ticked-off feelings. It could be a recipe for disaster."

"Could be," James agreed, turning his empty cup in his hand. "But it doesn't have to be that way. There are plenty of family businesses out there that make it work. Why couldn't we be one of them?"

"Well, what if one of us doesn't want to be a partner?"

He froze. Narrowed his eyes at her. "You don't want to be a part of Montesano Construction?"

"I don't know. That's the thing. What if Neil stays

in Seattle or gets traded to a team in Florida or the Predators in Nashville? What if Bree and I want to move to be closer to him?"

"Things that serious between you two?"

"I wouldn't have gotten involved with him again, wouldn't have done that to Bree if things weren't serious. It's not like we're engaged yet, but we have discussed getting married. And if…when…we make that commitment, call me crazy, but I want to live in the same state as my husband. Preferably the same city."

James hadn't considered that. Had assumed that Maddie would always work for Montesano Construction, that she and Bree would always live in that tiny house across from their parents. That they'd always be here. Would always be close, part of his daily life.

Nothing stayed the same, he reminded himself. Not even the things you wanted to.

"I don't think it's something you'll have to worry about," James told her. "Dad's set against bringing us in as partners. Because he is, I've been thinking over my options."

Maddie's leg stilled. "I don't like the sound of that."

He stood, tossed the cup into the garbage can. "I'm considering going out on my own."

"Please tell me you're talking about taking a year off to go into the wilderness, living off the land and using nothing but your wits and handmade tools to survive."

"I'm considering starting my own contracting company."

"Go into business by yourself? Against Dad? Be his competitor?"

"There's more than enough work in a town this size for another contracting company. Besides, I don't think there'd be much competition," he said drily. "I'm not talking about running a company this size. Mine would be a small operation, me and maybe one or two other carpenters." He looked at her meaningfully.

"Oh, no. No way." She jumped to her feet, whipped her long, dark ponytail over her shoulder. "I would never do that to Dad. I can't believe you're even suggesting it. That you'd leave Dad because you're…what? Not getting your own way?" She stormed up to him, her hands on her hips. "I've said it before but it bears repeating—you really need to get your head out of your ass."

And with a sneer, she brushed past him and stomped out.

James pressed his fingers against his temple in an attempt to ward off a brewing headache. "Anything you want to add?" he asked Eddie.

Eddie raised a shoulder. "Hard to follow that." He shut his laptop. "But I am wondering what brought all of this on."

"Haven't you ever thought about it?"

"Becoming partners in the business? Sure. I figured we'd do like you said—take over when Dad retires."

"I don't want to wait any longer. I want a say in my own future instead of sitting around taking whatever comes my way. I want to make the decision. I want a choice."

"Funny thing about choices," Eddie said quietly, his eyes watchful. He tucked the laptop under his arm. "We always have them. Even when we think we don't."

SADIE DIDN'T WANT the night to end.

Because when it did, when the sun came up proclaiming the dawn of a new day, she had to go back to work.

She had to face James.

Maybe she could call in sick.

Thank God today had been Labor Day, giving her an extra day to hide. To recover from the colossally stupid mistake she'd made Friday night. The bigger one she'd made Saturday morning.

I can't stop thinking about you.

Yes, that was the perfect way to get them back to being friends. Way to muck everything up even more.

She padded into her mother's neat, contemporary kitchen with its stainless-steel appliances, light woodwork and glass-front cabinets. Elvis followed, settling down on the rug in front of the door. Without turning the light on, Sadie got herself a glass of water and chugged it down.

The worst part was that it was true. She couldn't stop thinking about James and in a much friendlier way than just...well...*friends*.

Way friendlier.

Groaning, she let her forehead bump against the side of the refrigerator. Let it rest there.

No more tequila, she vowed. It killed too many brain cells. Made smart women do incredibly idiotic things.

The lights came on and she turned, startled.

"Sadie," her mom said, surprised. "It's almost midnight. What are you still doing up?"

Contemplating her messed-up life. Wondering how soon she could escape it, escape Shady Grove. Wishing it was sooner rather than later.

"I was hungry," she said, opening the refrigerator and staring at the well-stocked contents, as if the answer to all her problems was tucked between the leftover potato salad and freshly squeezed lemonade.

Sadie pulled out the leftover risotto with pesto sauce and shrimp, just one of the many dishes she'd helped her mother prepare yesterday for the small picnic they'd hosted that afternoon. She dumped some into a bowl and grabbed a clean spoon from the drawer.

Sat at the table and dug in.

Irene looked scandalized. "Don't you want to heat it up first?"

"Why?"

Her mother sighed. "Never mind."

Sadie grinned a little, feeling better for some reason. "Sometimes I eat dinner leftovers for breakfast," she said as Elvis abandoned the rug to sit under the table, always hopeful for a dropped crumb or two. "And I don't even heat them up first."

"Stop," Irene said, holding her hand out, "I'll have nightmares."

"Is that why you're up so late? Bad dreams?"

Her mom turned the flame on under her teakettle. "Actually, I haven't been to bed yet. I was finishing up some paperwork for the store. I thought a cup of tea would help me unwind."

"You were working? This late?"

"Hmm." She retrieved a teacup and saucer from the cupboard, got a tea bag from the canister on the counter. "My hobby does keep me busy."

Though it was said lightly, Sadie winced. "About that…I never should've said that."

It wasn't even true. These past two weeks, Sadie had witnessed how hard her mom worked to make WISC a success, how many hours she put in, not only at the store itself, but also in the home office she and Will shared. She'd been at the store just that morning working the Labor Day sale before coming home and hosting the picnic.

Sadie had brushed aside her mother's business as

nothing more than a way for Irene to fritter away her time, a way to spend her husband's money.

Sadie swallowed, but it felt like a shrimp was stuck in her throat. "I'm sorry," she whispered, her voice breaking. "I'm really sorry."

"Oh, honey," Irene said, bending to give her a hug. "What—"

"What on earth is wrong with me? What did I do now?"

It was what her mother always asked her. The first thing she'd asked when Sadie returned to Shady Grove.

"I was going to ask what was wrong," Irene said, brushing back a loose lock of Sadie's hair like she used to do when Sadie was a little girl.

She leaned her head against her mother's shoulder. "I've made such a mess of things," she admitted. "I've screwed it all up."

"Screwed what up?"

Everything. Charlotte still wasn't talking to her, hadn't said one word to her since that night at O'Riley's. She'd even skipped the picnic today, had told Irene and Will she had to work.

Sadie would bet money Char had volunteered to stay at the E.R. just to avoid her.

Plus, Sadie had barely begun to save enough money to get across Ohio, let alone the country. She'd gotten drunk in front of her boss and then there was the whole James debacle... She sighed. She'd made a complete idiot of herself in front of him.

"I've screwed up my life," she said. "God, you must think I'm such a joke."

"I think no such thing."

Sadie snorted.

"I don't," Irene insisted. "I just wish you wouldn't jump into things without thinking them through first, that's all. Sometimes it's safer, more practical to have a better sense of where you're going before you head out on that highway."

Sadie stared at her mother as if she was a stranger. Well, in a way, she was. They'd never understood each other, not the way Irene and Charlotte did with their common love of lists and schedules and goals and plans.

"That's just it. I'm not practical. Even the thought of being so gives me the heebie-jeebies. Sometimes I wonder where I came from. I mean, look at us—" She gestured between them. Though it was almost midnight, Irene's hair was smooth and glossy, her freshly washed face shiny with moisturizer, her silk pajamas and matching robe expensive and demure.

Sadie touched her messy ponytail. She didn't own a robe, had on fuzzy pink socks and bright green-and-white polka-dotted shorts. And James's T-shirt. "Are you sure I wasn't adopted? Or switched at the hospital?"

Irene's mouth twitched. "I'm sorry to disappoint you, but no."

"I'm not disappointed."

Irene watched her in that way moms had, as if

they had some sort of window into your soul simply by virtue of being a card-carrying member of the mom club. "Are you sure?"

Sadie dropped her gaze. She wasn't disappointed. She loved her mom. Loved Will and Char, too. So much. She just wanted more out of life than they did.

The teakettle whistled and Irene shut it off, poured the hot water over her tea. "You came from me, and though you resemble me, you are and always have been your father's daughter in every way that matters."

"I know." Sadie picked out a shrimp and nibbled on it as her mom sat next to her. "I guess I've never been sure if that was a good thing in your eyes."

"I loved your father, oh, Lord, I fell for him so hard. He was so…alive. So full of life and charm. No one could resist him." As if remembering, she smiled. Dipped her tea bag up and down. "When he set his sights on something, he was unstoppable, nothing could deter him. You get that from him."

"He always seemed so huge to me, bigger than life. I always thought it was because I was so little when he died."

Irene laughed. "No, he really was bigger than life. Always on the go, always smiling and ready for the next adventure. He was…hypnotizing. When we first met, he scared me to death. He was so much. Too much. He wanted me, came after me with a single-minded determination that was—"

"Flattering?"

"Frightening," she said softly. "'Here,' I remember thinking, 'here is a man who could make me give up all my carefully thought-out plans, all my goals. A man who could change me. Who I am, what I want...'"

Recognition slid along Sadie's skin, raised goose bumps on her arms. Those were the same thoughts, the same fears she had about James.

Maybe she and her mother had more in common than she'd ever realized.

Irene sipped her tea. "Victor must've asked me out—for dinner, a movie, drinks, coffee, any number of endless activities—a hundred times before I finally said yes."

"Well, as I'm here living and breathing and eating some really good leftovers, can I just say how glad I am you gave in?"

Irene patted her hand. "Me, too."

"Though, to be honest, I can't imagine anyone refusing Daddy."

Victor had been so charming. So persuasive. Why would anyone want to refuse him?

"It wasn't easy, believe me. And it wasn't just his looks, though he certainly had those to spare. It was everything about him. His easy smile, his Southern charm, the way he looked at you, as if you had his entire focus, as if there was nowhere he'd rather be other than with you, listening to every word you had to say."

"I remember that," Sadie said. "How he'd sit on

the floor listening to me tell him about my day, as if the goings-on of a third-grader were the most exciting things he'd ever heard."

"He loved you so much. I'm sorry you didn't have him in your life for long, but I am so very, very glad he gave me you."

Sadie's throat tightened. "Thanks, Mom."

"Goodness, I almost forgot," Irene said, setting down her cup with a soft clink. "I have good news."

"You found Will's secret stash of dark chocolate and are going to split the loot with me?"

"Please," Irene said regally, "I've always known where he hides his chocolate. As long as he thinks I don't know, I can monitor how much of it he's eating." She leaned over, lowered her voice. "If he knew I knew, he'd go off and cheat on his diet some other way."

Sadie grinned. "Mom. I'm impressed."

Irene inclined her head in a small bow. "No, my good news is that I might have found a home for Elvis."

Hearing his name, the dog stood, walked over to press against Irene's legs. "I...I don't understand. You found his family?"

"I'm not sure that's ever going to happen. It has been several weeks after all. But, this morning when I was at the store, Molly Snow came in—you remember Molly, don't you? Her daughter Janine was in your dance class? Anyway," Irene continued when Sadie just shook her head, "Molly and her husband recently lost their dog—cancer. She was crushed and had sworn she'd never get another dog, but when I told her about Elvis, she was intrigued enough to ask if she could meet him. Isn't that wonderful?"

Sadie glanced down at the dog, her chest tight. "Yeah. That's…that's great. I mean, it would be great, except we can't just give him to someone. What if his family contacts us? They could be out of the country and not know he's missing."

She couldn't give him up. Not yet.

"It's an option. One we need to consider. It's not as if he can stay here after you're gone." She stilled. "Unless…unless you plan on staying here…permanently?"

She sounded hopeful. Excited.

The thought of it, the idea of never getting out of Shady Grove, of living her mother's life, made Sadie break out in a cold sweat. Her fingertips tingled then numbed.

Of course she couldn't stay. She'd spent most of her life trying to escape this town. Desperate to escape the type of existence that killed one's individuality and dreams. She had to leave. If she didn't, she would fail herself.

Worse, she would fail her father.

But for the time being she was stuck. She glanced at her mother, noted the way the diamonds in Irene's wedding band caught the light. Sadie straightened. She *was* stuck, unless…

Unless she did the one thing she'd never done before. The one thing that was so humiliating she'd never, not once, stooped so low.

She could ask her mother for help.

It would mean admitting that she hadn't been strong enough, smart enough to find a way out of this mess on her own. That she was terrified and desperate. It would mean swallowing her pride. But for the sweet taste of freedom and the possibility of getting her life back on track, she'd gladly choke down that damn pride and ask for seconds.

"Actually..." Sadie said, "I'm thinking of heading out to California. I have a friend out there who owns a winery."

"A winery? What would you do there?"

"I'm not sure. I could manage the office. Or work in marketing." Both of which she was good at and had experience. "The thing is..." She traced her fingertip over the table, made a figure eight then another one. Forced herself to stop and meet her mom's eyes. She clasped her hands together in her lap. Inhaled deeply. "The thing is, I don't have enough money to get out there, won't have enough for weeks." Possibly months.

And that would not do.

"I hope you know you're welcome to stay here for as long as you like."

Sadie smiled weakly. "I appreciate that but...it seems silly to prolong the inevitable. Especially as Phoebe—that's my friend—could use my help sooner rather than later."

She waited, held her breath, but her mom remained silent. As if she had no idea what Sadie was trying to ask. As if she had no desire to fill in the blanks, make this easier on her daughter.

Crap.

"If I had the money now—just a few thousand dollars," Sadie said, "I could leave right away. I'd pay you back," she added. "Every cent. Plus interest."

Irene sat back, her shoulders snapping against the chair as if someone had shoved her. "You want me to give you money so you can go to California?"

"Loan me some money. *Loan.*" Not give. God, *give* was too close to a handout. "Like a…a business transaction." She leaned forward, laid her hands on the table, palms up, beseeching. "We could draw up papers if you'd like, make it legal… Anything you want. Whatever you need."

Whatever it would take.

"You know Will and I want to help you in any way we can," Irene said, clasping Sadie's hands in her own. Relief flowing through her like a balm, Sadie shut her eyes. "Any way," her mother repeated, squeezing Sadie's fingers, "except that."

Sadie's blood went cold, her fingers went lax. "What?"

"I won't give you money."

She yanked her hands free. "Why not?"

Sadie stared at her mother's back as Irene stood and carried the teacup to the sink. What had just happened? She'd lowered herself, had gone against her principles and none of that even mattered? Since walking away from this house all those years ago, Sadie had never, not once, asked her mother for anything. And the one time she did—the one, single time she needed her mother's help—she was turned down without ceremony, without care.

Her stomach burning, her chest aching, Sadie slowly stood, the sound of the chair's legs against the tile floor scraping across her already-raw nerve endings. "I don't need much," she said, not caring that she sounded angry. Frantic. "Just enough to tide me over for a few weeks. I could probably make due with a thousand. Fifteen hundred at the most. That's nothing to you and Will."

But to Sadie it was everything. Enough for her to start a whole new life. Again.

To escape this life.

Irene, her back still to Sadie at the sink, just shook her head.

Sadie shoved her hands through her hair, only then remembering it was pulled back. She yanked the band out and threw it onto the table. "I don't understand. You spent almost one hundred times that on Charlotte's education."

Now her mother turned, her eyebrows raised in that condescending way Sadie hated so much. "If you want to go back to school, Will and I would be more than happy to finance your education."

"Sure, you'll drop over a hundred grand if I decide to become a teacher or a nurse but you won't give me a lousy fifteen hundred dollars to do what *I* want?"

"What you want?" Irene asked with a humorless laugh. "Do you even know what that is?"

"I want my own life. That's the problem, isn't it?" Sadie's voice rose, her shoulders tightened. "I don't want to live in Shady Grove, I don't want the life you have and this is your way of punishing me. Of keeping me here."

Irene sighed, hung her head for a moment. "I'm not trying to punish you, honey. And I can't stop you from leaving. I never could stop you from leaving. But I refuse to enable you."

"Enable me?" Sadie asked, her eyes wide. "It wouldn't be enabling. It would be helping me to go after my dreams."

"If I thought that was true, I'd write you a check this instant."

"It is true," Sadie cried, crossing to stand in front of her mother. "How can you even doubt that?"

"Because you're not following your dreams," Irene said with a sad smile. "You never were. I used to think you were running from us—from me and Will. From Shady Grove and small-town life…" She touched Sadie's cheek. "But over the years I've come to realize you're not running away at all. You're chasing after your father."

Sadie's head snapped back. "That's ridiculous. Dad's gone. He's not coming back. You think I don't understand that?"

"Understand it? Yes. But I don't think you've ever been able to accept it. Not fully." Her mother's voice was soft and filled with so much compassion Sadie's teeth hurt.

And she wasn't done yet.

"You're not following your dreams," Irene repeated. "And you're not living your own life. You're living his."

CHAPTER FOURTEEN

"SADIE," JAMES SAID flatly as he walked into the office Wednesday afternoon and found her sitting behind her desk. Max trailed in behind him. "You're here."

She didn't even look up from the computer. "Nothing gets past you."

He clenched his teeth. "It's after four."

"Yes. I realize that."

"Then why are you still here?"

Damn it, she wasn't supposed to be. She was supposed to be gone at four. Hadn't he spent the past fifteen minutes driving around before coming here, giving her plenty of time to finish her workday and be on her way?

She lifted her head long enough to give him a bland look. "I'm using the computer."

"What's wrong with the computer at your mom's house?"

"Not a thing." She looked up again, noticed Max behind him and grinned. "Hey, Max-a-million. What's shaking there, handsome?"

Max, shy and quiet as his dad around most people, kept his head down. Shrugged.

"What'd you do wrong to have to spend time with this guy?" she asked, jerking her thumb at James.

Max raised his eyes and stepped closer to James. Sent him a worried look.

"She's kidding," James said, grabbing the file with the order numbers he needed.

"Not even a little." But she winked at Max. "Don't worry about Elvis," she continued when the dog came over to investigate the boy. "He's a big old teddy bear. Do you have a dog?"

Max shook his head, held his hand out for Elvis to sniff. The dog licked his arm and Max looked up at James. "He's bigger than Zoe."

James nodded, pulled out his phone and dialed the number for the distributor. "I need a few minutes to call this place, then we'll get going. Okay?"

Max kept petting Elvis. Glanced up at Sadie then at the floor. "Does he like to play fetch?"

"Loves it," Sadie said. "But he hates when I play. Says I throw like a girl." She gave an exaggerated eye roll and Max grinned.

He scuffed the toe of his sneaker along the concrete floor. Scratched the back of his neck. "Uncle James has a brand-new pack of tennis balls in his truck."

Sadie clapped her hands onto her thighs and stood. "Well, how about we break into them? I'm sure Elvis would be grateful to have someone throw the ball who can actually aim it properly."

Wide-eyed, Max stared up at James. "Can I?"

James almost told him no, but then realized that response was only because he was still angry with Sadie. Because he didn't want to be around her.

"Sure," he said, unable to think of a good reason to keep his nephew in the shop with him while he worked. Max ran off, calling the dog while Sadie followed more slowly. "Don't let him run into the road," James told her as she reached the door.

"I'd never let a dog run into the road."

"I meant Max."

She looked over her shoulder at him, blinked innocently. "Oh? I thought I'd have him play in traffic, but if you say not to, well, then…" She shrugged and sashayed out the door, her hips swaying under her long skirt.

James hoped like hell she was kidding. Hoped even more the kid made it back alive.

To be on the safe side, he crossed to the window, relieved when Sadie led boy and dog down the knoll to the far edge of his parents' backyard. Couldn't tear himself away as Sadie said something to Max that had him laughing, Elvis running around them. A breeze picked up, lifted the ends of her hair, molded that skirt to the roundness of her thighs, the slight, feminine curve of her stomach.

His mouth dried and he swallowed. Hard. He'd touched her there, had skimmed his hands over her legs, had trailed his lips across the incredibly soft skin of her belly. Had tasted her.

And now, after finally telling her what was in his heart—only to have her rip that heart from his chest and grind it under her heel as she walked away—he was still mooning over her like some goddamn love-struck teenager.

The more things changed, he thought, deliberately turning away, the more they freaking stayed the same.

He called the distributor and ordered doors and windows for a job they were starting next week, then returned a few customer calls, all the while pacing the small confines of the office. All the while avoiding that window.

Sliding his phone into his pocket, he glanced at her desk and cringed. What a mess. How did anyone work that way, with files stacked haphazardly and papers scattered across the surface? It was enough to make his hands shake with the need to straighten those piles, to organize the papers.

Though Sadie was messy, that disorganization didn't seem to affect her work. As much as he hated to admit it, she'd done a good job for Montesano Construction. It shouldn't piss him off even more.

But it did.

He slid to the right, glanced at her computer. The screen was blank. Frowning, he rubbed his fingertips together, reached for the mouse only to snatch his hand back. Whatever she'd been looking at wasn't his business.

Except, it was. Sort of. As her boss's son and part of Montesano Construction, he had every right to know what she'd been doing on a company computer. More than that, it was his responsibility...no, no...more like his duty to—

The hell with it.

He moved the mouse, bringing the monitor to life. A website popped up.

Amtrak's website.

She was checking prices, he noted, feeling as if some silent, invisible vortex had sucked the breath from his body. Checking to see how much it'd cost to take the train from Pittsburgh to Napa Valley.

As always, she was planning her escape.

Good. That was what he wanted. Her gone. Out of his life, out of his thoughts. Out of his dreams. He wanted to be free of her, once and for all.

Cursing viciously, he swiped his hand over the mouse, had it flying off the desk to hang by its wire. Damn her.

He went outside. Found Sadie and Max laughing like loons at Elvis, who was showing off, leaping into the air, waiting for Max to throw the ball.

"Ten more minutes, Uncle James," Max called, spying him walking across the parking lot. "Please?"

"Ten minutes," James said, stepping up beside Sadie. She stiffened. He ignored it. "Then we have to head to practice."

"Practice?" she asked.

"Hockey practice. Eddie's finishing up with the bookshelves in the living room at Bradford House so I told him I'd take Max to practice, get him fed after."

They watched boy and dog, the silence tense and uncomfortable. It never used to be that way, James thought as he stuck his hand in his pocket to stop himself from touching a strand of her hair that blew in the wind.

This was their new normal.

He hated it.

But he wouldn't do anything to change it. He'd always been the one to make things right—with his friends and family. To make things comfortable. Easy. Peaceful. It was past time someone else took over that role.

He glanced at Sadie's profile. A small smile played on her mouth as she watched Max and Elvis; the sun caught the pale strands in her hair. She was beautiful. So beautiful it hurt to look at her. To realize he still wanted her.

That he might always love her.

"When do you leave?"

As soon as the gruff words left his mouth, he cursed himself for even asking. For caring enough to ask.

"What?" she asked, squinting as she looked up at him.

"You were looking at train tickets on the office computer. When do you leave?"

"I was just pricing them," she muttered. "Seeing if it would be worth it to sell my Jeep...."

"But?"

She sighed, tucked her hair behind her ear. "But Phoebe says I'll need a vehicle out there and seeing how high the cost of living is in California, I'd be money ahead to keep the car I have. So it looks like I'll be here a few more weeks at any rate."

She didn't sound happy.

"Jesus, you make it sound like a prison sentence."

"It's no fun being somewhere you feel trapped."

Trapped. That was how she felt being in Shady Grove. Being with him.

Son of a bitch.

"I could already be gone," she continued, crossing her arms, her tone petulant, "out of your hair and your life. You can blame Mom for me still being here."

"Irene?"

"I asked her for a loan. Promised I'd pay her back, offered to have legal papers drawn up, but she wouldn't give me so much as one cent."

"That must've been rough."

Her gaze flew to his, startled and suspicious. "What do you mean?"

"It must've been rough," he repeated. "You swallowing your pride and asking her for money only to be turned down."

She blushed, lowered her head. "Yeah, it pretty much sucked. But that's okay. I've always made it just fine on my own. I'll continue to do so. And don't worry, I've already called the employment agency about finding a replacement for me. You won't be left hanging."

He snorted. She always left him hanging. Always left him wanting more than she was willing to give. He wanted to blame her for it—and did. To a point. But he was honest enough with himself to admit he shouldered part of the blame for expecting too much from her.

For keeping his feelings to himself all this time.

They fell back into silence. After a few more minutes, James checked his phone. Opened his mouth to call to Max.

"Is this as weird to you as it is to me?" Sadie asked before he could speak.

"This?"

"This." She waved between them, her brow lowered, her movements agitated. "This. You and me not talking. It's—"

"Weird," he put in. "So you've said."

"Not just weird but…wrong."

"It's the way I need it to be."

"Right. The way you need it to be." Her voice was quiet. Sad. It killed him. "Never mind that I miss you…that I miss us. That I'll be leaving and I'm—" Snapping her mouth shut, she shook her head.

"You're what?" he asked hoarsely, telling himself it didn't matter, that *she* didn't matter. Knowing he was a liar.

She met his eyes, her chin lifted in a look of complete defiance. Of strength. But when she spoke, her words were low. Unsure.

"I'm scared," she said, surprising the hell out of him. "Scared our friendship really is over. Terrified of living the rest of my life without you in it."

He was, too. But there was no other way. "You'll get through it," he said, not unkindly. They both would. "Finish up, Max," he called to his nephew.

Max waved to let him know he'd heard. James hesitated. Everything inside of him screamed at him to leave before he gave in to his need to comfort her, to try to make things right between them. But, as always, walking away from Sadie was impossible.

"No matter what's happened between us," he said, pitching his voice so his words didn't carry to Max, who threw the ball for Elvis again, "I wish only the best for you, and I...I hope you're happy. Wherever you go."

Not looking at him, she nodded. Swallowed visibly.

His truck keys in his hand, he turned.

"My mom thinks I'm trying to live my dad's life," Sadie blurted before he'd taken more than a step.

"What?"

"She accused me of not accepting his death, of trying to hold on to him by...I don't know...following in his footsteps, I guess."

"Are you?"

"No." She frowned. Shrugged irritably. "I don't know. Maybe. And if I am," she asked quietly, "is that so wrong?"

He was too stunned to speak. He'd always thought she moved from town to town, job to job, for the thrill of it. Because she loved nothing more than the next challenge, a new adventure.

For so long, he'd been confident he knew Sadie better than anyone else. That he understood everything about her—what made her tick, why she lived her life on the run. Her thoughts and fears and hopes and dreams. But now he wondered how much of that was true and how much was just his wishful thinking brought on by his feelings for her.

"You're following in your father's footsteps," she continued. "I don't see anyone holding that against you."

"I'm not sure the two are the same."

His father was a community leader, a well-respected businessman. More importantly, he was a good family man, a loving and devoted husband and father. From what little he'd heard, Sadie's dad had been a charming jack-of-all-trades who'd dragged his family from town to town, state to state, in search of his next big break.

James frowned. But then, he'd always been more than happy to pretend as if her life hadn't started until she'd moved to Shady Grove, to think that the only father she'd ever had was Will Ellison—

because that was the only father James had ever known her to have. Sure, Sadie had told James stories about Victor Nixon, but they'd been the tall tales of a child, offered when she'd first moved here. As they'd grown, Sadie had talked less and less about her dad, sharing only the occasional, casual remark about him.

"What was he like?" James asked. "Your father."

Her eyes narrowed. "Why?"

A lie settled on the tip of his tongue, ready to be said. But this was Sadie. She may have hurt him, may have broken his heart, but she still deserved the truth. "Because I never asked before," he admitted quietly. "And I should have."

SADIE STUDIED James, his gaze warm—like it used to be when he looked at her—his expression honest and open. What it must be like to be that free with one's emotions. To be able to share your thoughts and feelings so easily.

The idea of it terrified her.

"I'm sure you've asked me about him," she said.

"Possibly." Though he didn't seem to believe that. "Indulge me anyway."

She couldn't. She rarely shared her memories of her dad with anyone. Those memories belonged to her, her and her mother. They were special. Private.

They were all she had left.

But more than that, worse than that, they weren't as clear as they should be. Each year they dimmed, fading like a brightly colored painting left out in the sun.

As if reading her mind, James shook his head. "Never mind," he said. "I need to get Max to practice anyway."

"I don't remember much." Her words kept him there, talking to her. Listening to her. "Not nearly as much as I wished I did. And of the memories I do have, I'm never certain if they're real, or a figment of my imagination. Was he really as tall as I remember? As handsome? Or am I projecting onto him the person I want him to be?"

"Why don't you tell me what you know for sure?"

Inhaling deeply, she nodded. "I know he was funny. Fun. He could juggle and was great with animals, horses especially. He grew up privileged but felt stifled by the responsibilities that came with being part of a wealthy Southern family. The expectations." *Money,* he used to tell her, *does not buy happiness.* "He left home when he was seventeen and never looked back, preferring to make his own way in the world."

Preferring to be free.

"He met my mother one night at a club in Raleigh," she continued. "He was working at a horse farm there, Mom was attending the University of North Carolina and had gone out with some friends. He asked her out, she said no. It took him weeks, but he finally wore her down. Two months after their first official date, they were married and had moved to St. Louis where I was born." Sadie stared at James's parents' house. "He loved R & B music, made pancakes every Sunday morning and was so claustrophobic he couldn't even ride in elevators." She smiled. "I remember clinging to his back like a monkey when I was five or six as he carried me up the nine flights to our apartment."

"In St. Louis?"

"No, we left there when I was a few months old. This was in Baltimore. Or was it D.C.?" She shook her head. "After that, we only took apartments that were on one of the first three floors."

"How many times did you move before you and your mom came to Shady Grove?"

"A dozen at least, though I only clearly remember living in Baltimore, D.C., Memphis and Tallahassee. I thought we were going to stay in Tallahassee for good. My mom did, too. But Dad had a lead on a construction job outside of Baton Rouge. I remember them arguing about it when they thought I'd gone to bed." It was the first—and last—time Sadie had ever heard her parents fight. "When I got up the next morning, Dad was gone. He'd wanted an early start so he'd left without even telling me goodbye."

James touched her shoulder, let his hand linger there for a moment before trailing down her arm, his fingertips cool against her skin. She wanted to grab his hand, to press her mouth against his palm. She wanted, more than anything, to hold on to him in any way possible.

Except she was afraid it was already too late. She'd already lost him.

"We got the call about the car accident the next day," she said. "Two days later we had a private, graveside service for him in the morning. That afternoon we were on our way up here. As we crossed the Florida state line I started crying." Sobbing, really. She clearly recalled her body racked with so much grief she couldn't take a full breath, had felt as if she was drowning in her sorrow. "Because even though we'd just put Dad's body in the ground, even though he was never coming back, all I could think was that we were leaving and he wouldn't know where to find us. That he'd be looking for us, searching for his family. His home."

"You were just a kid," James said. But he didn't offer her the comfort of his touch again, no matter how hard she wished he would. "Death's hard enough to understand as an adult."

Her hair blew in her face; she let it go, let it hide her for the moment. "Eventually I stopped thinking he was looking for us. I missed him, but I also got used to him not being there anymore. Life kept moving, kept right on going, day in, day out. By the first anniversary of Dad's death, Mom was already remarried and pregnant with Charlotte."

"You seemed happy. I remember how excited you were that you were going to have a little brother or sister—no matter how many times I tried to warn you having younger siblings wasn't as much fun as you thought it was going to be."

"It was fun," she insisted, though it'd taken some getting used to, not having her mom's full attention. But Charlotte had been such a sweet baby, Sadie had fallen in love with her immediately. "Life was good. Mom was happy. And Will never treated me like anything less than his own daughter."

"He's a good man."

"He is. One of the best. He's not my dad—God, I don't think you could get two men who were more different." Except maybe James and Victor. "But he's been a really good father to me."

"And that made you feel guilty," James said, knowing her well. Too well. Able to see things she'd rather keep hidden.

"It was part of it. But it wasn't just loving Will, it was everything. We'd gone from living this gypsy existence, no ties, no commitments except to each other, to being surrounded by family and friends. Tethered to this town in ways I'd never experienced before." She and her mother hadn't just been welcomed into the community, they'd been absorbed by it. Irene had slipped seamlessly back into her life in Shady Grove with her parents and brother, her friends.

"It changed even more drastically when Mom and Will got together," Sadie continued. "No more secondhand clothes and sneaking out of town in the middle of the night because we couldn't pay rent. We had it all. And I loved it. I loved having a stepfather who could afford to buy me everything I wanted. I loved our big, fancy house and the security of knowing that if I asked for some toy or a new dress, I could have it. I was living a life my father would've hated, the type of life he himself had walked away from."

James bent and picked up a small rock, tossed it onto the weed-choked bank to his right. "That was his choice. What he thought was best for him. It's okay to want something different for yourself."

She wondered if he was talking about her...or himself. All of Montesano Construction's employees knew about the tension between James and Frank. It hurt that James hadn't confided in her about his problems with his father, that he wasn't happy with his place in the company.

It hurt even more to realize that she'd probably been the catalyst of those problems.

"Maybe, but I still felt like I'd let him down. That if he was watching over me like all the grown-ups told me, he was disappointed in what he saw. But the worst day came the summer I was thirteen and I realized I couldn't remember the last time I'd thought of my dad. That I couldn't picture his face without the help of a photograph, could no longer hear the sound of his voice, his laugh."

A chill racked through her. She wrapped her arms

around herself, but it didn't help. "Ever since Dad died, Mom and I were completely focused on moving forward. The only problem with looking ahead all the time is you stop looking back. And that's where my father was. In the past."

"You said it yourself," James said, so gently tears pricked her eyes. "Life moves on."

She cleared her throat, blinked away the moisture. "Yes, but we should still remember. I let him go." The memory of it still shamed her. "I let him slip from my mind, from my life. So maybe my mother is right. Maybe I am chasing his ghost or trying to live his life instead of my own. But it's the only life I know. The only way I can hold on to him. To not lose him again."

CHARLOTTE'S HAND SHOOK as she lit the last candle. She was nervous.

She rolled her eyes, used her other hand to steady the first. More like terrified—though nervous sounded a hell of a lot better.

Finally the wick caught and she blew out the match. She surveyed the room with a critical eye. Not bad. Not bad at all, if she did say so herself. The dining room was one of her favorite spots in the house—in what would be *her* house in a matter of mere weeks, she thought, more than a tad giddy. Wooden floors, huge windows to bring in tons of light and a view of the river, it was the perfect spot for family meals and holiday get-togethers, for Sunday brunches and kids' birthday parties.

And tonight, it was ideal for a romantic indoor picnic.

She'd scoured her mother's huge collection of home decorating magazines for ideas, then went out and spent a good portion of her week's pay on the necessary supplies to set the scene. Red candles, dozens and dozens of them in every shape and size imaginable, were scattered around the room, their flames flickering in the twilight. Fat ones clustered together in the corners, narrow tapers and squat votive ones set on black iron holders. The new dishes and stemware she'd bought were laid out on the thick blanket she'd spread in the middle of the floor. A bottle of champagne chilled in a silver ice bucket and in the background Jason Mraz's "I'm Yours" played over her iPod speakers, loud enough to hear but not so loud as to impede conversation.

The air smelled of roses and the dinner she'd picked up—pasta with vodka sauce, fragrant garlic bread and a side salad. For dessert, what could be more decadent, more sensual than chocolate-dipped strawberries?

He would feed them to her, of course. Sitting close enough that their knees brushed, he'd hold one to her lips and, after she'd taken a delicate bite, he'd cover her mouth with his own. They would share their first kiss right here in the house where they would someday make love for the first time.

Where they would raise their family. Grow old to-gether. It was that thought, the rightness of it, that had her nerves settling and anticipation building.

It was going to be perfect. Absolutely perfect.

Someone knocked on the door.

"Oh, God, oh, God," she whispered, skirting the blanket. Her heels echoed loudly in the emptiness as she crossed the room. Wiping her damp palms down the sides of her dress, she shut her eyes for a moment. When she opened them, she reached for the handle. Smiled.

And opened the door.

"James," she said, her voice husky and, she hoped, sexy. "Hi."

His eyebrows drew together and she had to fight to keep that smile in place, to not fidget or rub her fingertip under her lip to make sure her lipstick hadn't smudged.

"Thanks so much for coming over," she contin-ued, holding the door open wider, staying close enough that his hip brushed against hers as he stepped inside.

His gaze swept over her then skittered away. He swallowed visibly.

She made him nervous. Had rendered him speechless.

How simply wonderful.

It was nothing less than she'd expected, though. She'd tried on at least twenty outfits at WISC before choosing this silk blue dress with white polka dots, an open back and supershort hemline. The three-inch heels of her beige sandals made her legs seem endless, and she'd pinned her hair up, showing off the long line of her neck.

Clearing his throat, he tapped a mechanical pencil against his clipboard as she shut the door. *Tap. Tap. Tap.*

If he didn't knock it off, she was going to stab that pencil in the wall.

"Is this where you want it?" James asked in his deep voice.

She blinked. "Excuse me?"

"The mudroom." He looked around the small foyer and frowned. "It's either going to cut into your square footage here," he said, unclipping a tape measure from his belt, "or the porch."

"Why don't we discuss it over a drink?" she said, linking her arm with his and tugging him toward the dining room. She pressed against his side. "You must be thirsty. And famished."

"Actually, I grabbed a burger on the way over here."

She stumbled, catching her balance before he could do more than reach out a hand to steady her. Her face flamed.

He wasn't supposed to have already eaten. She'd bought supper. And now it would go to waste. Pouting only a little, she snuck a glance at his profile. His hair was mussed and dark stubble covered his cheeks, blending with his goatee.

He could have put a little effort into his appearance, she thought grumpily. Not that she minded that he'd obviously come straight from a job site—she appreciated a man with a strong work ethic, after all. But it would have been nice, considerate, if he'd changed out of his old jeans, taken the time to shower off the scent of sawdust, to shave.

The important thing was that he was here. That tonight was going to be special.

They stepped into the dining room and he stiffened and stopped like his feet had been set in cement. She let go of his arm and went over to the champagne.

"If this is a bad time," he said quickly, looking panicked, "I can come back tomorrow. Or the next day."

"What? Why?"

He waved vaguely at the candles, the blanket. "You must be expecting someone—"

She laughed, the sound as bubbly as the champagne she was pouring. "Don't be silly." Taking the clipboard from him, she tossed it to the ground before handing him a crystal flute. She laid her hand on his chest, gratified and emboldened when his heart skipped a beat. "I've been waiting for you."

He leaped back so quickly, champagne sloshed over the rim of his glass. "Charlotte, I—"

"To my first house," she said, determined to get this evening on track. On *her* track. Her schedule. She tapped her flute against his, the light peal of it ringing in the air. Holding his gaze, she stepped closer. "And to new beginnings."

He averted his gaze, didn't touch his drink.

She sipped hers to hide a frown. Had to remind herself that he was just nervous, too. Hadn't she been glad of it not a few minutes ago? This was a big moment for them. Huge. He must know that. Sensed it.

She took his drink, then crouched and set both glasses on the hardwood floor near the edge of the blanket. Straightening, a mix of courage, fear and anticipation tumbling inside of her, she reached for him.

Only to die a little when he bolted to the other side of the room and stared out the window. "Great view."

"Yes," she said slowly. "You mentioned that when you were here before."

With his back to her, he nodded, his hands in his pockets. "That's because it's great. Really great."

She closed the distance between them. "James, is something wrong?"

He turned slowly, his gaze serious, his mouth a thin line. "Charlotte, I—"

Desperate to stop his words—words she instinctively knew she didn't want to hear—she lunged at him, pressed her mouth against his. He jerked violently, hitting his head against the wall with a dull thud. She wound her arms around his neck, linked her fingers together there and plastered herself against him—breasts, hips and thighs.

Tears stung her eyes. She didn't understand. It should have been the best moment of her life so far, a magical moment, one she could look back on with a fond smile. The first kiss with the man she loved, the man she planned on spending the rest of her life with. But it wasn't.

Because he wasn't kissing her back.

He grasped her upper arms and pushed her away from him. Panic and confusion suffused her.

Holding her at arm's length, he watched her. She wanted to see longing in his eyes, wanted to imagine he was being noble and honorable, not wanting to take advantage of her despite his feelings, his attraction to her.

But it wasn't attraction she saw in his eyes, it was regret. Affection, yes, but not burning desire or love.

"Charlotte," he said in his lovely, deep voice, "I…" He shook his head.

Humiliation washed over her, coated her mouth and throat with a bitter taste. Oh, God. She didn't understand. What had she done wrong? It should have been perfect. Hadn't she done everything to make sure it was? She'd set the scene, had planned it all out. This was supposed to be the night when everything changed between them, when he realized he couldn't live without her.

When he realized how much he loved her.

"I…I don't understand," she said, trying to smile,

because surely she could still turn this around. "Don't you find me attractive?"

"You're beautiful."

But he didn't sound like a man in the throes of passion. He sounded like a big brother assuring his awkward sister that someday the boys were going to be lining up for her. Just like he had all those years ago.

She couldn't give up. Not when she was this close to getting what she wanted. "Look, I know what you're thinking. There's the age difference and the fact that you and Sadie are friends, but none of that matters to me. It doesn't," she insisted as he cursed under his breath and let her go to start pacing. She twisted her hands together. "We would be so good together. We'll take it slow, of course, to start. It'll be a shock to some people, us getting together, but once they see how we're meant to be—"

"Charlotte," he said with a sigh.

"No," she rushed on. "They will. We both want the same things. Marriage and kids and life right here in Shady Grove. It'll be perfect. Perfect," she repeated, sounding more irrational than she would have liked.

"Both of us wanting that isn't enough to make a relationship work," he said carefully. "It doesn't take the place of real feelings, the kind that will last a lifetime."

Her feelings were real, damn it. They had to be.

"Couldn't we—" She swallowed. "Couldn't we

at least try? We could date, get to know each other better." That had been her mistake, she realized. She'd gone too fast. Hadn't taken enough time for him to know her as an adult, as a person other than simply his best friend's little sister.

Once he did, he would realize he should be with her.

He swiped up his clipboard. "It wouldn't work."

"Is there someone else?"

His gaze flicked to the floor before he met her eyes again. "No."

Her shoulders sagged in relief. "Then there's no reason we can't—"

"Charlotte, I care about you," he said.

She shook her head, hugged her arms around herself as if that alone could protect her from what she clearly saw coming. "Don't," she whispered, her throat painfully tight. "Please—"

"I'm sorry," he said, whether in response to her plea or a preemptive apology for how he was about to rip her heart out, she wasn't sure. "But I don't think of you that way." His voice was low. Compassionate. Kind. "I don't feel that way about you."

And, oh, God, but that kindness, that compassion made it worse, so much worse.

"I'm sorry if I gave you the wrong impression," he said, reaching out as if to touch her, to pat her on the head like a child.

She lurched back blindly, kicked the glasses with enough force to have them airborne before crashing to the floor. Champagne sprayed her bare ankles, shards of crystal flew.

"Careful," James said, tugging her away from the mess.

She stared pointedly at his hand until he dropped her arm. "I need to clean this up," she said, but instead of coming across as strong, angry, she sounded hollow. Broken.

He opened his mouth, but then nodded. Slapping his clipboard against his thigh, he walked to the doorway. Stopped and faced her. "I really am sorry, Charlotte."

She didn't look at him. Could never face him again. He'd been so damned nice about it, so sympathetic. She would have preferred him laughing at her.

Unmoving, she stared at the burning candles until she heard the front door close. Until the flames wavered through her blurred vision. Until she slid to the floor, curled her knees to her chest, laid her head down and cried.

CHAPTER FIFTEEN

"WHAT THE HELL are you doing here?"

Sadie looked up with a start, her heart racing to see James standing in the doorway to the Montesano office, looking like some thundercloud. "James. God, you scared me." She glared at Elvis, who was lying next to her, his head on his front paws, his tail swinging back and forth. "Some watchdog you're turning out to be."

Scowling, James stepped into the office. "Damn it, you're not supposed to be here."

She stiffened at his angry tone. "I wanted to finish typing up these estimates for Eddie." Plus, ever since her mother had refused to give her the money to leave town, she avoided being at the house as much as possible. "What is your issue?" she asked, her own irritation growing. He had no right to come in and interrupt her, to growl at her this way.

He paced the short length of the room. "Nothing."

"Fine," she said, standing. "I'll just get out of—"

He was already storming into the kitchenette. Sadie rolled her eyes. She shut down the computer and grabbed her purse while James muttered to himself, opening and slamming cupboard doors.

"Where is it?" he demanded.

Putting her sweater on, she barely glanced at him. "Where's what?"

"My mug." He stormed over, glared at her desk where the blue mug she'd sent him from Texas a few years ago sat, complete with the remains of her afternoon tea and a lipstick smudge. "Goddamn it," he said, grabbing it and shaking it at her, "this is my mug."

"I realize that, seeing as how I gave it to you."

"Mine," he repeated, getting closer, stalking her until she backed up a step. Then another. "Don't you ever use it again."

"You," she said pointedly, "have lost your ever-loving mind."

He whirled around, threw the mug across the room. Tea arced out, splashed onto the floor, splattered the metal filing cabinet. The cup hit the wall, the ceramic exploding into dozens of pieces that rained to the floor.

Eyes wide enough to pop right out of her head, Sadie could only stare at James.

"You were right," he said, his body vibrating. "Damn it, you were completely right. I saw it, too late, but I did see it. I tried to stop it…"

"Jamie, what has gotten into you?"

"Charlotte. She kissed me. Told me we were meant to be together."

Oh, poor Charlotte. And poor James. Even more upsetting was the jealousy gnawing at Sadie's gut, the urge she had to go to her little sister and tell her, in no uncertain terms, to keep away from James.

He plopped down on the chair near the filing cabinet, laid his head in his hands. "Why me? I'm ten years older. She's surrounded by doctors and firefighters and police officers…why the hell did she have to pick me?"

Sadie kneeled next to him, the cold concrete seeping through the thin material of her skirt. "Oh, James," she said softly, laying her hand on his thigh. "How could she not? You're honest, hardworking and so damned good."

He was perfect. The perfect man for someone like Charlotte, someone who wanted nothing more than to stay in her small hometown, who wanted to make a family there, live the rest of her life with the same hills for a view, surrounded by the same people she'd known since she was born.

"I messed up," he admitted on a soft exhale, his eyes bleak. "I thought I could handle it, could handle her. That it would be better to ignore it, but I walked right into it, like an idiot. She had a picnic set up, a romantic picnic, with champagne and candles. I could've stopped it, tonight, days ago, but I didn't want to hurt her feelings. But I did. I hurt her. I embarrassed her."

And both of those would weigh heavily on James, with his kind heart. Be the cause of his anger. His frustration. "I'm sorry, James. But you can't be too hard on yourself. She's young. She'll get over it."

"I kept telling myself that as I walked out. I know you're right. It's just…" He shook his head. "I let it go on too long. I told myself it was because I didn't want to jump to conclusions or hurt her feelings, but part of it was that I didn't want to face it. She's Charlotte, your little sister, the girl we used to baby-sit, for Christ's sake."

"She's a grown woman. One with her own mind, her own feelings, who makes her own choices. She chose to try something, to go after something with no guarantees of how it would end. I think that's incredibly brave."

He nodded. "I'm not deluding myself that I'm her great love and she'll never get over me, but I feel guilty for not putting a stop to it earlier."

"Like you said, you didn't want to hurt her."

"Is that why you kissed me back?" he asked, his gaze intense. "That night at my house. Is that why you made love to me, because you didn't want to hurt my feelings?"

"The two situations are totally different," she said.

"Are they?"

"Yes. For one thing, you and I were friends. You and Charlotte were more…friends by proxy. For another, her feelings for you were remnants of a childhood crush. She took it too far, that's all."

"Maybe that's what I did," he said, as if to himself. "That night. Maybe I took old feelings too far. Made them too important."

She was too stunned to speak, too scared to move. What was this fear building inside of her? Why did it feel as if he was trying to make what had happened between them meaningless? Why couldn't she let him? She should. It would be better for them both if she did.

Easier for them both to move on.

This might even be the way for her to salvage her friendship with him, a way to guarantee he'd always be in her life. Always be there for her.

But he was looking for the truth from her now. He needed her.

He. Needed. Her.

For the first time, he was turning to her. This was her chance to give back when before, she'd always taken.

He started to stand, but she shifted so that she kneeled in front of him, pressed her hands on his legs to keep him seated. "No. I wasn't pretending. Not that night. Not when I came to your house last weekend and kissed you. I wish I was."

"Why?"

"Because I've already done so much to screw this up. I don't want to hurt you, Jamie. It's the last thing I'd ever want to do. But when you kissed me on your birthday…it wasn't one-sided." She admitted what she'd kept from even herself. She slid her hands up his thighs, felt his muscles tighten under her fingers. "This isn't one-sided," she whispered, leaning forward.

Their gazes held, the air charged around them until all she could hear was their harsh breathing, all she could feel was the erratic thumping of her own heart, the warmth of James under her hands.

They came together at the same time, their mouths voracious, the kiss heated and hungry and desperate. He yanked her onto his lap, shoved her skirt up to her hips. His jeans were rough against her bare inner thighs, his hands hard and seeking as they roamed over her body. She latched onto his shoulders, felt the hard ridge of his arousal at her center. Rolled her hips.

He moaned, his fingers tightening on her waist.

Feminine power rushed through her, made her light-headed that she could make this strong man, this good man, the best she'd ever known, moan and tremble. He didn't touch her like he had when they'd made love before. Gone was the careful, reverent lover. In his place was a man starving for her. Desperate. Needy.

He shoved her shirt up, did the same with her bra, freeing her breasts. His mouth on her was hot and wet as he sucked on her nipple, his tongue swirling, driving her mad, his beard scraping her skin, heightening her pleasure.

His passion, his need for her, inflamed her own and she squirmed, trying to get closer, trying to ease the ache in her core. Lifting his head, he slipped his hand between them, rubbed his thumb over her. She gasped.

"That's it," he murmured in his familiar voice. "I'm going to watch you come, Sadie. Come for me."

She couldn't tear her gaze from his, couldn't ignore his commanding tone, the heat and pressure building inside of her until she thought she'd go mad if he didn't stop. That she'd go mad if he did. He shifted slightly, tugged her underwear aside and slid his finger inside of her. She bucked against his hand, her orgasm spiraling through her.

He was watching her so she left herself open to him, let him see what he did to her. Let him see in her eyes what she truly felt for him.

Let him see what she was afraid to admit, even to herself.

JAMES HAD NEVER seen anything as beautiful as Sadie, her face flushed from her orgasm, her gaze holding his, pleasure darkening the blue of her eyes. He slid his hand from her, felt her heat on his fingers, smelled her sex, the scent making him even harder.

He wouldn't push her, wanted this to be her choice. He wanted...he needed...this to be her idea. What she truly wanted.

She leaned forward, her bare breasts brushing his chest. Somewhere in the back of his mind he heard the dog whine, didn't even bother glancing over to see what had happened to Elvis. How could he think of anything when Sadie was kissing him, her soft hands cupping his face?

Her tongue flicked over his lips and he opened his mouth for her; when her hands went to his jeans, he lifted his hips so she could unbutton them, slide the zipper down. She straightened and took off her panties while he shoved his pants and underwear to his knees. He grabbed a condom from his pocket and sheathed himself.

Holding his gaze, she settled on him, her eyes shutting on a soft groan as she took him into her body. His heart stopped. She took his breath. She'd stolen his heart years ago and he knew, without a shadow of a doubt, that no matter what happened between them, he'd never get it back.

He'd never love anyone the way he loved her.

But he had to keep his words, his feelings, to himself so he didn't scare her off again. So he didn't push too hard, too fast and send her running.

Her back bowed and she kept her hands on his shoulders as she moved, taking him higher and higher. He gripped her waist, his fingers digging into her skin, his breathing growing ragged. Sweat coated their skin, her bare breasts swayed with her movements, the delicate skin pink from his beard.

She was so tight and hot and wet, and he slid into her deeper. Harder. Faster. She moaned, one long pull that seemed to wrap around him, pushed him into sliding to the edge of the chair and quickening the pace. She braced her feet on the back of the chair, taking him in to the hilt.

It wasn't enough, not nearly enough. He stood, lifting her easily. Her eyes widened, her grip on his shoulder tightened.

"Wrap your legs around me," he ordered roughly, walking the two steps to the desk.

As she did as he commanded, he swept a hand over the desk, clearing enough room to set her ass down on the edge. He stood, pumping into her, her ankles digging into his lower back, her weight resting on her elbows, her head thrown back.

She tightened around him, her body growing even hotter. She shuddered as she came, her body milking his until he went over the edge and emptied himself, giving her everything he had, everything he was.

As always, loving her more than was wise.

"I THINK WE'VE traumatized the dog," he muttered later—it could have been five minutes or five hours. Who knew? He was boneless and weightless, his muscles relaxed.

Sadie glanced over at Elvis, who was lying in the corner, facing away from them. She laughed. "Poor baby. Guess his previous owners did these things behind closed doors."

James forced himself to straighten, then, because he wanted to hold on to her, quickly dropped his hands after helping her to her feet. "I'm pretty sure it's the first time it's been done behind this particular door."

"I doubt that. I've seen your parents. They still act like newlyweds. Remember that one time we walked in on them making out in the kitchen? Your dad had his hand on your mom's—"

"I've spent all these years trying to forget," James muttered, pulling his pants up as she readjusted her clothes.

"I'm just saying they've probably already broken this room in. So to speak."

He went cold all over, stared horrified at the desk, the chair. "I may never have sex again."

"Now that would be a real shame," she said with a small, shy smile.

She was adorably mussed, her hair a tangled, golden mass around her face, her cheeks flushed, her shirt wrinkled. His heart ached with longing. He wanted to ask her to come home with him, to spend the night in his bed. He wanted to make love to her again. And again.

Most of all, he wanted to make her his. Forever.

Keeping his words inside, his feelings to himself, he turned his back on her then crouched and scooped up a pile of papers from the floor, chagrined to realize his hands were unsteady. He felt her watching him, her gaze boring a hole into the back of his head, trying to dig into his thoughts. Trying to figure out where they stood now.

He wished he knew.

Holding his breath, he kept focused on his task, exhaling only when he heard her footsteps retreat into the kitchen. He shut his eyes, hung his head. By the time she returned, a roll of paper towels in her hand, he was in control again. In control of his body and, more importantly, of his emotions.

"Sorry about the mess," he said, setting the papers on the desk.

"That's okay." She wiped the tea from the filing cabinet then tossed the soggy towels into the trash before ripping several more from the roll and using them to sweep up the chunks of broken mug. Elvis, finally over the trauma, crossed over to sniff at the floor by Sadie's feet. "I'm sorry I used your cup."

James's face warmed. He scratched his chin. "That may have been a little overkill."

"You think?" She straightened. "I've never seen you that angry. I didn't think you could *get* that angry."

"Right. Because I'm usually such a Boy Scout."

"Nothing wrong with being a Scout."

"Maybe not, but being a good guy hasn't exactly gotten me anywhere. I thought I'd try something different."

"Is that why you threatened to quit Montesano Construction if you didn't get the partnership? To prove you're not a pushover? You shot yourself in the foot if you ask me."

"I didn't ask you," he said coolly. "Now, if you'll excuse me, I have work to do."

He went into the shop, the lights he'd turned on when he'd first arrived glowing brightly. Damn it, he wasn't about to discuss his personal life, his problems with her. They weren't friends anymore. Even after what had just happened—maybe because of what had just happened—that much was clear.

He put on his tool belt. He'd come here to work on the frame of the kitchen cabinets for Bradford House. Though Eddie usually did the finish work, James, Maddie and Frank all pitched in when they were behind schedule.

Or, like tonight, when one of them needed work to keep busy, to keep their thoughts occupied.

Sadie came out, her purse over her shoulder, her hand on Elvis's head as they walked side by side. "Look, I know you don't want my opinion—"

He grunted.

"But I'm going to give it to you anyway. You love Montesano Construction."

"Thanks for the insight."

"You love it," she repeated. "Until your father hired me, you were happy with your place in the company. Do you really want to leave? If Frank doesn't agree to bring you in as a partner, will you be able to walk away from the company you've spent half your life with?"

He shrugged, though it felt as if he was lifting one hundred pounds on his shoulders. "Guess we'll find out."

"I hadn't realized how completely stubborn you

could be," she said, not sounding impressed by that fact.

"Maybe we didn't know each other as well as we thought."

"I know you've always been a part of Montesano Construction, no matter who is listed as the owner. But you convinced yourself you were being somehow slighted. Now you've worked yourself into a corner—and you're stuck there because you issued that stupid ultimatum. If you don't do something to fix this—and soon—if you walk away from the company, you'll spend the rest of your life regretting it."

"You were right the first time. I don't want your opinion."

She looked hurt. Worse, she looked disappointed. In him.

It cut him to the bone.

He turned on the table saw, the loud whine of it making it impossible to hear any response she might give. Hell. He didn't need her harping at him. He already wondered if he'd made the right choice— or if he'd let his anger and frustration over Frank hiring Sadie push him into making a rash decision.

One his pride wouldn't let him take back.

"YOU'RE ALL PROBABLY wondering why I asked you to be here," Frank said Saturday evening.

"Don't tell me," Maddie said, helping herself to

another scoop of their mom's pasta salad, "Colonel Mustard did it in the pantry with a wrench."

When James's mom had invited him for dinner that night, he'd almost refused, hadn't wanted to spend that much time with his father, not when things with the business were still up in the air. But when Rose had mentioned that the rest of the family was coming—with the exception of Leo, who was working—James had relented.

It was better than staying at his place alone, reliving making love with Sadie. Hearing her voice in his head.

You've always been a part of Montesano Construction, no matter who is listed as the owner.

If you don't do something to fix this—and soon—if you walk away from the company, you'll spend the rest of your life regretting it.

Damn her for voicing his own silent fears, for making them impossible to ignore any longer.

Now he and his family had finished eating—he eyed Maddie putting away the pasta salad—almost all of them were done eating, he amended, and Bree and Max had gone downstairs to play video games.

Frank leaned back in the dining room chair, linked his hands on his still-flat stomach. "We need to clear the air about this partnership business. Montesano Construction can't go on like this. Neither can this family." He looked around the table. "I'm proud of you, all three of you, and you have no idea what it means to me to know you all want to work for the company, to be a part of it forever, to take it into the future and possibly hand it down to future generations."

"But?" James prompted quietly.

Frank sighed, seemed to age in front of James's eyes, which was ridiculous as his father was only fifty-six. Not some old man. "I've seen it too many times. Families fighting once they're brought on board a business. They're torn apart."

Eddie frowned. "The companies?"

"The families. I don't want that to happen to us. The infighting and arguments. Things will change if we're all owners. It's already started."

James sat back. So Maddie had been right. He'd been so sure his dad had been trying to hold on to his power, to keep complete control of the company, that this other stuff was an excuse. Clearly James had had it wrong.

Maybe Frank was just trying to hold on to his family.

"Things will change," James said slowly. He thought of him and Sadie, of how they'd gone from friends to lovers to…what, he had no idea. "They're meant to. But that doesn't mean things will be worse. We don't want to shove you out or take over the business, but we do want to be fully invested in it. We love it. We all love it. And we want a say about how the company is run, how we take it into the future. We deserve that."

"I'm sorry," Frank said, sounding as if he really

meant it. But it did little to appease James. "I can't risk this family. I won't."

Disappointment settled heavily on James's shoulders. But he nodded. He'd asked his father to make a decision and Frank had done so. James didn't have to like the end result. "Then I guess we have nothing left to discuss," he said as he rose to leave.

His father opened his mouth but Maddie spoke before he could.

"You," she said, pointing her fork at James's jugular, "are seriously getting on my last nerve. I suppose this is where you make some dramatic statement, quit and then storm off, your lofty ideals and this sudden need for recognition intact."

Sudden need for recognition? Was that really what she thought of him? He scanned his parents' faces, Eddie's. Christ, was that what they all thought?

Worse, could they be right?

"This isn't about my ego," he said, his voice stiff. "It's about me finally choosing what happens in my own life. I've never, not once, considered doing anything with my life other than working for Montesano Construction."

Maddie shrugged. "So? Neither did I. At least, not seriously."

"Shouldn't we have?" he asked. They should have explored their options, seen what else was out there for them. Instead, they'd drifted into their jobs, taken the easy route. Settled.

He'd settled.

"Seems to me," Eddie said, "you need to stop worrying so much about what you did and didn't do in the past and figure out what you want in the here and now."

"And that," Maddie said, nodding at Eddie, "is why he is the wisest of us all. He may not say much, but when he does, it's pure gold."

Rose's eyebrows lifted. "Except when he disagrees with you."

Maddie nodded. "Except when he disagrees with me."

"Your father and I have discussed this," Rose said, her back ramrod straight, her hands flat on the table on either side of her plate. "And if you—" she sent Maddie a pointed look "—could keep your thoughts in your head where they belong, perhaps he could tell you about our decision. Please sit down, James."

"Mom, I—"

"Sit. Down." This from Frank, said in such a no-nonsense tone, James found himself moving to sit, but he locked his knees. "Please," his dad added gruffly.

James sat.

Frank pushed aside his empty dinner plate, clasped his hands together on the table. "As your mother said, we've discussed this and we've come up with what we feel is a good solution, a fair one for all involved." He cleared his throat, seemed nervous. "But, if after you hear our proposition, you still feel it's in your best interest to go out on your own, to start your own company," he said to James, "then we want you to know, you'll have the full support of this family."

"He will?" Maddie asked incredulously.

"The full support of this *entire* family," Frank said, frowning at his daughter.

She slouched in her chair like she used to when she'd been a taciturn teenager. "Fine."

James was stunned. "That means a lot to me," he said. "Thank you."

Frank rubbed circles on the tablecloth with his palms. "Yes, well, we're hoping that once you hear what we're offering you won't want to go anywhere. But it's important to me for you to know—" he swept his gaze around the table "—for all of you to know that nothing means more to me and your mother than our family. I'd dissolve the company before I'd let it come between any of us. What we're hoping is that you three will take Montesano Construction into the future, that you—and possibly your children—will keep it running long after I'm retired. If that's what you want," he added quickly. "In the meantime, we'd like to bring you all in as shareholders."

James narrowed his eyes. "You want us to buy into the company?"

Most owners used shareholders as a way to raise capital in order to grow their business. But Montesano Construction was sound and could easily afford any type of expansion ideas Frank might have.

"We want to give you the shares," Rose said. "Ten percent each."

James and Eddie exchanged a surprised look. Their parents—their father—was willing to give them 30 percent in his company. It wasn't a partnership, wasn't even close to what James had wanted. Had thought he wanted. He still wouldn't have a say in how the business was run.

But he would have ownership in it.

It was a compromise.

Sadie had been right. James had let his anger and pride push him into a corner. This was his way out.

"That's very generous," Maddie said, sending James a glare when he remained silent. "But I don't feel right accepting. Not when I can't guarantee where I'll be a year from now."

"You're part of this company," Frank said firmly. "You've helped Montesano Construction grow, have put your heart and soul into it. We want you to always be a part of it, whether you're here or across the country."

Maddie, her eyes wet, rose and went over to Frank to kiss the top of his head then press her cheek against his. "In that case, I accept your offer."

Frank reached back and patted her upper arm. "Eddie?"

Eddie nodded.

Everyone's attention turned to James, their gazes expectant.

It could work, James realized. They could make this work. But there was still one problem....

"What about Leo?"

"What about him?" Maddie asked.

"He may not be part of Montesano Construction," James said, "but he's part of this family."

And James didn't want him to feel as if he'd been slighted. Didn't want to cause any bad blood between Leo and the rest of them because Leo had chosen a different path.

His dad was right—nothing was worth risking their family's future.

"I want Leo to have half my shares," James said.

Maddie straightened, kept her hands on Frank's shoulders. "Why not just split the thirty percent by the four little Montesanos? Seven and a half percent each."

A proud grin lit Frank's face. "Looks as if we have an agreement then."

"Another family crisis averted," Maddie said, returning to her seat. She piled more food onto her plate then glanced at Rose. "What's for dessert?"

As Rose and Maddie discussed the cake Rose had made and Frank asked Eddie a question about Max's hockey team, James couldn't stop from smiling. He was in for God knew how many more years of long hours, of listening to Maddie bitch about one thing or the other, of trying to get Eddie to meet with customers instead of hiding out in the shop. Years of endless customer calls and complaints, of dealing with distributors and employees.

But, for the first time in a long time, it didn't feel as if he was stuck. It felt as if he'd finally set himself free.

"Hey, there, Red. Can I get you a sod-y pop?"

Charlotte glared at O'Riley's owner. "Whiskey and diet cola. Please," she added through gritted teeth.

He raised his eyebrows and she fisted her hands so she wouldn't be tempted to slap that condescending smirk off his too-handsome face. Jerk.

"Drinking with the big girls tonight?" he asked, fixing her drink.

Was that what the big girls drank? She had no idea. She usually stuck with a beer or two.

"Here you go. Take it easy on those," he said with a wink.

She took a huge gulp, just to prove she could, just to prove she didn't have to listen to him. Dear Lord, it was strong. Her eyes watered; her throat burned. "Did you forget the cola part?" she asked on a wheeze.

Amusement shone in his eyes and in that instant, she hated him. "Maybe you should stick with beer."

She worked up a sneer. "Maybe you should go to—"

"Hello, Lottie," Sadie said, hurrying out from

behind the bar. Char hadn't seen her yet, but Sadie must have noticed her boss was giving Char a hard time.

Did she mention he was a jerk?

"Sadie." Char tried to glare, but it was a weak effort. Even though she was mad at her sister, she still missed her.

She'd been so upset after James left the other night, so embarrassed, she'd stayed at the house, watching the candles burn down for hours. When she'd finally been able to get up and go to her apartment, she'd fallen onto her bed and slept for twelve hours straight, then had to work a double shift at the hospital. This was the first chance she'd had to track down her sister.

"What's up?" Sadie asked. "You okay?"

Char opened her mouth to say she was fine, but what came out was, "No. Not really."

Sadie studied her, looking more serious than her sister usually did. "Come with me," she said, taking Char's hand and leading her back behind the bar. "I'm taking a break," she told her boss.

He scowled. "You've been working only twenty minutes."

"And now I'm taking a break." She glanced pointedly at the only two patrons at the bar, the couple seated at a booth near the pool table. "I think you can handle the early-Saturday-night crowd."

She kept going, pulling Charlotte into a small break room off the kitchen. Either her sister was extremely brave or she had reason not to fear her scary boss. "Are you sleeping with him?" Char asked.

Sadie twitched in surprise. "Who?"

"Scary man. Your boss."

"Please. Even I'm not that stupid." She handed Char a bottle of water from a small fridge, opened one for herself. "Now, what's going on?"

Char took a sip, put the lid back on. "I...I need you to talk to James for me." When she'd come up with this plan, it had seemed like a good idea, but saying it aloud made it seem a little too...middle school. But she'd come this far and Char didn't like to go backward. "Please. He'll listen to you."

"What do you want me to talk to him about?" Sadie asked, sounding hesitant.

Well, she probably didn't want to get involved between her sister and her best friend. Char could understand that, but this was important. "I love him," she said quietly, then again, louder, because it was the first time she'd said it out loud. "I love him. But he's afraid to be with me because of the age difference or...I don't know why. I just need you to talk to him, ask him to give me, to give us, a chance."

Sadie was staring at her, stunned. She shook her head. "You...you love him. James? My James? I thought it was just a crush."

Something in the way she said *my James,* the second time she'd slipped like that, had Char's eyes narrowing. "I love him," she repeated. As if she didn't know her own feelings. She was a grown woman, for God's sake. "We'd be so good together. But I need to know I have a chance. He said he wasn't seeing anyone. Is that true?"

Sadie was white. "Char, honey...I don't know how else to say this, so I'll just spit it out." She inhaled deeply. "He's seeing me. Sort of."

"No, no. I mean, is there some woman he's romantically involved with?"

"Me. James and I are...together. Well, we have been...together."

Char went hot then cold. Her skin crawled, as if someone had poured hundreds of tiny spiders over her. "What?"

"Break's over," Sadie's boss said, sticking his head into the room. "A bachelorette party just came in."

"In a minute," Sadie said.

"You...you're seeing James?" Char asked, stepping closer to Sadie, her big sister, the woman she'd always looked up to, whom she'd admired and loved so much. "You're with James?" The more it sank in, the angrier she got. How dare Sadie take James from her? "You're screwing him?"

Sadie flinched, but then her expression hardened. "Watch it, little girl."

"I am *not* a little girl." And if she wanted to add a foot stomp to that proclamation, no one had to know but her. "How could you do this to me?"

"Believe it or not, me getting together with James had nothing to do with you."

Of course not. She hadn't even thought of Char, of how this would affect her. "God," she said, stepping closer, "you are unbelievable, you know that? You just waltz back into town after years, *years* of being off—" she waved her arm wildly, forcing Sadie to take a step back "—finding yourself or whatever it is you tell yourself you're doing while you run away from being a real grown-up—"

"Seriously starting to tick me off," Sadie warned tightly.

But Char didn't care. Why should she? Sadie never cared about anything, not her family, not the havoc she wreaked on people's lives. "Oh, please, it's the truth. You're so selfish. All you care about, all you've ever cared about, is yourself."

"If you two are going to keep at it," O'Riley's owner said drily, "mind if I hose both of you down and charge a cover fee? Might as well get something out of this catfight."

"Shut up," Char said, whirling on him.

"Hey," Sadie said, pushing Char's shoulder. "Don't tell my boss to shut up."

Char used both hands to shove Sadie back two steps. "Don't push me."

"Back up, little sister," Kane said, grabbing her arm and pulling her away as if he sensed she was gearing up to punch Sadie's nose.

"Don't touch me," she said lowly, not bothering to try to free herself, just giving him a withering glare.

It didn't bother him in the least. Figured. "If you

don't calm down," he said in his flat voice, his grip on her firm, but not tight enough to actually hurt, "I'm going to personally escort you out of here. You get it?"

Tears threatened. She choked them back. "I'm leaving anyway. I don't want to be in the same building as her."

He opened his fingers and she headed for the door.

"Okay, enough of the drama-queen routine," Sadie said, blocking what had been a very regal exit on Char's part. "Look, let's just calm down and—"

"I won't calm down," Char snapped, slapping at the conciliatory hand Sadie reached toward her. "You stole the man I loved."

That may have been a little over-the-top, but it was heartfelt and true.

Impatience crossed Sadie's experience. "You don't even know him. You had a crush. It's understandable. He's a great guy, the best, but, honey, you don't love him. Not really."

She did. Didn't she? He was perfect for her, for her plans, for what she wanted for her future. But Sadie had taken that away from her. "And you do?"

Sadie looked as shocked as if Char had given in to that urge to pop her one. "James and I are...we're... friends. We care about each other."

"Friends?" Char sneered. "Friends with benefits? How convenient for you, and just how you prefer things. No strings. No promises, certainly no ties to strangle you. God forbid you actually commit to anything or anyone. But while you're having this easy, no-strings-attached affair, did it ever occur to you that you're holding him back? James deserves a woman who's going to love him forever, who wants to get married, have children and raise them here in Shady Grove."

"Someone like you?" Sadie asked.

"Someone exactly like me," Char snapped. "You only came here because you messed up your life. And once you get bored or something more interesting—*someone* more interesting—comes along, you'll drop James and take off like a rocket. It's what you do. It's who you are." Char stepped closer, couldn't stop her voice from shaking. "You'll hold him back from finding true happiness, but worse than that, you'll hurt him. You'll leave him alone with a broken heart, and that's something I never, never would do."

Sadie was white, her lower lip trembling, but Char didn't take her words back. Couldn't. They were true. And it was past time someone told Sadie exactly what she was doing wrong instead of always letting her charm her way out of things.

Sadie turned and walked away.

Because she couldn't defend herself. Because she knew damn well every word, every single one, was true. But if she was in the right, and Char assured herself she was, why did she feel so horrible?

CHAPTER SIXTEEN

"SADIE!" IRENE CALLED, waving her arm frantically as she jogged across the backyard toward Sadie and Elvis.

"Mom?" Sadie raised her eyebrows and, wrapping the leash around her hand, picked up her pace, causing Elvis to trot to keep up. "What's the matter? What's wrong? Is the house on fire?"

They'd just returned from their evening walk, had only been gone an hour. What could have possibly happened? She glanced over her mother's shoulder but there was no smoke billowing from the windows, no flames shooting from the roof.

"Nothing's wrong." Irene grabbed Sadie's hands, clutched them tightly. "You're not going to believe it. You were right!"

"Yes, that is a shock," Sadie said drily. "As I'm usually completely wrong."

Irene laughed, squeezed Sadie's hands once more before dropping them. "No, no. That's not what I meant. It's just such a shock…after all this time who would've thought…" She bent and rubbed Elvis's head—the first time Sadie remembered her petting the dog. "Wait until you see who's here for you," she told him.

Why that made Sadie nervous, she had no idea. "Mom, what is going on?"

"Jo Jo!"

At the shout, Sadie looked up. Elvis barked, hopped into the air. Barked again.

Then took off like a shot.

Which wouldn't have been a problem except he practically took Sadie's arm off. Running to keep said arm attached to her shoulder, Sadie grabbed the leash with both hands and struggled to get Elvis to show a little decorum, but he was out of control. He lunged at the last moment and Sadie used all her strength to yank him back before he knocked over a lanky teenager with short brown hair and a chin covered in acne.

She opened her mouth to apologize only to choke on the words when the kid fell to his knees and held out his arms.

And her dog raced into them.

"Hey, boy," the kid said, rubbing Elvis's ears, then holding the dog's face in his large hands. "Did you miss me?"

"I...I don't understand," Sadie whispered when her mom joined them.

But she was afraid she did.

Irene put her arm around Sadie's shoulders and steered her toward the edge of the yard where a smiling

Will stood with an equally cheerful-looking middle-aged couple. Everybody was all happy-happy.

Sadie wanted to cry.

"Sadie," Irene said, "this is Kent and Tracy Jackson. And that—" more smiles, this time accompanied by a head tilt toward the kid "—is their son Jason. They're Elvis's—" Rolling her eyes, she laughed. So glad to see everyone was having such a fabulous time. "They're Jo Jo's owners."

Sadie's blood chilled. "How… Why…"

"It's such an amazing story," Irene said. "You're not going to believe it."

"Try me."

"Well, you see, six months ago, we moved from Pittsburgh to York," Tracy, a heavyset woman with round cheeks and kind hazel eyes, said. "About two months ago, Jo Jo dug a hole underneath the fence in the backyard and took off. We searched for days." She moved closer and lowered her voice. "Poor Jason was heartbroken. We thought for sure we'd never see Jo Jo again."

Kent nodded. "We'd even started checking into getting another dog from the shelter—Jo Jo was a rescue."

"But Jason would not give up hope," Tracy said, her lower lip quivering. "And then yesterday, one of his friends from his old high school messaged him on Facebook—"

"And told him he'd seen an ad in the paper about

someone finding a dog that looked like Jo Jo," Kent
said. "So we looked up the ad online—"

"And Jason was so sure it was Jo Jo he wouldn't
even let us call first to warn you all we were coming," Tracy said. "So we hopped in the car and here
we are."

"They got here right after you left for your walk,"
Irene told Sadie. "They've been waiting ever since."

Sadie couldn't speak. All she could do was stare
at Jason and Elvis—at Jason and *Jo Jo*. She wanted
to scream, to demand these people show proof that
this was their dog. She wanted to rip Elvis—damn
it, Jo Jo—from the kid's arms. Run inside and lock
the doors until they went back to York.

But she didn't need proof. Not when the dog and
boy were obviously crazy for each other.

She had to let Elvis go.

Her eyes pricked with tears and she blinked rapidly. "I'll just…" She frowned. Wasn't sure what to
do. What do say. "Uh…get his things."

"That's not necessary," Will said, watching her
carefully, the only one of the original happy camp-
ers who seemed to suspect she wasn't as thrilled
with this development as everyone else. "We've already gathered up his things and put them in the
Jacksons' car."

"Did you get his squeaky toy? And his rope? He
loves that rope."

Will patted her shoulder. "I got them."

She crossed her arms. Her throat was tight, her chest ached. "Good."

Kent checked his watch. "Come on, Jas. We need to get on the road—it's a three-and-half-hour drive home." He turned to Sadie. "We can't thank you enough for taking such good care of Jo Jo."

She tried to smile but it wobbled around the edges. "My pleasure."

Jason had the dog's leash, walked over to Sadie and held out his hand. "Thank you for finding my dog."

He's not your dog. He's mine.

He was going to be mine.

She shook his hand. "You're welcome," she whispered.

She trailed her fingers over the silky fur on Elvis's head then turned and hurried into the house.

She was in the kitchen searching for her keys when Irene came in. "Honey, are you all right?"

"Fine. I just… I'm going out for a little while…." Where were those damn keys? She could have sworn she'd left them right here on the counter.

"It's Sunday night," Irene said with a concerned frown. "Going out where?"

Sadie spied her keys hanging on the key rack—right where her mother must have put them. "Just out." She gave her mom a quick kiss on the cheek then practically ran to her Jeep.

She drove aimlessly for an hour. Around town. Outside of town. One street after another. Finally, she pulled to a stop at the place she'd tried like hell to avoid.

The place where she'd known she'd end up eventually.

A minute later, she knocked on James's door.

JAMES OPENED the door, his heart tripping to find Sadie, once again, on his doorstep. Except this time she wasn't drunk, wasn't hanging on another man. She was simply heartbreakingly beautiful.

"Can I come in?" she asked, her eyes bleak, her lower lip trembling. "Please? I...I could really use a friend."

He couldn't turn her away. Had always had a hard time refusing her anything.

He stepped aside. In the great room, she stared at the cold fireplace, her shoulders slumped. She was dressed in bright orange jeans, her top was a kaleidoscope of colors ranging from black to deep red to pink that burned a man's retinas. But the long sleeves were loose, the wide neck falling down one shoulder to show the white strap of her bra.

"Everything okay?" he asked reluctantly, afraid to be drawn back into friendship with her, terrified of letting her get close enough to rip his heart out again.

"They took him."

"What?"

She faced him. "They took Elvis. The Jacksons."

He moved closer, wanting, needing to keep his

distance but unable to do so when she looked so lost, when she sounded so incredibly sad. "Who are the Jacksons?"

"Elvis's owners. Except, his name isn't Elvis. It's Jo Jo." She tossed her hands up. "Jo Jo! What kind of name is that for a dog?"

James glanced at Zoe, who watched him with her head cocked, one ear up. "Uh…"

"A stupid one, that's what," Sadie said, starting to pace. "They moved to York from Pittsburgh and it seems El—Jo Jo," she ground out the name, "ran away one afternoon, made it all the way back here where I just happened to pick him up one rainy night."

"You're saying you found Elvis's owners?"

"They found him. A friend saw the ad in the paper, contacted them. Isn't that great? A happy ending for everyone."

Except she didn't seem happy. She seemed angry. Miserable.

"That must have been hard," James said, watching her carefully. "Giving him up."

She lifted a shoulder. "Why would it be? It's not like I'm stupid enough to think I could actually keep him. You sure as hell didn't seem to think I was capable of taking care of him."

"That's not true."

She stopped moving long enough to throw him a hard glare. "Isn't it?"

"No." But maybe, just maybe, he thought, guilt

pricking him, it was. At least a little. "You've just… never been the type to want any commitment. No pets. No long-term plans."

"You're right. You're absolutely right." Arms crossed, she stormed past the sofa, Zoe following her. "I don't like anything to tie me down. Nothing." She swallowed. Her chin quivered. Her eyes glittered with tears. "Nothing."

Aw, shit.

"Come here," he said gruffly, opening his arms.

With a sniff, she went into them. He lifted her, cradled her against his chest as he crossed to the couch and sat, settling her on his lap. She pressed her face against the crook of his neck, her tears wetting his skin, dripping down to the collar of his shirt. Her sobs shook her body. He felt helpless. Inept. He wanted to take away her pain, to go after the Jacksons or whoever the hell they were and get Elvis back for her. He wanted to make sure nothing and no one ever hurt her again.

But all he could do was smooth back her hair, kiss her forehead.

And hold her while she cried.

SADIE WOKE WITH a start. Her heart racing, she clutched the blanket covering her and glanced around frantically, trying to figure out where she was, why her mouth was dry, her eyes burning. It came to her in a flash. Elvis was gone.

She'd been upset and had done what her instincts

demanded. She'd come to James. He'd held her while she cried, gotten her some water then held her some more. She'd finally drifted off, exhausted and emotionally spent. It was dark now, though she had no idea how late. James had obviously left her to sleep on the couch, covering her with a blanket.

She wiggled her toes. He'd even taken off her shoes.

He'd taken care of her.

She wanted more from him. It was selfish. But she wanted more.

Not bothering with the lights, she slipped across the room, undressing as she went. She slid her shirt off by the chair, dropped it on the table. Reaching behind her, she unhooked her bra, left it on the floor outside James's bedroom.

She opened the door quietly and Zoe padded over. Sadie shooed the dog toward the kitchen then crept inside the bedroom, shutting the door again. She unzipped her pants, pushed them and her underwear down, stepping out of them as she approached the bed.

James slept on his stomach, his bare back visible, his right leg bent, his left arm stretched out over his head. He was beautiful, his tanned skin smooth, his back sculpted with muscles.

James deserves a woman who's going to love him forever, who wants to get married, have children and raise them here in Shady Grove.

He did, he absolutely did. She wasn't that woman.

From the moment she'd set foot in Shady Grove, her one goal had been to get out. To live the life she was meant to live, the one she'd lived before her father had died and her mother had become a totally new person. A life filled with freedom and endless choices. She wasn't cut out for the routine of small-town life, the drudgery of the same job year after year. The normalcy of marriage and kids and Friday-night dinners at the same restaurant and weekends spent by the pool or the ice rink.

There were too many places she had yet to see, too many things she had yet to do to ever be tied down.

But instead of feeling excited about those adventures, thinking about them made her anxious, as if they somehow weren't enough for her anymore. And that scared her to death.

She slid under the covers and he stirred. His scent, the soap he used in the shower, his laundry detergent, tickled her nose, would always remind her of him, of them as they were now.

Friends to lovers.

She pressed against him, seeking his heat, his strength. Smoothed her hand down his back. He rolled onto his side.

"Everything okay?" he asked, his voice husky from sleep, his first thought, as always, of her and how she was.

"Fine," she whispered, not wanting to break the tranquillity of the moment. "I want to be with you."

Nudging his shoulder, she pushed him onto his back, made quick work of the boxers he wore, then straddled him and leaned down to speak directly into his ear. "I hope you don't mind."

His erection pulsed between them, nudging her lower belly. "I guess I don't."

Smiling in the dark, she trailed her hands over his shoulders and down his chest, felt the ridges of his ribs then moved lower to the muscles of his stomach. She shifted back, dragged her finger from the top of his penis to the base and back up again. It jumped.

"Are you sure?" she asked, encircling him and sliding her hand up. Then down. "Because I could always go back to the couch."

"No, no," he said, his voice breaking on a moan when she rubbed her thumb over his slick head. "That's not necessary."

"Good."

She bent her head and took him into her mouth. He exhaled a soft curse, his hands going to her head, his hips lifting in supplication, in a plea. She pleasured him, reveling in his sighs and moans, in how his fingers kneaded her hair. And when those hands fisted and he gently pulled her to him, she willingly slid up his body for his kiss. He reached into the drawer next to the bed and she helped him sheath himself with the condom. He flipped her over and entered her, his hands linked with hers.

She arched as he moved inside of her, so strong and hard. This, this was what she wanted. What was between them. Charlotte had been wrong. What she and James had was special and lovely and real. It was more than just a fling, more than friends with benefits.

You'll hold him back from finding true happiness, but worse than that, you'll hurt him.

Tears clogged Sadie's throat, blurred her vision so she shut her eyes. She would hurt him. She didn't want to, but she couldn't be what he wanted. What he needed. She should walk away, let him move on with his life.

And she would, she assured herself. But not to-night. Tonight she was going to hold on to him for all she was worth.

JAMES STROKED SADIE'S hair, watched as she woke. Her eyes slowly opened. She smiled at him.

She was his dream. One he wanted to hold on to.

He couldn't contain his feelings, what she meant to him. How much more right could it be, the two of them, wrapped together in his bed, their bodies sated after a night of lovemaking? He'd held her all night. He wanted to hold her every night.

He wanted all of her.

"I love you."

She went so still, he shook her hands to make sure she was still alive. She sat up, clutching the sheet over her breasts. "James...don't. Please."

He watched as she pulled away from him, crossed the room, naked, to pick up her clothes.

"Don't what?" he asked quietly. "Don't tell you how I feel about you? Don't tell you what I want?"

She flinched. "Look, we care about each other. Isn't that enough?"

"Not for me."

"Why not? Why can't we keep going the way we have been?"

They could, he realized, and that was the problem. He was terrified if something didn't change between them now, it never would. Maybe it was time to put that, to put them, to the test.

"Because I want to move forward," he said.

She yanked on her clothes. "Just because we're not moving forward doesn't mean we're moving backward, either."

"No. It means we're stopping. Is that what you want, Sadie? Do you want to stop?"

She didn't answer, didn't even look at him.

He climbed out of bed, pulled on a pair of jeans and went to take her hands in his. He leaned down, kissed her. "Sadie, I love you." Her fingers twitched in his, but he didn't let go. His own hands were unsteady, but he didn't mind. Not when this was so right. Not when it was so important. "I love you," he repeated. "I want you in my life always, I want us to have a future together. A home. A family. And I need to hear you say that you want that, too."

"I CAN'T," SADIE whispered, tugging free to hug her arms around herself. "You know I can't."

James frowned, but he didn't seem deterred, oh, no, not James. He stubbornly caught her hands again. "Why not?"

"Why not? Are you crazy? It'd never work. Please, James," she begged, "please don't push this. Let's just...forget this ever happened okay?"

His expression hardened. "Like you wanted us to forget the first time we made love?"

"Look, I'm not what you want. What you need."

"I think I'm capable of deciding what I want and need, Sadie. It's you. It's always been you."

"Only because you've never let it be anyone else," she said quietly.

"Just tell me why," he insisted.

"Because I'm leaving!"

Her heart thudded painfully, her breathing was as ragged as if she'd run five miles. James looked stricken. "What?" he asked. "What do you mean?"

She licked her lips. "I'm going to California. I'm not staying here, James. I can't."

"You can't leave," he said, shoving his hands through his hair. "What about your job? What about your family? What about me?"

She wanted to bawl, wanted to rail at him for putting this all on her, his hopes and expectations. Hadn't she told him not to? Didn't he know better? "What about them?" she asked, forcing her voice to be flippant. "I appreciate what your family's done for me, what with the job and all, but everyone knew it was only temporary."

He seemed stunned. "So that's it...you're just going to leave?" he asked, staring at her as if he'd never seen her before.

"You knew I wouldn't stay. I'm not meant for the whole...routine."

"Routine?"

"Yeah. Marriage. Family. Kids. Play dates and soccer games and weekly brunches with the parents?" She laughed, but it came out humorless. "God. Can you see me doing any of that?"

"Actually," he said, watching her with those deep, dark eyes, "I can see you doing all of it."

"No thanks. I've got better things to do. I've always been too big for this town, you know that."

She'd always wanted too much, more than what anyone could offer her here. Excitement, thrills and the adventure of never knowing what the next day would bring. That was living.

She'd die here. She'd suffocate under the expectations, the routines.

Nothing was worth that. Was it?

"You could have everything you want here," James said, sounding and looking so confused, it broke her heart. But if she stayed, it would only be worse for him. For both of him.

"You mean I could have everything *you* want if I stay. That's what this is all about, isn't it? Your plans."

He flinched. "I just wanted you to give us a chance. To see how good we are together."

"I bet you did. I bet you had it all worked out. Tell Sadie you love her, that you've always loved her and if she balks, well, just lie low and give her time to come to her senses."

His eyes flashed. "You came to me. You crawled into my bed naked, for Christ's sake!"

"And I bet you were just thrilled, weren't you? Things were working out better than you could have anticipated. God, I fell right into your lap," she said as she stormed toward the door. "And now, because of that, you think I'm finally the woman you always wanted me to be?"

"I never tried to change you."

She whirled around. "No? What do you call what you're asking me to do? You want to mold me into the perfect wife, the perfect mother material. Well, forget it. I'm not interested."

JAMES'S HEAD WAS buzzing, his blood boiling under his skin. Anger shot through him, had him chasing after her. When he caught up with her by the front door, he grabbed her arm, spun her around.

"You're not interested?" he asked, his voice low. Then louder. "All I wanted, all I've ever wanted, was for you to stop seeing me as your buddy, your old pal James. To start seeing me as a man you could be interested in. Could have a future with." He shook her once and Zoe barked. "You think you can treat people like they don't matter?"

Her eyes were wide, her face pale. "James, I—"

He shook her again. His dog went nuts, barking and barking. James ignored her. "You're so busy trying to prove to everyone how free you are. You're not free, Sadie. You're scared. You've been running scared your entire life. Scared to face your feelings. To take a chance on something real. Something permanent. You want everyone to believe you're fearless, chasing after adventures, but you're a coward." He let go of her, unable to stand touching her a moment longer. "You're nothing but a coward, too afraid to have anything true and meaningful in your life. You think I wanted to make you into my ideal wife? My ideal woman? You already were. You were who I wanted. You with your crazy clothes and frizzy hair. I didn't want to chain you to some life you didn't want, I wanted to love you. To have a future with you."

He paced away, spun back. "You say you're too big for Shady Grove, too big for a normal life? Fine. Go live your life on your own terms. Alone. Because I'll get over you. I'll move on. But you? You'll always be alone."

He reached past her, yanked open the door so hard it hit the interior wall with a bang. "Just go. I'm through with you, Sadie Nixon. You understand? I'm through being your friend. Through being your patsy, your shoulder to cry on, the guy you run to every goddamn time you mess up your life." He leaned in so they were nose to nose. "I am finally, and forever, through with you. But know this, I would've gone with you. If you had only asked, I would've given it all up—my house, Montesano Construction, my family and my dreams, all of it— to be with you. To go where you go. I never wanted you to give up anything for me." He stepped aside. "Now get the hell out of my house and my life, and don't you ever come back."

CHAPTER SEVENTEEN

"COME ON NOW," Irene said, her voice so bright and chipper it hurt Sadie's teeth. "Come to the store with me," she continued, walking into Sadie's room, the same bedroom she'd slept in as a child after Irene had remarried. "You've been moping around for over a week. It's time to snap out of it."

Moping. That was a good definition. She hadn't stopped thinking about James. But she wouldn't cry, Sadie told herself. No matter how tight her throat got, no matter how badly her eyes stung, she wouldn't cry over him. He was lying. It was all a trick to somehow make it seem as if she was the one in the wrong. She pushed her hair from her face, curled up in the chair where she'd been pretending to read a paperback.

She wasn't wrong. She couldn't be.

And while she wasn't exactly setting the world on fire here in her old room, she wasn't desperate enough to spend the day running the cash register at her mom's store.

Irene sighed and crossed to crouch next to her chair. "Honey." She brushed Sadie's hair back gently. "Are you going to look for a job today?"

"What's the point? It'll only be temporary. Kane said he'd give me more hours, and as soon as I get enough money saved I'm going to California. That was always my plan. What I want."

"But...I don't understand," Irene said. "I thought you were doing so well here. Did something happen between you and James?"

Sadie slammed her book down. She should have figured her mom would eventually ask what was wrong. But after days of nothing more than sympathetic looks, Sadie had begun to hope Irene would leave the subject alone.

Which just proved hope was for fools.

"Oh, something happened all right. He told me he loved me. He wants me to stay here. God, can you imagine that?"

Just thinking about it had fear sliding along her spine. He wanted to lock her in a cage. Not one with bars, one that trapped her with promises, with words of love.

"Well, of course he loves you," Irene said as if not surprised in the least. "He always has. Why shouldn't he want you to stay? Why shouldn't you want to?"

"Because that's just the first step. The next thing you know, he'll want me to move in with him. Then, someday down the line when he's decided enough time has passed, he'll propose. And I don't want to get married. Ever. I don't want to have kids or stay in this stupid, boring town." Her breathing grew ragged, panic and desperation ripped the words from her throat. "God, the last thing I want is to turn out like you. Same dinners every week, same friends, doing nothing more with my life than taking care of a house and raising a couple of kids, making sure my husband's life is easy and comfortable. No, thanks. I want more than that."

"How dare you?" Irene asked in a low, vicious tone Sadie had never heard before. Her mother's face was red, her hands fisted at her sides. "How dare you look down on me and what I've chosen to do with my life, with what I've accomplished."

Something in Sadie whispered that she'd gone too far, that she'd said too much. But she couldn't back down. Not when she only spoke the truth.

"What you've accomplished?" Sadie asked incredulously. "Such as chairing the garden committee? Running some store that caters to women who have more money than they know what to do with? A store your husband bought and paid for you to run? Oh, or how about being den mother? Yeah, those are quite the accomplishments."

Irene straightened, her movements jerky. "I suppose I should've spent my life like you spend yours? Chasing one fantasy after another? One dead-end job, one dead-end relationship after another?"

"At least I'm living my life for myself," Sadie said, getting to her feet. "Not waking up every morning only to make my husband happy, to take care of my children. I'm out there, experiencing life to its fullest, Mom. You remember what that's like, don't you?"

"Oh, yes," Irene said, her tone chilling Sadie to the core. "I remember exactly what it was like. The question is, do you?"

"Of course. You and Dad were free. No rules, no restrictions. You came and went as you pleased, but then he died and you gave up. You couldn't make it on your own. But don't fool yourself into thinking I'm anything like you."

"No, you're nothing like me. Is that what you want to hear? Does that make you happy, knowing you're exactly like your father?"

Tears burned Sadie's eyes. "He was a great man."

"He was a charming man. Fun. He could light up a room, was the life of any party, and boy, did he love a good party. If there wasn't one going on, he'd make one out of nothing. He was irresistible, and I fell for him so hard it didn't matter that he was spoiled and had no way of actually making his big plans come true. I was so dazzled by him, all I could see, all that mattered, was being with him."

"He loved us." But instead of sounding positive, right, she sounded unsure. Scared.

Irene sighed. "He did love us, but that doesn't take away from the fact that he was irresponsible, easily bored and unreliable. At first, life with Victor was exciting. We were always moving from city to city, town to town, searching for the next great adventure. It didn't matter that we didn't have a place

of our own or grocery money because we were together. And then we had a baby, and suddenly it all
mattered, too much to me, too little to him. I was
the one making sure you had enough to eat, that we
didn't sleep in the car. I was the one working part-
time jobs just so I could buy baby formula and ce-
real, diapers and laundry soap while Victor went
off searching for his next challenge."

Sadie shook her head, but deep down she was
afraid her mother was right. Her memories of her
father were of a tall, handsome, fun man, always
laughing and dancing. But other memories, of waiting, constantly waiting for him to come home, were
there, too. Of her mother, tired and stressed.

Oh, God. What had she done?

Irene dug through her purse. She pulled out her
checkbook, wrote something. "Here."

Sadie tucked her hands behind her back. "What
is it?"

"A check for five thousand dollars. Take it."

All Sadie could do was shake her head, wishing
her words back.

Irene set the check on the unmade bed. "There.
Now you have no excuse not to leave. As a matter of fact, I'd like you to be gone by the time I get
back from work."

Sadie's head snapped back. Irene was kicking her
out. No matter what she'd done, Sadie had always
known she had a home here.

She'd lost that, too.

Irene walked to the door. Sadie wanted to call her back. Wanted to rip the check up and beg her mother to forgive her.

She stepped forward but stopped when Irene turned to face her again. "Your father was always searching for something that neither you nor I could give him," Irene said wearily. "That wears on a person, on a marriage. I came home to Shady Grove, not because I couldn't handle life by myself but because I was tired, so very tired, of doing it all on my own. I was blessed to find another man to love, one who took care of me, who raised my child as his own. But that's never been good enough for you, has it? You act so superior to me, as if my choices were wrong, but I have a husband who loves me. Two healthy daughters. Family close by, friends I adore and work that's satisfying to me." She paused, as if weighing her next words, then softly said, "Tell me, Sadie. What do you have?"

AN HOUR LATER, Sadie stood outside the wooden door. Making a fist, she pounded, the sound reverberating through her body. She waited. Knocked again. What if he was sleeping? A distinct possibility given that it wasn't even noon yet. Or maybe he was downstairs at the bar—

The door opened.

Relief rushed through her, made her knees weak. "I'm sorry." The words rushed out. "Did I wake you?"

Kane, barefoot and shirtless, wearing only a pair

of undone jeans, his hair wild around his shoulders, scowled. "I run a bar that doesn't shut down until 2 a.m. What do you think?"

"I'm sorry," she repeated, pretending her voice wasn't reedy and pitiful. That she wasn't a pathetic mess with her tangled hair and pale face. "I didn't know where else to go."

He flicked his cool gaze from her face to the suitcase in her hand and back to her face again. "I hear the Holiday Inn off the highway has affordable rates."

And he started to shut the door. She stuck out her foot to block it. "Please. Just for a night or two."

Or however long it took her to figure out why she wasn't already on her way to California. The check her mom wrote burned in her pocket.

"You don't want to come in here."

"I do." She didn't have much choice. "I really do."

His expression darkened but he stepped aside, scratched his flat stomach. "Don't say I didn't warn you."

She tried to smile but it was too much effort. "Thanks," she said, brushing past him. "I promise not to—"

"You have *got* to be kidding."

Sadie bristled so hard she was surprised she wasn't vibrating. She slowly turned toward the sound of that familiar voice.

"What are you doing here?" she asked Charlotte, her eyes widening as she took in her sister's tight jeans and clingy, low-cut top. "Where did you get those clothes? I didn't realize Nordstrom had a tart department." She whirled on Kane. "And you. You should be ashamed of yourself. She's just a child!"

"I probably should be," Kane said. "But I'm not."

Charlotte stalked toward her—though how she could even move in those pants was beyond Sadie. "How dare you? I'm a grown woman, damn it."

"Then I suggest you act like one," Sadie said, sounding so much like her mother she almost did a double take to make sure Irene hadn't somehow magically arrived and spoken over her.

"I don't need to stand here and listen to this." With a toss of her hair, Charlotte snatched her purse from a small table next to the door. "You're in my way," she told Sadie, who had yet to move from the doorway.

"You're not going anywhere until you tell me what, exactly, you're doing here."

"I'm not telling you anything. Now move. Or I swear, I will move you."

Sadie narrowed her eyes. "I'd like to see you try."

"And I'd like to see the backs of both of you as you leave me in peace so I can get some more sleep," Kane said.

"Blame her—" Char jabbed a finger at Sadie, stopping just shy of drilling a hole through her sternum.

He yawned. Rolled his shoulders, took them each by the upper arm and tugged them out into the hallway then stepped inside his apartment to face them. "Let's not cast blame," he said.

And he shut the door, the soft click of the lock being engaged echoing in the stunned silence.

"Jerk," Charlotte muttered, looking as if she wanted to give the door a solid kick.

Sadie could relate.

"Well, there goes my plan for bunking with him for a few nights." She glared at Char. Tightened her hold on her suitcase. "Thanks a lot."

Char's eyes narrowed. "Why would you want to stay with Kane? Unless James isn't enough for you now. Moving on to the next guy already?"

Sadie opened her mouth to blast her sister, but what came out sounded closer to a sob than any snarky comment. Horrified, she covered her mouth with her free hand. But that didn't stop the tears from forming in her eyes, from tickling the back of her throat.

"James and I are… Whatever we were—" Friends. Lovers. Something more, something infinitely more frightening. Something rare and special. "It's over," Sadie said, firming her mouth. She sniffed. She would not cry over him. She would not cry. "Completely over."

Tears leaked from the corners of her eyes. With a sigh, she sank to the top step, crossed her arms on her bent knees, lowered her head and gave in to them.

She sensed more than saw Charlotte shift uncomfortably. "Are you okay?" she asked, her tone hesitant. Still belligerent.

"I'm great," Sadie said, her voice muffled by her arms. "My dog is gone, you hate me, I had to quit my job so I didn't run into James who, by the way, never wants to see me again. And to top it all off, I got into an argument with Mom this morning where I said some really horrible things right before she wrote me a check for five thousand dollars and told me to get out of her house."

"Ouch," Char murmured. "Well, if it makes you feel any better I just threw myself at a walking, talking sex god only to be told he wasn't the least bit interested."

Sadie rolled her head to the side. "He is a jerk."

"I know." Char sat next to Sadie. "And for the record, I don't hate you. I was just angry. Really, really angry."

Sadie straightened and wiped her eyes on the edge of her sleeve. "Back at ya."

But she'd missed her sister. Had wanted to call her more than once during the past week, but her pride wouldn't let her.

"Five thousand dollars, huh?" Char asked. "That seems like more than enough to get you to California. So what are you still doing in Shady Grove?"

"I don't know," Sadie whispered. All she'd known was that she couldn't leave. Not with her mom so upset with her. Not after everything that had happened with James.

"I don't think I ever told you this, but I always envied you."

Sadie snorted. "Me? Why?"

"You were…free. Independent. God, I thought you were so amazing, the way you weren't afraid to take risks, how you'd pick up and start your life over somewhere new. You've been to so many places, seen and done so many things. I used to look up to you."

Used to.

Sadie's chest felt hollow. "Guess you outgrew that."

"Not so much outgrew. More like I realized that while your life seemed so exciting, so adventurous and, well, brave, I guess, it wasn't. You never seemed happy. Not really. It's as if you're endlessly searching for something."

Her words echoed what Irene had said about Sadie's father. Sadie really was following in her father's footsteps in more ways than one.

Maybe, just maybe, it was time for her to make her own way.

And that thought was thrilling and terrifying all at the same time.

Her life was filled with new people, new places and the constant fear that if she didn't keep moving, she would lose the most vital part of who she was. She was searching. Always searching.

She had a feeling, a deep-seated fear, that she'd

found what she'd always been seeking right here in Shady Grove. And she'd tossed it away.

"I don't know what to do," she admitted.

Char stood. "Damned if I know," she said, but she softened her words by holding out her hands. When Sadie clasped them in her own, Char tugged her to her feet. "But you can stay with me until you figure it out."

EVERYONE GAVE HIM a wide berth.

Good, James thought on Monday morning. He preferred it that way. He'd had a tough week since sending Sadie on her way. But maybe he'd snapped at his sister and brother a few too many times. They'd banished him to hauling debris from the site to the Dumpster, a job meant for the high school kids who worked after school and on Saturday mornings, but James wasn't going to complain. He didn't want to be around people, didn't want to answer any more questions about where Sadie was and why she wasn't at work and when she'd be back.

He wasn't sure if she'd left town yet, hadn't let himself ask anyone if they knew what was going on with her. All he knew was that she'd called his father, told him she quit and no one in his family had seen her since. She'd leave. Maybe today. Maybe next week. All he knew for sure was that when she did, she wouldn't come back. That, too, was for the best. He was done living his life waiting for her. Wanting her.

He was through loving her.

Despite the mild temperatures, he was sweating, his jeans and T-shirt clinging to his skin, his hair damp at the nape and forehead. It was quiet behind Bradford House, the only sounds the occasional power tool or the shout or laugh of one of the workers. Zoe trotted alongside him as he made trip after trip from the rear of the house, where the ripped-up flooring and baseboards were piled, to the flatbed truck.

He didn't need Sadie. He had his work, his family and a job he loved. He had friends. Maybe he'd call Anne, apologize for not getting back to her after their date. They might not have immediately clicked, but they'd had a decent time. And maybe, eventually, their feelings for each other would grow.

If not, he would eventually meet a woman who made him feel the same things Sadie did, who wanted the same things he did out of life. A home. A family.

He smelled her first, the familiar light scent reaching him on a breeze, on a sigh. Walking toward the house, he lifted his head like a wolf sniffing for his mate. She was here, standing by the kitchen window, wearing one of her flowing skirts and a short jacket over a floral-print top.

He didn't slow, couldn't even look at her.

She stepped forward. "James—"

"Don't." *Don't talk to me. Don't look at me. Don't remind me of what I've lost, what I'll never have.*

He lifted boards, set them on his shoulder and took them to the truck. Damn her. Damn her! Why did she have to come back? Why did she always have to come back? When he returned to the house she was still there, Zoe sitting by her side.

"They should've sent your final paycheck to your mother's house," he said, wanting—needing—her gone.

"I didn't come for my paycheck," she said quietly. She sounded nervous, looked so beautiful it hurt just to breathe. "I came for you."

"Don't," he repeated, harsher this time, and she flinched. Good. She'd better goddamn well flinch. "I'm not yours to come back for, so why don't you do what you're best at and just leave?"

This time when he took the boards to the truck she followed, her steps quick, the ends of her hair lifting. "James, please, just hear me out—"

"No."

What did she want from him, blood? He picked up his pace, wiped the back of his hand across his forehead.

She hurried to block him. "James, please." He almost ran her over, but she scooted out of his way. "Please. Five minutes. That's all I ask."

"If I say yes, will you promise to leave after that?"

"I swear."

She looked like hell. Her face was pale, her eyes rimmed red with dark circles underneath. He should find satisfaction in that, but he didn't. Couldn't. "Fine. Five minutes."

He checked his watch, then grabbed a bottle of water from the cooler in the back of his truck, sat on the tailgate.

She swallowed hard and began to pace. He forced himself to look somewhere over her head, anywhere but at her. "Did you ever..." She inhaled deeply and started again. "Did you ever tell yourself you wanted something only to realize later that what you really wanted you had all along?"

He took a long drink. Put the cap on. "No."

She smiled softly and it broke his heart. "Of course not. You've always been so...comfortable in your own skin. I've always admired that about you. Envied it." She stopped pacing and stood before him, twisting her hands together at her waist. "You see, I thought I knew what I wanted. I thought that living a life defined by traditional roles and normalcy, I guess you'd say, would somehow make me disappear when all I've ever wanted was to stand out."

She stepped closer, her eyes pleading, her voice soft. "But with you, I always stood out. You always saw me as someone special. As someone worthy. That meant something to me. Means something to me. More than you'll ever know."

He felt himself soften. He hardened his heart. "Glad I could help your ego." He tossed the empty bottle into the back of his truck. Checked his watch again without really seeing it. "Time's up. Good-bye, Sadie."

He brushed past her, told himself that the sheen of pain in her eyes wasn't real. That she wasn't hurting, couldn't be hurting nearly as much as he was.

"You saw the real me," she called. "From the time we first met, you've always accepted the real me, and I was so stupid, so blind I couldn't even see it. And when you kissed me on your birthday, it was like...God, James, it was like coming home. It was like I knew, finally, where I was meant to be for the rest of my life, and that scared me.

"I'm not as brave as you are," she went on, persistent and, if her tone was anything to go by, determined. "You were right when you said I was a coward. I am. But I want to change. I want to be brave, but more than that, I want to spend the rest of my life proving to you how much I love you."

Her words were like a knife to his heart. "If this is one of those let's-be-friends speeches, I've heard it before. I'm not interested."

She hurried over to him, blocked his way so he couldn't pick up any more boards. "I don't want to be your friend. I mean, I do. You're my best friend, but I want to be more than that. I want to be your lover and your wife. The mother of your children and the woman you grow old with. I want to be the one who brings color into your world and into that brown house of yours. I want to get a dog, a friend for Zoe, and teach them both how to play dead and

I want to spend my days working at a job that I love that fulfills me creatively, my weekends making your house our home and my nights in your arms. I want," she continued, her voice shaking, her eyes wet, "to have your babies and dance with them in our living room and make love to you after they're put to bed. I want to be your life, your future. Please, please say you still want that, too. Please forgive me and I promise I will never, ever hurt you again."

Could he believe her? Could he afford not to? James wasn't sure. All that he was sure of was the truth shining in her eyes, the hope he saw on her face. It was the same hope trying to build in his chest. Hope he couldn't deny.

He lifted a hand, trailed the tip of his finger down her cheek. "I want that, too," he whispered.

She shut her eyes. "Thank God."

And she leaped into his arms and kissed him, a kiss filled with promise and friendship. But most of all, a kiss filled with love.

* * * * *

*Look for the next book
in the* IN SHADY GROVE *series
by Beth Andrews!
Coming in December 2013
from Harlequin Superromance*

LARGER-PRINT BOOKS!
GET 2 FREE LARGER-PRINT NOVELS PLUS
2 FREE GIFTS!